THE GARDEN PARTY

THE GARDEN PARTY

A Harry Vicary Mystery

Peter Turnbull

This first world edition published 2012
in Great Britain and in the USA by
SEVERN HOUSE PUBLISHERS LTD of
9–15 High Street, Sutton, Surrey, England, SM1 1DF.
Trade paperback edition first published
in Great Britain and the USA 2013 by
SEVERN HOUSE PUBLISHERS LTD

British Library Cataloguing in Publication Data

Turnbull, Peter, 1950-
  The garden party.
  1. Vicary, Harry (Fictitious character)–Fiction.
  2. Detective and mystery stories.
  I. Title
  823.9'2-dc23

ISBN-13: 978-0-7278-8216-5 (cased)
ISBN-13: 978-1-84751-456-1 (trade paper)

All Severn House titles are printed on acid-free paper.

Severn House Publishers support The Forest Stewardship Council [FSC],
the leading international forest certification organisation. All our titles that
are printed on Greenpeace-approved FSC-certified paper carry the FSC logo.

FSC	MIX Paper from responsible sources FSC® C018575
www.fsc.org	

Typeset by Palimpsest Book Production Ltd.,
Falkirk, Stirlingshire, Scotland.
Printed and bound in Great Britain by
MPG Books Ltd., Bodmin, Cornwall.

ONE

Once again, the man found himself drawn with horrific fascination to the note, and, once again, he pondered the clumsy, almost childlike scrawl that was the thickly lined handwriting, as though, he thought, the note had been written by someone holding a wax crayon or a marker pen in his, or her, fist. The man, who would be seen by an observer to be middle-aged, short, but stockily built, and would most likely judge him to be 'working class', had read and re-read the note so many times he believed that he could accurately recreate it from memory; not just the simple recall of the wording of the note, but the misspellings and the pattern of the letters. So awed was he by the note that the man had taken not one but two photocopies of it, which he had consigned to the safety of separate places within his house. He read the note for the final time in the natural light of a Monday afternoon in mid-June just before the train on the Northern Line of the Underground system swayed gently as it entered the tunnel at East Finchley, which would take it beneath central London. Reading the note in natural light served to remind the man that despite being called 'the Underground' the majority of the track network is on the surface. As the train was swallowed by the tunnel the man folded the note and placed it inside a clear cellophane envelope, and then placed the envelope within the black bin liner which had tightly encased the note when he had discovered it. The man glanced briefly and discreetly at his fellow passengers, who were four in number, it being shortly after midday during the working week, and as always on the 'tube' no one spoke, not even those people who were travelling companions, although the man who was carrying an urn of human ashes smiled sheepishly as he and the man carrying the black bin liner caught brief eye contact. Two men, each with a story on his lap.

The man would normally have undertaken the journey into central London by bus, always preferring to be above ground rather than below the surface, and also subscribing to the view that the best way to see London is from the top deck of a double-decker bus, but he also knew that nothing beat the 'tube' for speed and efficiency, and on this day he felt that the speed of his journey was a factor to be considered. He changed from the Northern Line at Embankment and caught a westbound District Line train, alighting from it at St James's Park. From the underground station he walked along Broadway, which he saw was lined with solid-looking medium-rise commercial premises, and entered New Scotland Yard's public entrance, close by the permanently revolving triangle which read 'Metropolitan Police' and beneath being the legend 'Working for a safer London'.

The man felt nervous and wholly overawed as he entered the pleasantly cool interior of the building and walked timidly, cap in hand, up to the enquiry desk. His feeling nervous was not at all helped by the serious-looking, white-shirted constable who stood behind the desk, and who seemed to the man to be looking at him with a curiosity which verged on suspicion. The man, fighting the strange urge to turn and run, eventually reached the enquiry desk and said, 'To let you understand, sir.'

A smile. A wholly unexpected smile cracked open the constable's stern countenance. 'Scots,' said the constable. 'Another Scotsman.'

'Aye,' the man returned the smile. 'Long time down here right enough, but Scots . . . yes. We get about, so we do.'

'Whereabouts?' the constable asked.

'Barrhead,' the man replied, pronouncing the name of his native town as 'Barrheed'.

'Livingston,' the constable replied. 'I don't see myself as staying down here much longer; it's not for me. It was interesting at first, exciting even, but the travelling gets to you, such a long journey in and a long journey home.'

'Aye . . . doesn't it just,' the man said, 'but careful though, I said the selfsame thing. Not for too long said I . . .' he glanced to his left and then a note of regret entered his voice as he said, 'To think it was thirty years since I said that . . . thirty years . . . thirty long years and here I am, still here. Married a London lassie you see and you know the problem with Londoners?'

'Tell me.' The constable leaned forward.

'The problem with Londoners is that they have got this invisible chain which connects them to the River Thames, just like a Glaswegian has an invisible chain that connects him to the Clyde. Anyway, I am from Barrhead, not Glasgow, so of the two of us, me and our lassie, I was the one to relocate. She had this chain you see, kept her fastened to the river. So I came south and the best I could negotiate was summer holidays and each New Year in Scotland. So take a tip, sir, London girls are lovely, but don't take one for your wife, not if you want to live in Scotland again, Jim.'

'I'll remember that.' The constable smiled. 'So what can we do for you, sir?'

'Well . . . it's about this.' The man glanced about the spacious reception area as he took the note from the black bin liner and handed it to the constable. 'I really do not know what to make of it, I really don't. Might not be anything, but it's not really my place to say whether it is or not. I put the note in the clear cellophane, but I found it in this.' The man dropped the black bin liner on the desk.

The constable read the note but did not remove it from the cellophane. He read the note again and then looked at the man. 'I see what you mean, sir,' he murmured, 'I really do see what you mean.'

'It was in the black bin liner which was in the wall . . .'

'In the wall?' The constable queried.

'Yes . . . yes, sir. It was in the wall cavity,' the man explained. 'The wall has two vertical walls of brick, it was wedged between the two walls that make up the whole wall.'

'I see.' The constable reached for the phone which stood on the enquiry desk to his right-hand side, and in a slow but confident motion he pressed a four-digit number. 'Hello,' he said when his call was answered, 'Murder and Serious Crime Squad . . . Yes, hello, sir, PC McMichael here, enquiry desk. Can the duty CID officer please attend? I have a member of the public here with me. He has produced something which seems to be a matter for the Murder and Serious Crime Unit. Yes . . . yes . . . very well . . . yes, I will, thank you.' PC McMichael replaced the handset with the similar calm that he had picked it up. 'I'll have to keep hold of these items.' The constable picked up the bin liner and the cellophane envelope containing the note.

'Yes, sir.' The man nodded. 'I understand.'

'If you'd care to take a seat just over there, sir.' PC McMichael took the bin liner and the envelope and placed them on a shelf beneath the surface of the enquiry desk. 'An officer is coming down to take a statement from you, sir.'

Frankie Brunnie read the man as he approached him. He saw him to be weather-beaten, muscular about the shoulders . . . ruddy complexion, and thought that he probably enjoys a beer or two, if not something stronger . . . he noted the red patterned shirt, dirty denim jeans, heavy shoes for the time of year, a man seeming to be more comfortable in industrial work wear . . . rough, very rough hands. He introduced himself as the man stood, and he and the man shook hands. The man, Brunnie found, had a pleasing handshake, not vice-like nor offensively loose, just pleasantly firm. He took the man to an interview room set off of the main reception area of New Scotland Yard. The room was decorated in a soft pastel shade of cream with a hard-wearing brown carpet. A polished wooden table and four matching upright chairs were the only furniture. Brunnie read the photocopy of the note the man had produced, the original plus the black bin liner having been carefully filed away for later forensic analysis. 'Well . . .' Brunnie smiled and adopted a relaxed body posture, 'if we could start at the beginning, please, sir?' He held his pen poised over the writing paper he had brought with him. 'I am, as I said, Detective Constable Brunnie of the Murder and Serious Crime Squad. You said your name was Mr Brady?'

'Yes, sir, Alan Brady, just plain Alan Brady.' He glanced nervously about him but for the most part he kept his eyes downcast. 'I live in Finchley; not the posh part. I am fifty-seven years old and am a builder by trade.'

'Thank you, sir.' Brunnie wrote on the notepad. 'I understand from the constable at the enquiry desk that you removed the note from a brick wall?' Brunnie asked.

'That is correct, sir.' Brady gave a brief nod. 'Found it inside the wall, so I did.'

'So what's the story there?' Brunnie grinned broadly. 'I confess

I have heard of strange things being found in strange places, but a note within a brick wall . . . that really is a new one; a new one on me, anyway.'

'It's a new one on me as well, sir,' Brady returned the grin. 'I have been sticking bricks together all my days and finding something in an old wall is a new experience for me, but I have heard of such.'

'Oh . . .?' Brunnie queried.

'Well, occasionally you get a dismantling job, or a renovation, and in such cases a builder will come across a sort of time capsule, something left behind by accident or something deliberately placed there for someone to find years from then . . . an old tobacco tin full of coins, for example; that's what a pal of mine once found, but I have never found anything until last Saturday . . . two days ago.' Brady looked up at Brunnie and saw a large, well-built man with shiny, jet-black hair and a neatly trimmed black beard. He found DC Brunnie's attitude to be warm, gentle and affable.

'But two days ago you were unsticking bricks,' Brunnie clarified, 'rather than sticking them together?'

'Yes, sir,' Brady replied, 'that's correct. The job came by word of mouth, as it often does. Strange it is; one job comes to an end, nothing in sight, you're looking at being idle—'

'Idle?'

'Oh yes, sir,' Brady explained, 'it's an old word for "unemployed" . . . it lasted longer in Scotland than it did in the rest of Britain, I just picked it up.'

'I see,' Brunnie smiled. 'Carry on . . .'

'Well, it is the way of it, sir,' Brady continued. 'You work your way into the building trade, into the building community. Over the years I have got to know chippies and sparkies as well as other trowels.'

'Trowels?'

'Bricklayers, sir,' Brady explained, 'they're called "brickies" or "trowels", and we put work each other's way. Anyway a chippie . . . a carpenter—'

'Yes, I know that.' Brunnie grinned. 'A sparkie's an electrician.'

'Yes, sir.' Brady found himself relaxing in Brunnie's company.

'Well, it turns out that the chippie is putting up shelves for this geezer over in Barking, so he is.'

'All right.'

'It's a bit out of my way; plenty of local brickies over in Barking; but things were a bit quiet and you never ever turn down work.'

'So I believe.' Brunnie stroked his beard.

'Well . . . it's fatal if you do.' Brady cleared his throat. 'So, anyway, the chippie is working away up in the attic of this geezer's house and there is this almighty rumble from just outside, and the wife of the gentleman, who is having a study built in his attic, is downstairs and she lets out this almighty scream, so Martin—'

'Martin?' Brunnie queried.

'Martin Phelps, my mate the chippie.'

'Ah, yes.' Brunnie nodded.

'So Martin – good lad is Martin – he runs down the stairs like all the fiends in Hell are chasing after him and he's thinking that an aircraft has crashed or something, so he is, but what he finds is that a coach, a small one . . . you know the ones that can carry twenty passengers and you only need a normal driving licence to drive?'

'I know the type,' Brunnie said. 'Carry on, please . . .'

'Well . . . yes . . . well one of those has crashed into the wall. See, beside the house, to let you understand, sir, is a path which runs from the pavement to the back garden of this geezer's property.'

'Yes.'

'And then there is the wall . . . like a boundary.'

'Yes.'

'And on the other side of the wall there is a small hotel with a car park in front and the motor coach was about to pick up passengers, and it was trying to turn round.'

'And the driver crashed into the wall?' Brunnie anticipated Brady.

'Yes, sir, that's what happened.' Brady hunched over the table as if getting into his stride of telling the tale of the motor coach and the brick wall. 'And, anyway, the police, you guys, were called because Martin Phelps says the coach driver didn't just strike the wall a glancing blow when he was inching forwards; it was more in the manner of crashing into it at ninety miles an hour. Well, that's a bit of an exaggeration.'

'All right.' Brunnie nodded. 'I get the picture.'

'So the police smelled drink on his breath and he is taken away.'

'He would be.' Brunnie chuckled.

'Fortunate in a sense, he hadn't picked up any passengers, but he demolished the wall and the motor coach is a tow-in job . . . probably a write-off.'

'Yes.'

'So . . .' Brady continued with what Brunnie sensed was a developing relish, 'the geezer what Martin Phelps is putting up shelves for now has half a wall blocking the pathway at the side of the house, which is not good news, not very clever at all . . . and the owner of the motor coach hire company is full of liability but he is not wanting to claim on his insurance which, if he did, he reckons would skyrocket his old premium, so he is offering to pay for the rebuilding of the wall out of his own piggy bank.'

'I follow.' Brunnie spoke softly.

'So Martin, the chippie – he is right on the ball is old Martin – he says to the coach operator that he knows a builder, a good builder . . . bit of a brown envelope merchant but a good man.'

'Being you?' Brunnie smiled. 'The brown envelope merchant?'

'Yes . . . I only work for hard cash . . . just cash in hand.'

Brunnie held up his hand, though he smiled broadly, 'You'd better not tell me that, just stick to the story, you're doing well.'

'OK.' Brady looked sheepish. 'Thank you, sir, I hadn't thought . . . but I do declare it to the Revenue.'

'Just not all of it,' Brunnie grinned. 'It's OK, I am not bothered about that, not unless it is a million pound fraud . . . then I might sit up.'

'Yes, sir.' Brady held eye contact with Brunnie for a fraction of a second. 'Thanks anyway. So Martin bells me and tells me what has happened, and asks me to motor over there and take a butcher's, so he does. So over I go, it was quiet, like I said . . . give the damage a quick gander . . . give a fair quote to the coach operator and we shake hands . . . all that was about a week ago, a bit more in fact.'

'OK . . . carry on,' Brunnie replied encouragingly.

'The wall is not a tall wall. It's about six feet high . . . two metres . . . and twenty feet long, and there is a gap in the middle of about ten feet where the coach crashed into it, so I went to work putting the bricks back together and it was when I was doing that that I found the note.'

'All right.'

'But I can't fathom it, neither I can, because you see the wall is Victorian, glazed brick, but the note is on modern writing paper . . . in a plastic bin liner. The note was well in the wall between the two lines of bricks; two vertical lines topped off with heavy coping stones. See, sir, think of a ham sandwich on its side . . . the bread is the two walls . . . the ham is the narrow space between the two walls.'

'The cavity?'

'Yes, sir.' Brady nodded. 'That's the word; just a very narrow cavity between the two walls; that was where I found the note. So I took the note home. I have a niece and she is wed to a police officer . . . so I phoned Nettie, my niece, her name is Annette but we call her "Nettie", so we do, and I asked her advice and she asked her husband, and he said to take it to New Scotland Yard.'

'And here you are.' Brunnie raised his eyebrows.

'Yes, sir, and here I am –' Brady shrugged his shoulders – 'and here I am. Don't know what I have started . . . if anything. But, yes, sir, here I am.'

Harry Vicary leaned forward with a furrowed brow as he read the photocopy of the note which lay on his desktop. He re-read it and then he focussed his attention upon the handwriting. He noted the large and clumsy, childlike scrawl and he also noted the very evident spelling errors. 'Semi-literate,' he commented softly.

'Probably and possibly, sir.' Brunnie reclined backwards in the chair in front of Vicary's desk, with arms folded and legs crossed. 'But only probably and only possibly.'

'Probably? Possibly?' Vicary looked up at Brunnie with a brief smile. 'Why do you say that, Frank?'

'Well, sir, it is simply that disguising your handwriting by writing a note with your subordinate hand – pretending to be semi-literate – is another way of throwing the hounds off the scent; another way of hiding your identity. It is not easy for a genuinely semi-literate person to give the impression that they are literate . . . such a person would have to know that they are semi-literate, and would have to check the spelling of each word using a dictionary. That is not easy for a semi-literate and is also very time-consuming.'

'Yes . . .' Vicary once again looked at the note. 'I take your point and so we won't jump to the conclusion that we are dealing with a semi-literate person. "The bodies", which he has spelled "b-o-d-y-s", "is here" . . . which I assume means "are here" . . . "one day they will get a right burial" . . . spelling burial as "b-u-r-y-a-l", by which we can assume the note writer means a proper funeral, do you think?'

'Yes, sir.' Brunnie unfolded his arms and clasped his hands together in front of him. 'That would be my reading of it. The writer is notifying the authorities in some time to come of the location of the possible unlawful burial of two or more bodies in the hope that they'll get a proper funeral and their souls will be released. Proper burial confirms, I think, that we are talking about human remains; we are not going to dig up a pair of much-loved dogs or cats or a couple of hamsters.'

Vicary chuckled softly.

'And,' Brunnie continued, 'the note seems to have been written by someone with a conscience, and a male of the species because of where it was found.'

'Inside a brick wall you mean?' Vicary asked.

'Yes, sir, as if placed there by a bricklayer. Women get every-where these days, even flying fast jets and being in command of battleships, but I have yet to come across a female brickie. It's hard to see a woman surviving on a building site . . . but working alone and building a brick wall, well . . . it's feasible,' Brunnie suggested, 'it is feasible.'

'Yes . . . just,' Vicary growled, 'but I think you are right, we must assume that we are looking for a male . . . and someone with a conscience . . . and . . . and also someone who assumed that he'd be well out of it by the time his note was found, but he left the note in a plastic bin liner . . . which is?'

'With forensics, sir,' Brunnie replied promptly, 'along with the original note.'

'Good. So, the wall . . .' Vicary brought the conversation back on track. 'It is described as being of the Victorian era but contains a note written on contemporary notepaper wrapped in a plastic bag. The only conclusion we can draw is that the wall was rebuilt some time in its recent history, in addition to the rebuilding of the present time, and it was rebuilt by someone who knew about what might be two shallow graves or some other form of conceal-ment, and –' Vicary leaned back in his chair – 'rebuilt by someone who knew there would be some fallout upon the discovery of said concealment and who wanted to ensure that he was not going to get in the way of said fallout. He knew about the bodies and he knew that his head would be for the chopping block if and when they were discovered, but he also wanted to ensure that they were discovered at some point. A villain with a conscience.'

'Seems so, sir . . . or somebody trying to protect another living person; wanting to ensure that another person is well out of it by the time the remains are found.'

'Yes . . . dare say we'll find out at some point.' Vicary held up the photocopy. 'And the map . . . well, hardly a map . . . simple diagram . . . clear as a bell; two lines which join each other, and close to the join is a cross . . . and from the note there is a line leading to the cross.' Vicary paused. 'There is, though, no indication that this map shows a location within the Greater London area.'

'I thought that also, sir.' Brunnie once again glanced out of the window of Vicary's office. He saw blue sky and high, wispy white cloud . . . summer over London Town.

'If it isn't of London, we'll broadcast it nationwide to all the provincial forces, but for now we'll assume it shows a location within London.' Vicary placed the photocopy back on his desktop and re-read the note. 'There won't be many Monkhams, quite a few Orchards though . . . whether Avenue, Street, Road, Drive or any other name . . . but there will only be one place where a Monkham something will join an Orchard something.'

'Shall I get on to that, sir?' Brunnie stood. 'I just need an *A to Z.*'

'Yes, please, if you would, if you would.' Vicary smiled. 'Who is in the unit right now?'

'Just Tom Ainsclough and Penny Yewdall, sir; they're both addressing paperwork at the moment, which –' Brunnie opened his right palm – 'may well be important . . . if not vital . . . but I don't doubt for a second that they will mind being torn from it.'

Vicary grinned. 'I don't doubt it either. Ask them to go out to the address in question, will you, and obtain any information they can about the earlier rebuilding of the wall, then pick up a trail if they can, see where it takes them.'

'Very good, sir.'

'Then open a file, get a case number from the collator and write up what has been reported so far.'

'Yes, sir.' Brunnie stood and reached for the handle of the door of Vicary's office.

'Well, as you see this is the wall –' the man indicated the wall with his left hand – 'one wall, brick, boundary definition, for the purpose of. It is at least the wall in its present condition. Most of the middle section, as you see, is in the form of loose bricks on the ground.' He was a tall man, slender, round-lensed spectacles, T-shirt, trimmed beard, wispy hair, jeans and sports shoes. He had, thought Tom Ainsclough, a warm and a confident manner about him. Ainsclough also noticed clipped vowel sounds in his speaking voice which emerged occasionally within his apparent Received Pronunciation. He might, Ainsclough thought, be a man who could initially be taken for a native of the Home Counties until he felt the need to bathe, whereupon he would announce his intention to take a bath rather than a 'barthe'. For this man there would be no 'R' in bath, or path, or many other words in which the southern English clearly believe there to be one. Neither Yewdall nor Ainsclough were surprised when the man gave his occupation as that of 'university lecturer'. 'Lovely glazed brick, as you see . . . gorgeous . . . really gorgeous . . . they could afford such luxury in Victorian times.'

'Yes.' Ainsclough nodded his agreement and smiled. 'I too appreciate glazed brick; it glows in the sun on occasions, like Northern Red Brick.'

'Yes, this brick has to be kept clean to do that but Northern

Red Brick will glow even if caked with industrial fallout . . .
but, yes, glazed brick is quite a luxury and we do appreciate it.'

'We?'

'My wife and I,' the man explained.

'Ah, yes,' Ainsclough replied with a note of apology in his
voice. 'Sorry, I should have realized.'

'No matter.' The householder smiled. 'But, glazed brick . . .
You know I went to an awful school – a terrible place which
was new built and was constructed out of soft, unfaced brick –
and I was the first pupil to carve his name into the wall, and
another lad who was with me at the time did the same. The staff
were not best pleased, the Education Department had, we were
told, wanted to build the school in glazed brick to prevent pupils
carving their names or their initials into it, but were told by the
Council that it would be too expensive, so they had then asked
to compromise and have the lower six feet of glazed brick, but
even that was out of the question, financially speaking. The school
lasted for twenty years without such vandalism, "Then one boy
had to come here and now the school is ruined." They couldn't
take action because I wasn't caught in the act and I was not
going to admit to anything. Also, I wasn't the only boy in the
school with the initials C.B. and the other boy wasn't the only
boy with the initials D.H., but they knew I had done it. I was
just that sort of boy . . . Fifteen years later I took my wife-to-be
to show her my roots and I took her to the school. The initials
of other boys had spread out like a virus from where me and
D.H. had carved our initials . . . all over the wall and round the
corner.'

'You don't feel guilty about doing that?' Yewdall commented.
She was unimpressed and allowed a note of disapproval to enter
her voice.

'Nope.' The man shook his head. 'No reason why I should
feel guilty, it was just that sort of school; it invited contempt. I
mean, we were told that Victorians ventilated coal mines by
lighting live fires underground to cause an updraught – apparently
methane did not exist then – and that the Romans owed nothing
to their weapons. What nonsense. We had a maths teacher who
did not know what interpolation meant, and that was in the final
year. We had a physics teacher whose idea of teaching was to

copy the text book on to the blackboard . . . I mean, word for word, and have us copy it into our exercise books . . . and a religious instruction teacher who was so out of his box that he could be goaded into a very satisfying fist fight . . . and you know, quite frankly, in hindsight, I am surprised it took twenty years before a pupil saw the appeal of all that non-glazed brick, and if they had taken action against me I would have returned under cover of darkness and carved my initials below the head-master's study window. As I said, I was just that sort of boy.'

'You seem to have done well despite a poor start.' Ainsclough cast an envious eye over the man's house, and having also survived a similar-sounding school he did not share Penny Yewdall's disapproval of the man's early teenage actions and attitude.

'Yes, I have degrees from three universities. I feel that what I achieved in life I achieved despite my school, not because of it. I am a school governor and read the Old Testament lesson at our church's Evensong Service . . . I am part of our neighbourhood watch team . . . so I dare say that I have evolved out of all recognition from the fifteen-year-old boy with a penknife, but I do not regret doing what I did. But the wall: Mr Brady is repairing it . . . doing a good job. He phoned us this morning to let us know that he wouldn't be attending today; he did not say why and now the police have arrived and have an interest in it. Is it something I should know about?'

'Yes,' Yewdall replied. 'I mean, yes, we have an interest in it.'

'Why?' the man asked.

'We can't say at the moment, but I can say that it seems unlikely that it is anything that you need worry about, sir.'

'That's a relief.' The man breathed deeply. 'When the police call it can only mean trouble in one form or another.'

'Trouble for somebody,' Yewdall replied, 'but not necessarily for the person being called upon, as in this instance. We have reason to believe that the wall was also rebuilt some years ago, but not a long time ago.'

'Yes.' The man looked inquisitively at Yewdall and then at Ainsclough. He saw two plain-clothes officers in their late twenties. 'Yes, it was; it was a bigger and a more expensive job than we had anticipated. It was leaning you see . . . about ten degrees out of true.'

'Which is quite a lot,' Yewdall commented, 'quite significant.'

'Oh yes, and it was leaning inwards towards our house, not outwards and thus towards the hotel car park. That is inwards from our perspective.'

'Yes . . . yes . . .' Ainsclough replied, 'I knew what you meant.'

'It was like that when we moved in and would probably have stayed like that for the next fifty years, but the children had arrived and since it could not have leaned any more without collapsing, there was no decision to take; it had to be demolished and rebuilt.' The man looked at the pile of bricks. 'It really was at my wife's insistence; she had a near death experience when she was about five years old; a brick wall collapsed on top of her and her parents were told that the only reason she survived was because she had a very strong will to live . . . but it haunts her.'

'It would do,' Yewdall said drily, 'those sorts of experiences never leave any of us. I have a few such memories – we all have – they come unbidden to mind when you can't sleep or are triggered by an unexpected sight or sound or turn of phrase.'

'Yes, it is like that, and for my wife it's a leaning brick wall with children in close proximity, and so she was nothing if not insistent. So down it came.'

'Very understandable,' Yewdall nodded.

'So I negotiated with the hotelier, he's not a bad sort, and I negotiated access to six foot of his land for six weeks because the builders needed access to both sides of the wall in order to take it down and rebuild it. They reckoned the job would take three weeks but I negotiated for six weeks' access. I was just being cautious, you understand.'

'Sensible.' Ainsclough glanced at the hotel car park and the hotel itself which was clearly once a very large family home. Its white paint was at that moment gleaming in the sun.

'So we hired a builder. We hired the one who gave the lowest quote and he came and he started work. He was very thorough, painstakingly removing each brick and then chipping away all the old Victorian mortar. These houses were built in the 1890s . . . so very late Victorian . . . and the wall is contemporary with the house; it is mentioned in the deeds. So, once they had all the bricks in a neat pile, they rebuilt it again. This was five years ago.'

'That is one of the questions we were going to ask.' Yewdall interrupted the householder. 'You are sure it was five years ago?'

'Yes.' The householder smiled. 'Because if you would care to follow me . . .' He turned and led the officers to the far end of the wall near the back of the house where he pointed out the year carved into a wider than usual area in the cement between two bricks. 'Dare say old habits die hard.' He grinned sheepishly. 'But there is the date when the cement was still wet. Five years ago this summer.'

'Good enough,' Ainsclough murmured.

'Very good enough,' Yewdall also murmured in reply. Then turning to the householder asked, 'Who were the builders?'

'Oh, they were an outfit called Seven Kings Construction.'

'Quite local in that case?' Yewdall commented

'Not far at all,' the householder agreed, 'this being Barking, where we are all mad.'

Ainsclough gave a gentle, diplomatic smile at the householder's joke.

'Just two geezers in the main,' the householder continued, 'with the occasional extra man. They seemed to have a pool of bricklayers to call on. Once the rebuilding commenced there was just one bloke set to the task, sometimes two, but mainly the one fella. It seemed that the labour was required during the controlled demolition and the chipping away of the old cement. Once that was done and dusted the rebuilding was just a one or two man job.'

'I see,' Ainsclough replied. 'Do you have their phone number?'

'I did,' the householder said flatly. 'I phoned them up again when that drunken halfwit of a coach driver insisted on driving his vehicle into my wall at fifty miles an hour, but they are no longer trading. Fortunately for me the carpenter who is putting up shelves in my study was able to recommend Mr Brady. He's a good man, a good, steady worker. I don't mind that he has taken a day off; he'll get paid when the job's done but as I say, he's a good, methodical worker. I can tell you that the business premises of the Seven Kings Construction Company have been taken over by an outfit of glaziers . . . same overall line of work, I dare say.'

'Glaziers?' Ainsclough repeated.

'Yes, Montgomery Glazing.'

'Montgomery Glazing,' Ainsclough scribbled the name into his notebook.

'Yes. I remember the name; it's my sister's married name. So I dare say if anyone can help you trace the builders of the wall of five years ago it will be the people at Montgomery Glazing. It was they who told me that Seven Kings had ceased trading, suggesting they know at least a little of what happened to the proprietors.'

'Retired.' Alexander Montgomery of Montgomery Glazing Co. smiled in what both Yewdall and Ainsclough thought to be a knowing and a supercilious manner. It was, they thought, the sort of smile that is often displayed by criminals when they say, 'You'll need more than that if you're going to make this one stick, governor.' Alexander Montgomery was a large man, overweight, as well as being big boned rather than muscular, with thick black hair and a round, reddish face. He was dressed in a brown workman's smock over denim jeans, and wore industrial footwear, which both officers felt must make his feet uncomfortably hot in the present very warm weather. Montgomery received the officers in the small wooden hut which stood on what they both thought to be a large area of land for the premises of what evidently was a small business. It seemed that the premises of Montgomery Glazing were stuck in the corner of a large, uncultivated field. Further off, a second wooden hut, which appeared to be unused, stood in the centre of an adjacent, smaller area of land which was also uncultivated; the two plots of land being separated only by an ageing wicker fence, with a gate set in it.

'It's quiet here,' Yewdall commented.

Montgomery nodded briefly. 'Yes, it is . . . it's a little oasis of peace in the middle of Ilford but close enough to the town . . . farmland to the north . . . a clay quarry to the south and Painters Lane running between the two . . . east to west . . . straight as a die.'

Outside the hut stood a glazier's lorry with an inclined wooden frame on either side where a large sheet or sheets of glass could be placed and secured prior to transport.

'You don't seem to be very busy?' Ainsclough observed.

'Oh, the wagon you mean? It gets used but not often, not a lot of call for full-sized panes of glass for shop windows. We don't get much commercial work.' Montgomery leaned back causing the chair in which he sat to creak loudly under the strain. 'We mostly get called on to replace smaller panes of glass, house windows and greenhouse windows . . . boys with stones keep us in business. That and house breakers . . . vandals and burglars . . . they keep the nation's glaziers in business, they keep us well happy. Odd stuff glass, it's a liquid you know.'

'Yes,' Ainsclough replied, 'I have heard that in fact windows on medieval churches are thicker at the bottom than at the top because over time the glass has succumbed to gravity, it being a liquid, as you say. So, Seven Kings builders?'

'Yes.' Montgomery shuffled in his chair. 'They retired . . . we bought them out. That little patch there –' he pointed to the smaller field beyond the wicker fence – 'that was our property and that little old hut was our office. We had right of access over their land to reach ours. We got on well enough with them . . . two brothers . . . but they got to their mid-sixties . . . sold up . . . we bought the land.'

'We?'

'Well . . . I did . . . but me and my little business, we are a "we".'

'I see. Quite a lot of land.' Ainsclough glanced out of the office window.

'Five acres; eight if you include our original little plot.'

'OK.'

'Well . . . we have a plan hatching.'

'Expanding?'

'Could say that.' Montgomery grinned. 'Anyway, one of the brothers—'

'Brothers?'

'Yes, Roy and Tony Cole. Both retired. One in Spain—'

Ainsclough groaned. 'Don't tell me . . . Greece . . . Portugal?'

'Why, don't you fancy an overseas trip?' Montgomery smiled broadly. 'I have read about the Old Bill travelling the world to interview folk, and also to arrest them.'

'If we have to, then, yes, we travel,' Yewdall replied coldly, 'doesn't mean to say we enjoy it; we'd always rather stay closer to home. Travelling is no fun really. You can keep it.'

'Well, in that case I reckon you have just lucked in,' Montgomery sneered.

'We have?' Yewdall replied coldly.

'Reckon so, I reckon so,' Montgomery explained, then paused, 'but this geezer, Roy Cole, he's not in no trouble is he? I don't want to go grassing anybody up.'

'No . . .' Ainsclough said calmly, 'he's not a suspect.'

Yewdall remained silent but she could not help but glance at the small hut in the adjacent field. For some reason she couldn't identify, the small wooden structure seemed suspicious; in fact, she thought it was sinister. Even the jet-black crow which lighted upon the roof as she looked at the shed seemed appropriate.

'Only I don't want to finger no one.' Montgomery seemed to the officers to be very wary. 'There could be comebacks for me.'

'There'll be no comebacks,' Ainsclough spoke reassuringly, 'no comebacks at all.'

'OK. Well, he's living in Pilgrims Hatch.'

'Where on earth is that?' Yewdall returned her attention to Alexander Montgomery.

'Just ten minutes' drive to the north of here.'

'Suits us.' Ainsclough opened his notebook. 'What is the address?'

'Two brothers they were . . . still are . . . one went to Spain and the other, he wouldn't be dragged from England, wouldn't even be dragged from Greater London. "I don't need to travel because I have already arrived", that's his take on life.' Montgomery sat forward. 'Reckon I would feel the same; just know where my roots are.'

'So do you have his address in Pilgrims Hatch?' Ainsclough began to grow impatient.

'Not his address, just his phone number. I never phoned him, never needed to, but when we kept getting business for him I'd give the folk his number, though not for some years now. These days I just tell folk looking for the builders that they have ceased trading.' Alexander Montgomery turned to his right and opened an ancient card filing box which Ainsclough thought dated from the 1930s, recalling a similar one in the home of a very elderly relative when he was a child in northern England. Montgomery extracted a card from a drawer. 'Got a pen, governor?' he asked.

'We did all right me and young Tony, mustn't grumble. There's only a year between us but he was always "young" Tony. But mustn't grumble; never did anyone any good grumbling didn't, not ever . . . ever . . . ever.' Roy Cole had revealed himself to be a tall, sinewy man with a silver beard that reached down to his chest and which he stroked thoughtfully and lovingly when speaking to Ainsclough and Yewdall, with his long, slender fingers. His hair, also silver, had receded totally, leaving just a narrow band which ran from behind one ear, round the back of his head to his other ear, and which he had allowed to grow long so that it hung well over his collar. He could, thought Yewdall, who had rapidly warmed to the man, be taken for an artist or a sage in a university, rather than the retired builder he actually was. Roy Cole received the officers on the veranda of his house which projected from the front of the building. He sat in an inter-war period chair made of wicker and of the type which Yewdall had only ever observed in the bathrooms of elderly homeowners. Yewdall and Ainsclough accepted the invitation to sit on a wooden bench which was surfaced with faded varnish, and which also occupied a place on the veranda, but on the opposite side of the front door to where Roy Cole's chair stood. The veranda looked out on to the front garden of the bungalow, which the officers noted to have become overgrown in what seemed to be an accepting of nature in a generous-minded atti-tude. It was not uncontrollably overgrown, nor was it manicured to a lifeless perfection with every blade of grass cut to the correct length and all weeds plucked from the flowerbeds. Rather, Roy Cole's garden seemed to Yewdall and Ainsclough to have been allowed to develop into a powerful and confident declaration of the joy of life and of nature's bounty. It was abundant with colour provided by living things which sprang forth and bloomed in reds and blues, yellows and whites in the mid-June sun. Roy Cole's attitude served to remind Yewdall of a man she had once met who had said, 'What is a weed but a flower that nobody wants?', and indeed here she noticed bees pollinating the dande-lions as much as they pollinated the lupins and hollyhocks and roses. 'Thanks for the phone call,' Roy Cole said, 'letting me know that you were on your way, and thanks also for telling me it was nothing for me to worry about. Montgomery also phoned, telling me you were calling on me.'

'Did he?' Ainsclough observed the effect of a zephyr gliding across the garden, causing the flowers in the centre to sway gently for an instant, all under a vast blue sky.

'Yes . . . yes, he did. Just a courtesy call; probably didn't want the old boy to have a seizure.'

'We would have been more sensitive.' Yewdall relished the scent and fragrance which rose from the garden. She then explained the reason that she and Ainsclough had called upon him.

'Yes . . . yes . . .' Roy Cole seemed to the officers to be clearly relieved when he learned the reason for their visit; his head lifted noticeably and he began to look towards the officers rather than down at his feet or to his right and towards the garden. 'Yes, I do well remember that old job, four or five years ago now, I think. It was an interesting old job . . . a nice old job . . . dismantling took more time than the rebuilding, because it had to be dismantled brick by brick; couldn't put a sledge hammer to it.'

'So we understand.' Yewdall's eye was caught by a large honey bee flitting from blossom to blossom.

'Yes.' Cole pursed his lips. 'Glazed Victorian bricks with coping stones on top. They were caked in soot, mind, but would have made a splendid sight when newly laid, and after a hundred years of East End soot and grime . . . well . . . really quite dull by the time we saw the wall. Leaning dangerously, but it was still glazed brick, there to be rescued.'

'Can't carve your initials in glazed brick,' Ainsclough prompted.

'That, and they're longer lasting. Nice family in that house; kept us well supplied.' Roy Cole looked upwards.

'Well supplied?' Yewdall asked.

'With food and drink. You can fairly expect a mug of tea from householders, but that old geezer he brought us bacon sandwiches, a bowl of roast potatoes, broth in beakers. It was chilly weather, not like now, so the grub was especially well received and he talked to us like we were his equals, and him a university lecturer. He could have been a real toff with his nose well in the air, but he wasn't. He was just like an ordinary old geezer. We appreciated that and we did our best for him; a real down to earth sort of bloke. A nice job all round that was.'

'Good to hear,' Ainsclough spoke reassuringly, 'but we've met him and he told us that he had a working-class background, which might explain why he felt at home with a team of builders.'

'I didn't know that.' Cole glanced at Ainsclough. 'But he was still a decent geezer, all the same.'

'So,' Ainsclough asked, 'how many men did you have working on the wall?'

'Varied.' Cole stroked his beard. 'More on the dismantling, that's certain, just one or two on the rebuilding. The full crew was me, Tony, Gordon, Des and Keith.'

'Could you be more specific, please?' Ainsclough opened his notebook.

'Yes.' Cole continued to stroke his beard slowly and rhythmically. 'Des . . . Desmond Holst . . . Gordon, he was Gordon Owens . . . cocky little Londoner despite his Welsh name. Who else did I say?'

'Keith,' Ainsclough reminded Cole, 'Keith someone.'

'Keith . . . Keith Barnes, London bloke with a London name; all good, steady workers.'

'Where can we contact them?'

'In the wind, mate –' Cole made a sweeping gesture with the opened palm of his right hand – 'in the wind. They're out there somewhere. You see, that's the way it is in the building trade; it's all down to word of mouth. When a builder is setting on he'll put the word out and blokes who are not working will get in touch, and if they are good workers they'll be set on. So when I got the job of rebuilding the wall I put the word out that I wanted three trowels . . . but careful trowels, because it was a delicate job. That same day I got phone calls . . . and I was looking for blokes who were painstaking, not slap dash. If it was a demolition job that would be different, builders do demolish you know, but anyway we got the trowels we wanted within two days.'

'I see.' Yewdall enjoyed a blackbird's sudden burst of song. 'So you and your brother and Messrs Holst, Owens and Barnes did the job?'

'Yes.' Cole nodded. 'Just the five of us.'

'We are in fact more interested in the rebuilding,' Yewdall probed, 'who did that?'

'Me and Des,' Cole replied matter of factly, 'me and Des.'

'Just the two of you? You and Desmond Holst?' Ainsclough clarified.

'Yes,' Roy Cole replied slowly. 'I remember we got a big job that we knew was coming up and we wanted it bad . . . building a repair garage. We needed ten trowels for it, so Tony got on with that, leaving me and Des to rebuild the wall, and once or twice Des was by himself if Tony wanted an extra trowel on the garage just to get well on top of that job.'

'So,' Yewdall asked, 'tell us where in the wind might we find Desmond Holst?'

'Well, if he's still with us he'll be in his local, but I did hear that he took badly with pneumonia . . . hospital job . . . isolation ward . . . draining stuff from his lungs. A very bad way they said, so he might have gone before, as my old granddad used to say.'

'Fair enough,' Yewdall replied, 'we can but ask. Which is his local or which was his local?'

'The Neptune, Seven Kings High Road, near Goodmayes Railway Station.'

'Observations,' Yewdall asked, driving the car at a steady speed in a southerly direction towards London and towards Seven Kings in particular, 'observations and impressions?'

'Of Roy Cole?'

'Yes . . . and of Alexander Montgomery.'

'Well.' Ainsclough looked straight ahead. 'Confess I was surprised and disappointed for Roy Cole. A retired builder should have ended up with more than a run down little bungalow to show for a lifetime of self-employment in the building trade.'

'Yes, I felt the same,' Yewdall replied.

'And he was relieved when he found we wanted to talk about the building of the wall. Something was bothering him but he doesn't have form written on him.'

'His brother in Spain, possibly he nicked all the money . . . ran off with the family silver and doesn't want the police involved.' Yewdall kept her eyes focussed on the road.

'Possibly, but you know there's Spain and there's Spain.' Ainsclough glanced briefly to his left at the vast hole that was the clay quarry. 'I went to Benidorm once, for my sins, never again I tell you. Anyway, I soon got tired of the glittery seafront development and went walking behind the hotels, and I didn't have to walk very far before I was back in medieval Europe . . . people sharing their houses with farm animals . . . beasts of the field on the ground floor . . . humankind above them.'

'Point taken.' Yewdall slowed the car so as to negotiate a bend in the road. 'But I think you're right, there's a hidden agenda there. Roy Cole has been the victim of something he doesn't want the police to know about.' She paused. 'And Alexander Montgomery? Your views?'

'Well, he has form stamped all over him.' Ainsclough took a deep breath. 'I'll do a criminal records check when we get back to the Yard.'

The remainder of the journey to Seven Kings was passed in a comfortable and relaxed silence. It was the sort of silence that can only develop between two people who know each other well, who like each other on whatever level, and who work well together and who know exactly what the other is thinking.

The Neptune pub on Seven Kings High Road, Ilford, was easily located by Ainsclough and Yewdall, being where Roy Cole had described, to wit, close to Goodmayes Railway Station. It was found to occupy a corner site, as did many pubs of the Victorian era, which were built into terraces comprising a parade of shops with family accommodation above the business premises, and such was the location of The Neptune. It stood on the corner of a small street which joined Seven Kings High Road at right angles, with the front of the pub, and the main entrance, on the High Road. To the left of the pub, as viewed from the outside, there was a row of ten small shops until the terrace of buildings was interrupted by a junction where another side road joined the High Road. Ainsclough glanced along the row of shops, and noted a newsagent's, a betting shop, a café, a butcher's, a grocer's and a fishmonger's, with a military surplus shop occupying the other corner site. He ran his eye back along the row of shops to The Neptune, which had, he saw with some pleasure, retained many of the original Victorian features. It had stained-glass windows with a band of royal-blue above the windows with the name 'The Neptune' in large, gold letters. The wooden sign, at that moment hanging quite still above the doorway, showed a bearded male with the body of a fish from the waist down.

Having parked their car as close to The Neptune as they legally could, Ainsclough and Yewdall walked across the high street and entered the pub. It contained, they noted, few patrons at that time of day and what hushed conversation was being carried on instantly stopped upon the entry of the two police officers. Taking in the interior in a single sweep of his eyes, Tom Ainsclough noticed a pub which, just as on the outside, had retained many of the original features. It had the high ceilings favoured by the Victorians, with the solid wooden beams being covered in ornate plasterwork. It had a long bar of solid and polished wood, a dark blue carpet on which stood circular tables of wrought iron topped with polished wood and wooden chairs surrounding each table. It was, noted Ainsclough, only the electric lighting and a large, flat screen television mounted on the wall opposite the bar which showed that The Neptune was in the twenty-first century. The officers walked up to the bar where the publican stood, barrel-chested, with his hands resting on the bar, clean-shaven, and wearing an expensive-looking shirt and wristwatch. As the officers stood at the bar the low hum of conversation in the pub resumed.

'They're just a little suspicious of strangers.' The publican grinned warmly, showing gold-capped teeth. 'Especially if it's the Old Bill.'

'It shows?' Ainsclough returned the smile.

'It's stamped on your forehead, mate.'

'No matter,' Yewdall added, 'we don't take it personally.' She showed the publican her ID. 'May as well show you the warrant card anyway, just to keep things right and proper. We aren't here to arrest anyone.' She slid her ID into her handbag.

'Good, that really would not be good for business.' The publican continued to smile. 'Not very good at all.'

'We're looking for a geezer called Holst,' Ainsclough explained, 'Des . . . or Desmond Holst, works, or used to work as a builder . . . a bricklayer especially.'

'Used.' The publican stopped smiling. 'He used to be a good brickie so they say, a much sought-after trowel in his day.'

'Used?' Ainsclough echoed.

'Used . . . the Almighty called Des's name and number about a year ago . . . June now . . . so more than a year. It was the winter before last when Des was planted. Around Christmas time it was, because some old geezer made some remark about what a fine present it made for his old ball and chain . . . but Pearl . . . she's a foot soldier. She just planted her old man and got on with life. But Des, Des the builder, he was one of my regulars was old Des. He was a nice enough sort; seemed to get a bit quieter in himself in the last years of his life . . . not coming in as often, not drinking as much . . . but still a good regular and it's the regulars that keep a pub going. Regulars spend two hours in here, drink six pints and then amble home and never cause trouble . . . never cause no bother, like all my customers. Get very few strangers in here; nice local pub and we like it that way.'

'Good for you.' Ainsclough glanced once again round the pub.

'Yes, I'm still ticking over when other pubs are closing, so I don't complain.' The publican drummed his fingers on the bar. 'Don't complain at all.'

'Is his wife still with us . . . the foot soldier?'

'Pearl? Yes, she's still going strong, she just tramps on, Pearl does. She also nips in here for a vodka now and again. Saw her today, in fact, walking down the High Road just as I was opening up. She just took old Des's death in her stride, but she must have been getting ready for it; every woman has to G.S.M.W. as my old trouble and strife keeps saying. She tells it to our daughter.'

'G.S.M.W.?' Yewdall inclined her head slightly to one side. 'What does that mean?'

'It's a woman's lot, pet . . . according to my old lady anyway, unless she dies young or becomes a nun . . . Girlhood, Spinsterhood, Motherhood, Widowhood . . . no one escapes except by death or holy orders. It's a bit cynical but that's my wife, a cynic, but it's fair, at the same time; it's fair enough, men die young and women just keep going.'

'Or elective spinsterhood.' Yewdall straightened her head. 'That is another way out of G.S.M.W., at least the "M" and "W" bits.'

'Is that your status, darling?' The publican beamed at Penny Yewdall. 'An elective spinster?'

'Possibly. So where does Pearl Holst live?'

'She's not in any trouble?' The publican suddenly wore a solemn expression.

'None.' Ainsclough held eye contact with the publican. 'None at all, we assure you.'

'Hope you're right because publicans who grass up customers to the Bill . . . well, they tend to lose custom; tend to lose other things as well . . . like arms and legs, use of, if not completely . . . and Pearl, she's a small woman with a huge temper. She's a "pikey"; well not her, not now, but she comes from travelling people stock and they have their own way of settling things. You don't want to mess with those people. Pearl and I had a run in a few years ago and I took second prize, but I didn't slap her back because I was frightened of her relatives, not of her.' The publican wiped his hand across the surface of the bar, as if brushing away a fly that only he could see.

'Understood. Well, we know her name; we'll find her easily. A regular in here, woman in her sixties . . . Pearl Holst . . . old man was a brickie and she sounds like she'll have form.'

'Oh she has.' The publican raised his bushy eyebrows. 'She's got form, all right.'

'So if she comes in here wanting to go ballistic, you just say we found her because of her police record and we'll do the same,' Yewdall replied. 'That will cool her off.'

'Dare say that's true, but if she's not in trouble and her old man's in the clay, I don't see why I shouldn't point you in her general direction, don't see why not at all. Her old drum is just round the corner . . . five minutes' walk.'

Frankie Brunnie smiled. Harry Vicary had been quite correct. There were few Monkhams in London, just three in fact, one Avenue, one Road and one Lane, and there was a plentiful number of thoroughfares called Orchard something, but only one of the Monkhams, Monkham Lane, joined a thoroughfare called Orchard something. In this case it was Orchard Hill and they met each other in Woodford, north London.

*   *   *

Pearl Holst lived in what Yewdall and Ainsclough found to be a modest, neatly kept terraced house on Eynsford Road in Ilford. The houses along the length of the street had, they noted, a small area of land between their frontage and the pavement, and which the officers observed had either been retained as garden, or turned into a parking space for the family car, either one or the other, in equal measure. The houses were of a ground and upper floor design, with the occasional vaulted roof indicating the existence of attic space which could be developed into a living area. The complete absence of ventilation grills or small windows at ground level showed that the houses on Eynsford Road had no cellars. Yewdall and Ainsclough parked their car half on and half off the pavement where a space to do so was to be found, so as not to impede traffic flow along the narrow road, and walked up to the highly varnished door which was, they had been advised (and confirmed by means of a criminal record check) the home of Pearl Holst. Tom Ainsclough paused and then knocked on the door, twice, in what Penny Yewdall thought to be a soft, reverential, but yet authoritative tap.

The door was opened rapidly and aggressively by a short, strongly built woman, wearing a yellow T-shirt, faded blue jeans and sports shoes. She planted herself strongly on the threshold of her house in a manner which said loudly, 'This is my territory; no one comes in unless I say so'. She was, the officers guessed, in her sixties but had the muscle and facial tone of a much younger woman. Her blonde hair was worn back in a tight ponytail, further adding to a more youthful appearance for a woman of her years. The woman's face was small and pinched; her eyes seemed, to Ainsclough and Yewdall, to be cold and dark and piercing: the eyes of a raptor. 'The Old Bill?' she asked in a local accent.

'Yes.' Yewdall showed her ID card, as did Ainsclough. 'I am DC Yewdall, this is DC Ainsclough of Scotland Yard.'

'The Yard!' The woman seemed alarmed. 'Must be serious.'

'It is.' Yewdall replaced her ID in her handbag. 'But it is nothing for you to be alarmed about. All we need is a little information. Nothing more.'

'Just information? Well, I can't see what good anything I can tell you will be but you'd better come in . . . the curtains are twitching already.' Pearl Holst stepped aside and allowed the officers ingress to her home.

The two officers entered what they found to be a neat and cleanly kept living room with a television and a CD player on a shelf in the corner of the room. Net curtains prevented passers-by looking into Mrs Holst's living room. The air smelled strongly of furniture polish. Penny Yewdall's eyes were drawn to a line of framed photographs which stood on the mantelpiece above the fireplace, all showing a young woman dressed in swimwear and incongruously, in Yewdall's view, heavy wrestler's boots encasing her feet and calves.

'That's yours truly.' Pearl Holst followed Penny Yewdall's gaze. 'Me in my younger days,' she said proudly. 'I was a body sculptor.'

'A body sculptor?' Yewdall inclined her head and raised her eyebrows.

'Some people call it bodybuilding but we prefer the term sculpting, body sculpting. Building isn't an art form but sculpting is. I was runner-up in the North London finals, sort of one step short of the nationals. I was disappointed at the time because I wanted to be top of the pyramid, but looking back, well, it wasn't a bad achievement, especially since I never took no steroids, darling; I never used 'em. I seen the mess they can leave a woman's body in, so I left it out. I mean, I left it well out. For me it was all down to diet and pumping iron, that's how I did it. Dieting and pumping iron. If you ask me the women that used steroids were cardboard cut-outs . . . but me . . . me, I was the business.' Pearl Holst looked pleased with herself. 'I still work out . . . down the gym three times a week circuit training.'

'You are indeed very trim for your years, ma'am.' Yewdall once again inclined her head. 'Very trim indeed.'

'Thank you, pet, you can come again, even if you are the Bill. Take a seat . . . I'm going to.'

Once seated Yewdall began, 'It's actually about your late husband Des . . . or Desmond Holst.'

'Des?'

'Yes.'

'So it was the governor at The Neptune who told you where I lived?'

'We can't say . . . but you have form and we checked with CR.'

'He would have done, you can't protect him, he's got too much rabbit about him, just can't keep shtum. He doesn't know the meaning of this –' Pearl Holst drew her fingertip across her lips – 'he would have told you. Anyone looking for Des would go to The Neptune and talk to the governor.'

'We would have found you anyway, Mrs Holst.' Tom Ainsclough became suddenly very frightened for the welfare of the helpful publican of The Neptune.

'That's not the point.' Pearl Holst began to look angry, setting her jaw firm. 'Yeah, I've got form and I have lived in Seven Kings all my life . . . all my days I've been here . . . old Seven Kings. There's Seven Dials in the West End, there's Seven Sisters up Tottenham way and there's Seven Kings in Ilford . . . nothing to do with seven biblical kings or seven biblical kingdoms.'

'What isn't?' Penny Yewdall asked.

'Seven Kings, the name of this little corner of dear old Ilford, it's an old word . . . and I mean ancient. Seven Kyng meant a place where the gang of a geezer called Sootica lived; I looked it up when I was in the library, trapped in by the rain one day . . . over the years it became Seven Kings.'

'Interesting.' Ainsclough hoped to placate the angry Pearl Holst. 'You never stop learning.'

'You don't, do you? That day in the library I found out that Seven Sisters refers to a group of stars, possibly the plough . . . the sailors' stars . . . and Seven Dials in Covent Garden . . . nothing special there, just seven streets meeting at the same place, but I was always good at history when I was at school, that's when I went; I was a chronic truant.' Pearl Holst smiled at the memory. 'We used to go as far as Wanstead Park on hot summer days, do a bit of shoplifting on the way there and back. They used to larrup the living daylights out of the boys who truanted, but they couldn't or wouldn't touch the girls, so I was always all right. They just gave me a note to take home to my old man expecting him to do it, but he just laughed and said it showed I was adventurous, that I had an adventurous spirit. He said that that would take me further in life than anything I could learn in Ilford Secondary School. I think he was right as well, looking back. So Des; what's

Des done from the grave that could interest the boys and girls in blue?'

'He did us a favour,' Yewdall explained. 'At least we think he did us a favour.'

Pearl Holst looked up at the ceiling. 'That isn't like Des to do the Old Bill a favour . . . not Des. Mind you, I suppose you know him as Ralph Payne.'

'Yes, we do.' Yewdall nodded. 'Desmond Holst aka Ralph Payne.'

Ainsclough remained expressionless.

'Aka?' Pearl Holst queried.

'Police speak, Pearl,' Yewdall replied. 'You don't mind if I call you Pearl?'

'No, pet, so long as you don't want me to grass anyone up.'

'No, we don't want that. Aka,' Yewdall explained, 'it means "also known as". So Des is aka Ralph Payne.'

'I see. Well, you'll know he only went back to calling himself Desmond Holst towards the end. In the last few years he came over all Gandhi for some reason; just wanted to earn honest money for once. I mean, he got really Gandhi, full of the right and wrong of it all.'

'Honest money,' Yewdall queried, 'as a builder?'

'As a builder . . . as a bus driver . . . as a jobbing gardener, even working on old people's gardens for nothing . . . nothing! Can you believe it? Ralph Payne, now he was something, he was always very useful in a skirmish and a very useful geezer to have on your team. Well handy he was. A blagger's blagger and my dad liked him, but then a few years before the end he changed, Ralph did, went back to calling himself Desmond Holst, his real name, and only making honest money . . . and not very much of that.' Pearl Holst shook her head. 'He was a big old let down in the end; just not the geezer I married . . . now he was a wide boy, someone to be proud of.' She shook her head again in a despairing gesture. 'But Des, at the end, right at the end, last few months, he started to throw away all his possessions or give them to charity shops because they was moody goods, not bought with straight pennies . . . moody . . . so he says. He even tried to half-inch my jewellery for the same reason, but he got a slap for that and never tried it no more . . . but half his stuff went to the charity shops, like I said . . . right at the end he came over all Gandhi.'

'Did he ever talk to you about his honest work?' Yewdall asked.

'Stroll on, darling, stroll on . . . he never did. He knew I wouldn't have been interested. So . . . no . . . he didn't.'

'About five years ago,' Yewdall continued, 'he built a wall.'

'Did he? Well, I'll take your word for it, sweetheart. I'll take your word for it.'

'He never mentioned a shallow grave or some other form of hiding bodies . . . like under a pile of rubble?' Ainsclough glanced out of the window as an elderly man shuffled along the road. He thought the man seemed to be hurrying despite the shuffle.

'You've found one?' Pearl Holst sat back in the chair she occupied and crossed her legs in what both officers thought was a manly gesture, with her right ankle resting on her left knee and with her right calf parallel to the floor. 'So what's the big deal there? I mean, so what? They're all over London, darling . . . shallow graves . . . and iffy piles of rubble and up in Epping Forest, plenty of graves there.'

'And Desmond knew about them?'

'I'm not a grass, sweetheart, never was and I'm not changing now. Anyway, I think you'd better leave my drum, I've got a visit to make.' Pearl Holst's voice hardened.

'Oh . . .' Yewdall stood, as did Ainsclough.

'Yeah . . . I'm going to take a wander up to The Neptune. I'm going to slap the governor; he shouldn't have told you where my drum was . . . that was bang out of order.'

'We'd have found you anyway and we told him that. All we needed to do was to call the local nick . . . which we did.'

'Even so, I'm still going to deck him.' Pearl Holst stood. 'He was out of order.'

'He's bigger than you.'

'That didn't help him last time and it won't help him this time. That guy . . . he can't stop running his north and south off. I won't worry about him pressing charges against yours truly; he knows better than to do that. It'll be the end of him and the end of The Neptune if he does. It's not a bad old boozer but there are other battle cruisers in the borough, so we'll be all right.'

Penny Yewdall drove the car slowly along Eynsford Road and then turned right at the end of the street towards the main thoroughfare of Green Lane and the route back to Central London. Ainsclough glanced out of the window of the passenger seat. 'You didn't tell me he was a blagger.'

'Who?'

'Desmond Holst.'

'I didn't know, not till you did . . . not till just now. I also didn't know that Desmond Holst was aka Ralph Payne . . . nor did I know that Pearl Holst has contacts who can dissuade people from pressing charges and who can torch pubs. That is more than having distant relatives in the travelling community; that is being part of villainy, proper London villainy.'

'It is, isn't it?' Tom Ainsclough grinned. 'You know, it's astonishing what someone who isn't a grass and never was can tell you . . . it was very informative . . . very public spirited of her.'

TWO

Harry Vicary drove calmly and steadily out to the location following the clear directions contained in the note, which Frankie Brunnie had requested to be left for his urgent attention in Vicary's pigeonhole. Orchard Lane, Vicary discovered, was a short road with a surface of both concrete and tarmac which joined the much longer Monkham Lane at ninety degrees, thus creating a T-junction, and did so in an area of prestigious suburban housing set in and graced with rich foliage. Vicary slowed his car as he noticed the expected police activity and halted his car behind a marked police vehicle. He also noticed the other vehicles present at the scene: two vans from the Metropolitan Police dog branch, a black windowless mortuary van, a police minibus and two other cars, both unmarked yet both clearly part of the police presence. He got out of the car leaving his window wound down, thus allowing the interior of the car to 'breathe' in the summer heat, and then he strolled with effortless authority across Monkham Lane to where a lone constable stood. The constable, dressed in a short-sleeved white shirt and serge trousers, gave a half salute as Vicary approached and then stood aside and said, 'In the woods, sir,' indicating the area of woodland behind him. Vicary nodded his thanks and entered what he found to be the welcoming shade of the thick stand of trees. Once inside the treeline he immediately saw a blue-and-white police tape which cordoned off a small area of, he guessed, approximately ten feet by ten feet within the wood and, surprisingly, he thought, for a crime scene, quite close to Monkham Lane. The tall, black-bearded figure of DC Frankie Brunnie stood outside the cordoned off area, as did a number of white-shirted constables and two dogs, both resting, but both held on leashes by their handlers. Within the enclosed area, Vicary saw John Shaftoe kneeling on the ground, close to where a constable was slowly and carefully excavating a hole in the soil with a spade.

'Thank you for coming, sir.' Frankie Brunnie turned to Vicary as Vicary approached him. 'I thought that you would want to be here. I phoned the directions through as soon as I realized that there was something in this but you were out.'

'Yes, I was left a note in my pigeonhole. Thank you.'

'Sir . . . we're still finding bones, we are going very slowly.'

'So I see.' Vicary observed the careful, gentle manner in which the constable scraped away the soil, layer by layer. 'But bones . . . not bodies?'

'No, sir, bones, as you see.' Brunnie pointed to the bones which had been placed in a neat pile in one corner of the cordoned off area, and which at that moment were being closely examined by John Shaftoe, who glanced at Vicary and gave him a brief smile of recognition. He then returned his attention to the bones.

'We used dogs, as you see, sir, it being a wooded area; as you know, we can only use ground-penetrating radar in open spaces,' Brunnie explained.

'Yes.' Vicary brushed a fly away from his face.

'Dogs are preferable anyway if you ask me, sir. GPR images have to be interpreted, but a dog knows when he has picked up the scent of decaying flesh and they came up with the goods all right; two spaniels, as you see.' Brunnie nodded in the direction of the two springer spaniels. 'Alsatians have their uses in crowd control situations and in bringing down felons but you can't beat a springer when it comes to scenting . . . gun dogs, you see. Please meet Charlie Chan and Sherlock.'

'You're joking?' Vicary grinned.

'No joke, sir. Charlie Chan is the one lying down.'

'So . . .' Vicary looked at the pile of bones and then at the slowly deepening hole. 'What do we have?'

'Two adult males, according to Mr Shaftoe, sir,' Brunnie replied, 'two skulls and about the right number of bones to make two skeletons. They've been chopped up, I mean well chopped up.'

'Dismembered?'

'Yes, sir,' Brunnie replied, 'I dare say that that would be a better way of putting it. Mr Shaftoe is examining them at the moment.'

'So I see.' Vicary glanced at the figure of John Shaftoe, casu-ally dressed, kneeling on the floor of the woodland holding a long bone in each hand, and at that moment, Vicary thought, looking more like a man weeding his allotment than the Home Office Pathologist he actually was.

'Excuse me, sir,' the constable who was digging the hole stood and addressed Brunnie. 'I am certain that I have reached consolidated soil now; this soil hasn't been disturbed at all. I am coming across unbroken roots as well.'

'Very good.' Brunnie, accompanied by Vicary, walked to the cordoned off area and, raising the tape, walked to the edge of the hole in which the constable stood. The hole was, Vicary guessed, about four feet deep.

The constable drew the tip of the blade of the spade across the soil at the bottom of the hole. 'I've dug down about one foot deeper than the last piece of bone to be found, sir, and as I said, I am sure I am digging in undisturbed soil . . . totally consolidated. I am sure that nothing has been buried below this level.'

Brunnie glanced at Vicary who nodded. 'Very well,' Brunnie addressed the constable, 'thank you, that is a good job done. Get someone to help you and sift the soil as you refill the hole.'

'Very good, sir.' The constable's reply was prompt and attentive. Brunnie turned to a Scene of Crime Officer who wore a high definition yellow waistcoat. 'Can you photograph the hole, please? Perhaps you could use something to give the photograph scale?'

'Yes, sir, I'll use the spade, if I may.' The SOCO stepped forward and took hold of the spade as it was handed to him by the constable who was levering himself out of the hole.

'A hole with bones,' John Shaftoe grunted as he got to his feet and brushed soil from his trousers. He had rolled up the sleeves of his blue shirt and drew his forearm across his brow, sweeping away beads of sweat in the process. A white, wide-brimmed cricket hat sat upon the top of his head. 'It is quite a clever way of doing it,' he panted. 'You dig a hole, just a small hole . . . not as large as you would need for a body; place the bones neatly within said hole. You can place all the bones of the human body . . . an adult body that is . . . in the sort of cubic dimension of an old-fashioned television set, and two sets of bones both from adult humans could be placed in the sort of space that would be occupied by a small washing machine or a freezer . . . or in this

case a hole of that size; less in fact because the constable dug
down an extra foot or so, as he has just informed you, thorough
man that he is.' Shaftoe took another deep breath and shook his
head. 'I am not as young as I used to be . . . but all the flesh
has been removed, that is a necessity if you are going to conceal
bones in such a small area.'

'And that is what has happened here, Mr Shaftoe?'

'Yes, as you see, no flesh or muscle or any form of sinew
remain. I'll get the bones back to the Royal London as soon as
I can. There will be no pronouncements without prior examin-
ation under proper clinical conditions, but I can tell you that all
the bones show evidence of having been exposed to fire.'

'They've been burnt?'

Shaftoe inclined his head to one side and then the other. 'I
can't say for sure. I have seen similar scorching on bones in
archaeological sites where the ancients practised cannibalism . . .
or the remnants of animal bones round a camp fire. The scorching
is probably the indication of attempts to burn the flesh so as to
separate it from the bone rather than an attempt to burn the bones
themselves as a means of destroying them.'

'I see.' Vicary nodded. 'Understood.'

'I can also tell you that that could not have been done here.'

'No?' Vicary queried.

'No . . . well . . . just look around you, the proximity to a
very busy road and houses; leafy, well-set Ilford.'

'I see what you mean.' Vicary glanced around him.

'Space and time,' Shaftoe remarked. 'Both space and time
would be needed to reduce a corpse into a pile of bones; you'd
need quite a bonfire to burn the flesh away, then you would
separate the bones and possibly boil the remaining flesh away,
one or two bones at a time. This is not medical thinking, you
see, Mr Vicary, this is just honest to goodness logic.'

'Appreciate that, sir.'

'It would take a week from beginning to end, I would think.'
Shaftoe took off his wide-brimmed white cricketer's hat and
revealed a bald head. He wiped his brow once again and replaced
his hat.

'You think?'

'Yes, I would think so. A massive fire which would give off

the unmistakable smell of burning flesh, then isolating each bone and boiling it to remove the last remnants of muscle and sinew . . . where there is no danger of being disturbed . . . a few days' work there, I shouldn't wonder.'

'I see your point, sir.' Vicary glanced towards the road and nearby houses. 'It would not – it could not have been done here.'

'As to when.' Shaftoe shrugged. 'That will always be inconclusive.'

'We have information which suggests they have been here in excess of five years.'

'Oh?'

'Yes . . . it was a note in a wall which alerted us to the presence. The wall was built, or rebuilt rather, five years ago. It was in the form of a rough sketch map.'

'Very good,' Shaftoe murmured. 'Good enough, it got us here . . . it did its job.'

Besides Shaftoe, Vicary and Brunnie, two officers shovelled small amounts of soil into a sieve which was held by a third officer, whereupon it was gently shaken over the hole.

Shaftoe broke the brief silence. 'I do wonder why on earth they went to the trouble of burying them. I mean, if the felons had gone to all this trouble to separate flesh from bone, they clearly wanted their two victims to disappear.'

'That seems a reasonable assumption,' Vicary replied.

'So why then bury them in a shallow grave in woodland adjacent to a busy road and densely populated area? Seems to work against their apparent intention of permanent disappearance. If they had reduced the bodies to bones then it would be a simple matter to put the bones in one or two cardboard boxes and drop them off Richmond Bridge one dark, rainy night. Let the Old Father swallow them. But to go to the trouble of burying them in a wood, you'd have the devil of a job cutting through the root plate. I mean, any infantryman will tell you that you can't dig-in in a wood.'

'Because of the roots?' Vicary asked.

'Yes,' Shaftoe replied. 'This hole was much, much harder to dig than would have been a similar-sized hole dug in a field.'

Vicary turned to the constable who had excavated the hole. 'Did you encounter roots, constable?'

'Yes, sir, a few.' The constable held the sieve quite still as he answered Vicary. 'But it was all new growth. Any old roots had become mixed with the bones and had decayed.'

'You have a point, Mr Shaftoe. Why not just dump them in the river?'

'And why here?' Shaftoe added. 'Folk hereabouts would have called you blokes if they heard digging in the wood at night . . . and it would have been dug at night or over one or two nights because pedestrians or dog walkers would have heard it during the day, or even come across the man or men digging it. It's a puzzle, but one for you, not one for me.'

'Yes, dare say much will be answered if and when we identify the author of the note,' Vicary replied drily. 'I have two of my team trying to find him as we speak.'

'Good luck. Well . . .' Shaftoe brought the conversation back on track, 'what we have here is two adult males. They are most likely north-western European going by the skull shape, but they could also be Asian; European and Asian skull shapes being very similar, with the Asian skull being slightly more finely made, but that as a general rule of thumb.'

'Understood,' Vicary commented.

'Age at death.' Shaftoe pondered the skulls. 'Well, adult, probably older than thirty years. They both have fully knitted skulls and both have quite a lot of teeth missing, but both skulls still contain two or three teeth and that is all I need to determine their ages at time of death, within twelve months either way . . . I mean plus or minus a year.'

'Yes, sir,' Vicary replied.

'There do not appear to be sufficient teeth to be able to determine identity by means of dental records.'

'Can you tell how long they have been buried, sir?' Vicary asked.

'Nope.' Shaftoe smiled. 'The note you mentioned is probably a better indication than anything I can determine by scientific analysis. I'll take a soil sample back to the lab with me; send it by courier to the forensic science laboratory, they might be able to give some indication of when the soil was disturbed, though I do not hold out much hope. Frankly, I think DNA extracted from the bones will be the best avenue to explore to determine their identity and that may be your dateline. They were presumably murdered some time after they were last seen alive. Sorry I can't be more specific, but determining exact time of death by means of scientific analysis of remains is the stuff of television drama. So, we have a collection of charred bones, enough to make two male skeletons. I can't see any obviously missing bones nor are there additional bones from a third or fourth body. We do not have five femurs or six clavicles, for example. I am pretty sure we have all the bones from the two bodies. And the charring . . . it seems that they were burnt to aid concealment. It takes an awful lot of heat to turn bones to ash. Here they were burnt only to remove the flesh. Like a well-cooked leg of lamb, the meat just falls right off the bone on the serving platter at Sunday lunchtime, or any type of meat, really; it is just that leg of lamb is my favourite roast meat.' Shaftoe grinned. 'I am sorry but I am no vegetarian or animal rights activist.'

'Well said, sir.' Vicary returned the grin in clear agreement with Shaftoe's attitude.

'Rabbits are lovely, furry little animals,' Shaftoe continued, 'just perfect for the casserole dish.'

Again Vicary chuckled. 'So, in your opinion, the bones were burnt to aid their disposal?'

'I would think so; as I said, once the bones have been cleaned of all flesh and muscle and sinew, burnt and then possibly boiled to make them fully cleaned of flesh, then you can stack them neatly in quite a small space.'

'Rather than drop them into the river,' Vicary mused. 'It is a question to answer. This is not a hurried disposal, I think.'

'I would be inclined to agree.' Shaftoe brushed a persistent fly from his face. 'This hole took time and effort to dig.'

'Yes, the root plate and proximity to the road and to the houses, as we mentioned. It is strange that no one saw or heard the hole being dug or noticed it when it had been dug.' Harry Vicary glanced around him. 'On a quiet night the sound of a spade being driven into the soil would carry to the houses hereabouts and do so easily. Even allowing for the trees masking the noise somewhat, the sound would still carry and a light sleeper or someone lying awake—'

'Ah.' Shaftoe held up his right index finger. 'You have

probably just answered your own question there, Mr Vicary. You
see the remote location needed to burn the corpses, dismember
them and then possibly boil the bones until they were free of all
flesh suggests, as we have agreed, that the felons in question had
access to time and space.'

'Yes, we have agreed these,' Vicary replied.

'This further suggests that they had storage facilities to keep
the bones hidden while waiting for wet weather to arrive; I mean
waiting for the kind of storm cell that will bring the rain down
in stair rods, softening the soil, and then they arrive at the wood
with pickaxes and spades, dig said hole, with the rainfall dead-
ening any noise, place bones therein, fill in, place stones on top
and get away before it stops raining and dawn rises. But –'
Shaftoe shrugged – 'that is all speculation . . . Me, well, I have
to be scientific and confine my report to what made them stop
kicking, if I can. I'll have the bones removed to the Royal London
and commence the post-mortem as soon as I can. Will you be
observing for the police, Mr Vicary?'

'Yes.' Vicary nodded. 'Yes, I will.' Vicary turned to DC
Brunnie. 'We seem to be talking years buried, as the note indicated, but can you organize a search of the wood, please? You
have sufficient constables. Something of relevance may still be
here, still in the vicinity. I doubt you'll find anything though, but
if we don't look it will only be here waiting to be found . . . life
being like that.'

'Yes, sir.' Frank Brunnie smiled. 'I know what you mean.'

'Then do a house to house, again. I doubt anyone will
recall anything from five years ago in respect of the wood, but
ask anyway.'

'Very good, sir.' Brunnie nodded his understanding of the
instructions.

'I'm going to the Royal London Hospital to observe the post-
mortem. I'll be there if needed. Then I will go to the Yard.'

'Understood, sir.' Brunnie turned sharply away; he was a man
with a purpose.

The small terraced house was, Yewdall silently pondered, a sound
lesson to any person who might find themselves drawn to a life
of crime, who might be tempted by apparently easy pickings.

The house in question was on Perch Street in the appropriately, thought Yewdall, named area of Shacklewell in the London Borough of Hackney. Within the house there was a large area of living space which was divided into a kitchen cum dining area, a relaxation area comprising two armchairs in front of a television set which occupied the corner of the room, and a single bed pushed under the stairs which led to the upper floor rental. A toilet and shower cubicle were located beyond the kitchen and beyond that French windows looked out on to an overgrown garden that was enclosed by a six foot high brick wall and which was, thought Yewdall, about twelve feet square. Beyond the wall at the bottom of the garden the upper floors and roof tops of the next street parallel to Perch Street were visible. It was evident that the house had been originally a two storey house designed for occupation by an artisan and his family, and it was, by the time the officers visited, divided into two separate flats with certainly a long-term tenant on the ground floor and probably, guessed the officers, the same on the upper floor. A date set in the wall of an adjacent and identical house read 1885.

Inside the lower flat everything seemed to Ainsclough and Yewdall to be old and worn, very worn. The television set was a bulky item and sat upon a table which both officers thought was of the immediate post Second World War era. The twin high-backed and high-armed armchairs which stood side by side across the threadbare carpet seemed, to the officers, to belong to the same era. The decoration, apart from faded wallpaper, was confined to a print of a painting of a sailing ship contained within an inexpensive-looking frame which hung from the wall to the left of the television. Faded net curtains prevented passengers from seeing into the flat as they walked along the pavement, which was separated from the house by a very small area of personal space approximately two feet wide. All this was the home of Claude Bonner who, like his dwelling and the furniture and fixtures and fittings therein, could be best described as 'belonging to an earlier era', thought Penny Yewdall. Bonner, the officers noted, was short, with a protruding stomach, and was bow-legged, round of face, bewhiskered, with straggly grey hair which surrounded the bald crown of his head. 'Des . . . Des Holst . . .' Bonner spoke in a slow, croaking voice but he had, noted

Ainsclough and Yewdall, alert blue eyes and he stood square on
to the officers, in front of the television. He nonetheless gave off
the unmistakable musty smell of an elderly person. 'I heard he
went to Fiddler's Green, old Des; he went west did Desmond.
Nice old geezer but he kicked the bucket, so I heard, more than
a year ago now. Old Des, he left a gap behind him.'

'He did.' Penny Yewdall found herself breathing shallowly to
avoid the damp in the property gripping her chest. 'He died about
eighteen months ago. We have just called on his widow, Pearl.'

'Pearl,' Claude Bonner scoffed, 'you won't get nothing from
her, not from Pearl Holst. She keeps it well clammed, her old
north and south; well clammed when it comes to talking to the
police. She doesn't like the police, Pearl doesn't; she doesn't like
the Bill at all. It's her family see, there's not one of her family
that hasn't been banged up . . . not one . . . going back as far
as. It's like a right of passage for them, see, father, mother,
brothers, sisters, uncles, aunts, grandparents, great grandparents,
they've all been in prison. She was brought up to hate the police.
If I know Pearl she'll be friendly enough but she won't give
anything up; if she gave you the time of day it would be a couple
of hours short,' Bonner scoffed. 'Am I right or am I right?'

'Yes, you are so right, sir, so right.' Yewdall smiled at Bonner
sensing that he was a man who liked to be right because,
she thought, he has nothing else going for him. Yewdall also realized that she and Ainsclough needed Bonner's cooperation. It was
therefore very important to let Claude Bonner be right. 'We got
absolutely nothing from her,' Yewdall added, 'nothing at all.'

'See . . . I knew it . . .' Bonner smiled. 'You should have come
to me first; I could have saved you a trip out to Ilford.'

'Dare say you could,' Yewdall replied, sensing Tom Ainsclough
beside her, remaining diplomatically silent.

'That's Pearl,' Bonner continued, 'she was brought up to keep
shtum.' Bonner drew his finger across his lips. 'I bet she was ten
years old before she discovered that she had a mouth and a
tongue. She's a weightlifter . . . something like that. Des told
me she was Pearl Harley until she married and at school the kids
called her "Pearl Barley". It gave her a chip on her shoulder, so
she took up weightlifting or something similar. She got to be
very strong; she could punch above her weight and still come

out on top.' Bonner paused. 'So you've found me . . . you're my first visitors since before Christmas. Who told you where I was?'

'Wandsworth nick.' Tom Ainsclough also sensed the damp in the house and found that he too breathed shallowly.

'You've been there? Who's the Governor these days? I heard the last one retired.' Bonner smiled.

'Don't know,' Ainsclough replied, 'we phoned them . . . the old dog and bone . . . saves a lot of driving. They gave us your discharge address. We called on the off chance you'd still be in the same drum and you'd be at home.'

Claude Bonner glanced round his home. 'Well . . . what can I say? You put your roots down eventually, even if it is just rented; just half a house in Hackney. It's not much to show for my life is it? But the roof is good, it keeps the wet out, there's a boozer close by and some shops in Shacklewell Lane. I live on bread and cheese and what's put on the reduced items tray in the supermarket. I get meat there, sliced ham and stuff, and a beer when I have saved up enough. It's all the old state pension will run to, and it doesn't go very far.'

'No more crooking for you then, Claude?' Yewdall smiled.

'Not for me, miss, not any more. I'm knackered and look where it got me . . . half my old puff in the slammer and nothing to come out to. It's true what they say . . .'

'What's that?' Ainsclough wheezed as the damp in the house reached him.

'Prisons,' Claude Bonner sighed, 'they're full of the mad, bad and the sad. The real crims, the Flash Harrys, they rarely get nicked, and with me . . . with me it was all down to one nose-in-the-air posh cow of a chief magistrate back in the early days. It was only my second appearance before the beaks but she said I "needed catching for my own good" and that bench sent me down for three months. But that put me on the wrong path and I stayed on the wrong path. Prison does no good to no one. You know, even the copper who arrested me said that he thought it was a harsh sentence. I'd been fined once and he said he thought I'd get another fine or a period of probation, but not three months in juvenile detention.'

'For . . .?'

'Shoplifting.' Bonner looked up at the ceiling. 'Shoplifting.'

'It does sound a bit harsh, I have to agree,' Tom Ainsclough commented.

'And it was a pair of jeans. I just wanted a new pair of strides to impress the girl I had a date with that evening. I got arrested after leaving the clothes shop, then taken to the cop shop, charged and allowed to go to await summons to the Magistrates Court, and the richest thing was . . . do you know the richest thing of all? She didn't turn up for the date; she stood me up. I mean . . . is there justice? Me on the wrong track, and all for a girl who didn't turn up anyway. I mean, it was all for nothing, all for sweet Fanny Adams, and if someone had given that magistrate her raw meat that morning I wouldn't have been sent down. But she needed a victim . . . hungry people need victims . . . her and the other two beaks. Mind you, in the East End you're nothing if you're not a villain, so I would have gone down for something sometime, and I was running with the wolves. One old copper, not the one who nicked me for half-inching the jeans, a geezer called Carris, Mr Carris . . . Police Constable Carris . . . never got promoted, never got out of uniform. He was close to retiring when I was still a teenager. He was an old-fashioned copper and he would take me down an alley, clip me across the ear and he'd say, "Look here, Claude, I know you, you're not a bad lad so don't run with the wolves. Get home and take care of your old mum. No good will come of running with a pack like that . . ." and was he right or was he right?' Claude Bonner fell silent, then he said, 'He died, Mr Carris, the old copper. I didn't think his family would want me at his funeral but I went up to the cemetery the next day, I mean the very next day, and laid some flowers on his grave. I did that for him.'

'That was good of you, Claude.' Yewdall beamed at him.

Claude Bonner shrugged. 'There was a few of us did that; went to the cemetery the day after he was planted. We didn't plan it as a gang, just all acted as individuals, and we didn't buy the flowers anyway, we picked them from the park didn't we? But it's the thought that counts. Wrapped them in a rubber band the posties drop as they do their walk; if you want a rubber band they say all you have to do is walk along the pavement, before too long you see one. So that's what I did, left the house and walked towards the park and before too long I saw a rubber band.

Walked into the park and I picked a nice bunch of daffodils and carried them down the road to the cemetery. There were quite a lot of daffodils in the park the day of his funeral and not many the day after. All the lads who had had their ears clipped by Mr Carris and then sent home, they paid their respects to him. Nice old copper he was, Mr Carris, nice old geezer; based at Clapton Road Police Station.'

'So, Claude,' Penny Yewdall brought the conversation into focus, 'Desmond Holst aka Ralph Payne?'

'Yeah, Des or Ralph, two geezers in the same body but not like the lunatics, you know; those split personality types you read about, I don't mean that.' Claude Bonner paused. 'I mean he was born Desmond Holst and married Pearl Harley, then after that he began to call himself Ralph Payne, like it made some difference to him, and he became a blagger . . . like it made it possible to go ducking and diving with a new name . . . like it made it all right because it wasn't Desmond Holst that was doing it, it was Ralph Payne. Anyway, that pleased his old lady because she didn't want no council workman for a husband, she wanted someone she could visit in prison and that was Des . . . or Ralph, keeping Pearl happy by being a blagger. It gave Pearl street cred and made her family like her and her husband. It was just that sort of clan. Later though, Desmond . . . or Ralph . . . but later he wanted to make honest money, just honest money, so he did that; went against his wife and family and became Desmond Holst, honest Des Holst. Don't know what else I can tell you about him, poor old soul.'

'You are known to us as a criminal associate,' Tom Ainsclough explained, 'so anything you can tell us about him will be of interest. Where did you meet?'

'In the Scrubs; we met when we were in Wormwood Scrubs together. We were cell mates and we just clicked. You know how it can happen that two people meet and they just like each other from the outset?'

'Yes,' Ainsclough replied, 'I know exactly what you mean.'

'Well, that was me and Desmond. He called himself Desmond from the start, only later did I learn of his other handle. He just wasn't up to being a blagger, his heart wasn't in it, just did it to please Pearl, but he did it anyway. We kept in touch and did jobs together, got banged up together. Then, he went on a Government-sponsored bricklaying course and learned the trade, got work and got himself a reputation as a steady hand. Wanted to do it all the time but with a ball and chain like Pearl it wasn't easy for him, not easy at all. Pearl of the Harley crew . . . well, she didn't want no brickie for a husband, not if she was going to walk her manor like she wanted to walk it. So he kept going out on missions with some heavy boys, but no one can walk two paths forever and so one day he was a bricklayer and nothing else . . . and Pearl, well she wasn't happy with that but by then she was well past her sell-by date. Desmond told me she tried to be a cougar, but she was even too old for that so her old horizons came rushing in . . . Sorry I can't ask you to sit down,' Claude Bonner added, 'there's only two chairs.'

'Don't worry,' Ainsclough replied with a brief smile.

'Suppose there is one thing that might interest you. Me and Des went out for a beer one evening, early doors, when all the old gaffers go for a drink before the youth take over the pubs for the night and you can't get a seat or hear yourself think. Anyway, he was full of guilt; he had a wad of fivers and tens in his old sky rocket, but was full of guilt about where he had got it from.'

'Another job?'

'Something like that, but something different as well. He was calling himself Desmond full-time by then and had stopped crooking . . . but it was something that upset him badly . . . something that happened when Arnie Rainbird got out after a ten stretch.'

'Arnie Rainbird?' Penny Yewdall reached for her notebook.

'You'll have records on him even if you haven't heard of him yourself. Haven't heard of him myself for a while and I like to keep in touch, so he must be keeping his head well down, but that doesn't mean he's tending his racing pigeons.'

'We'll look him up when we get back.' Yewdall scribbled on her notepad. 'So what did happen when Arnie Rainbird got out of prison?'

'This is off the record . . .'

'Yes.'

'It didn't come from me,' Claude Bonner began to sound agitated, 'I won't be signing any statement.'

'All off the record,' Tom Ainsclough spoke in a calm, reassuring voice, 'it didn't come from you, Claude.'

'OK. Well they threw a party for him, didn't they?'

'Nothing unusual in that.' Yewdall looked puzzled. 'So why was Desmond upset?'

'Because it was not just any party, so Desmond said.'

'What did Desmond tell you about?' Yewdall pressed.

'That it lasted a full week . . . longer in fact; took in two weekends so Des said. It was held at a big house in Bedfordshire, as much as you can snort, and eat and drink, and they laid on the girls, as was normal when a blagger comes out after a long stretch.'

'Again . . . it's just the length the party lasted which is unusual, but why was he upset?' Yewdall tapped her pen on her notebook.

'Well, Des said the girls were cheated. They rounded up the girls from King's Cross, promised to pay them two hundred pounds for a night's work. It was Des that drove the bus that took them up to Bedfordshire . . . He had a public service vehicle licence as well as brickie's cards.'

'I see,' Ainsclough commented, 'handy sort of guy.'

'Yes he was.'

'A night's work for two hundred pounds,' Yewdall said, 'that's generous.'

'Yes, and this was some years ago as well when it had more . . . what's it called, than today?'

'Spending power?' Yewdall offered.

'Yes, that's the term. So, according to Desmond they got on the bus, and remember, two hundred pounds for a night's work about seven years ago, well that can buy a lot of quality, so these were the expensive ones, young and slender. About twenty, twenty-five of them, all serious-minded but all eager to earn good money, got on the bus, and then two minders got on . . . and Des starts the journey north, and the girls wonder where they're going and start asking questions and the minders are saying "It's OK, soon be there", but after a while they start getting worried and one of the minders snarls at them and threatens them with a slap, then they cool . . . but Des said he could begin to smell the fear in the bus.'

'I've heard of worse,' Yewdall commented. 'It still doesn't explain why Desmond was as upset as you say he was.'

'I'll explain.' Claude Bonner looked at the floor as if searching for inspiration or strength. 'In a nutshell it turns out that the night's work was a week's work.'

'They stayed for the whole of the party?' Yewdall gasped. 'So it was two hundred pounds for a week's work? That's cheap for a high-class girl.'

'More than a week,' Bonner replied, 'as I said, it included two weekends. The first Friday evening then the next eight days plus the second Sunday up to about seven o'clock . . . and then they got bunged fifty quid.'

'Fifty pounds!' Yewdall gasped.

'Yes, so the night's work meant the first evening and then an extra eight and a half days after that and the two hundred quid turned out to be fifty.'

'So why did they stay?' Yewdall asked.

'They didn't stay.' Bonner shrugged. 'They were kept against their will.'

'Imprisoned!' Yewdall gasped, once again.

'But there's more.'

'More?' Yewdall looked at Ainsclough.

'Seems so . . . it was the attitude of the girls . . . on the way up they were cooperative then they became frightened . . . on the way back they were just quiet, like they'd seen something, so Des said.'

'Subdued?' Ainsclough suggested.

'That's a good word for what Des described, they were subdued and as they got off the bus where it stopped they just accepted the fifty quid without a word of complaint, like they were just happy to be alive, so Des said. He said they all seemed like they just wanted to get home, and have a long, hot shower.'

'How were they kept against their will?' Yewdall pressed, feeling herself growing more and more angry. 'Locked in a room?'

'They had their clothes taken from them, so Des told me, no clothes and no shoes. You see, Des was just the bus driver, not invited into the house. He had to spend the whole time by the bus, sleeping in it, using the toilet in the coach . . . had his food brought out to him. He was the guy in the coach and all these flash cars around him, Rollers, Mercs, Range Rovers, Porsches . . . but he never saw anything of the party. But one night one of the girls walked out of the front door, just opens it and walks out, that's when Des knew they'd taken their clothes and shoes. The drive was long, covered in rough gravel, the girl wasn't escaping, she just wanted a bit of time to herself. She sat with Des and they had a fag together. She didn't tell Des anything but she said that there was an old brass in there keeping the girls in line . . . and this girl had a right shiner.'

'A black eye?' Ainsclough pressed. 'You're not telling us something . . . come on, Claude, you're doing well, don't string us along.'

'I'm scared of Pearl; she has very heavy connections, so this didn't come from me.' Bonner looked at Ainsclough.

'Agreed,' Tom Ainsclough replied reassuringly, 'fully agreed.'

'Yes,' Yewdall replied, 'also fully agreed.'

'Well, the last time I saw Des . . . we went out for a beer and he got depressed . . . and said something about "them having a bad end".'

'Them?' Ainsclough repeated.

'Yes, governor, "them", so more than one.'

'OK.'

'And then he said, "they should get a proper burial . . . eventually".'

'Should, as in the sense that they deserved a proper burial?' Ainsclough queried, 'Or should in the sense that with a bit of luck they will get a proper burial?'

'I thought the second way, guv.' Bonner ran his stubby fingers through his unkempt hair. 'Least, I took it to mean that . . . that's what it sounded like.'

'As if he had done something to ensure that they would get a proper burial?' Ainsclough clarified.

'That's what I thought he meant by the way he said the word "should" . . .' Bonner paused. 'He also said he had to keep the boxes hidden in the garden shed until the wet weather came. Dunno what he meant by that, guv.'

'And it was connected to the party?' Ainsclough asked.

'Yes, certain. Des was talking about the party and then said

"they should get a proper burial", as though he had done something to make sure of it. I didn't press him. So something bad
happened at that party. Des ran a bus load of high-cost brasses
from the King's Cross meat rack up to Bedfordshire, then ran
them back a week later with all of them too scared to complain
. . . and some geezers would get a proper burial some time in
the future.'

'But Desmond saw nothing?'

'That's what he said, so it was like part of his gofering meant
he had a mess to clean up, like bodies to get rid of . . . but
something definitely went down at that party; something really,
really heavy went down at Arnie Rainbird's getting out party.'

John Shaftoe pulled the anglepoise arm downwards so that the
microphone attached to the end of it was level with his mouth.
'Damn Dykk,' he muttered. 'Damn the man.'

'Sorry?' Harry Vicary stood against the wall of the pathology
laboratory wearing disposable green paper coveralls with
matching hat and slippers.

'Oh . . . nothing . . . nothing.' Shaftoe half turned to Vicary.
'It seems that Dykk has just taken against me. I don't mean "just"
in the sense of recently, I mean "just" in the sense that there
seems to be no reason for his hostility.'

'I see, sir,' Vicary replied, 'such things happen in all work
places.'

'I suppose, but with Dykk it's just plain snobbery if you ask
me. He took an instant dislike to me from day one. A working-
class, pigeon fancying coal miner's son from Yorkshire just
can't became a doctor . . . not in his hospital anyway. He's a
tall guy and one of his little tricks is to push the microphone
up out of my reach after he completes his post-mortems . . . but
he is the learned professor of pathology here and I am not, so
it is what it is and it is the way of it.' Shaftoe paused. 'Now,
dem bones, dem bones, dem dry bones,' Shaftoe hummed gently
to himself in an attempt to lift the gravity of the pathology
laboratory, but Shaftoe's attempt at humour only seemed to
succeed in making the pathology laboratory assistant, Billy
Button, tremble and whimper, not, thought Vicary, unlike a dog
which wants something. If there ever was a man more ill-suited

to his job, Vicary further thought, it was the quivering, slight figure of Billy Button.

'Not to worry, Billy, you won't end up like this.' Shaftoe smiled at the whimpering figure and once again Vicary observed Shaftoe extending more acceptance, more sympathy, more solace to the wretched Billy Button than he could ever muster. The small and retiring Button was, Vicary thought, more suited to pushing a lawnmower for whichever London borough he lived in, or some other lowly occupation. Watching Billy Button in the pathology laboratory, Vicary always felt, was akin to watching a claustrophobic in a coal mine or an agoraphobic in the middle of the tundra.

'No, sir,' was Billy Button's feeble reply.

'No worries, I am sure that both our lady wives will have us most properly interred or see that our ashes are placed in an urn.'

'Urn,' Billy Button whined, 'that would be better, sir, much better. It is the thought of being buried alive that is so frightful and my poor body being eaten by worms . . . oh . . . it is too horrible.'

Shaftoe picked up one of the skulls and began to examine it. Two of the six stainless steel tables in the laboratory had been utilized by Shaftoe, one full skeleton lying on each. 'The first did in fact used to happen.' Shaftoe replaced the skull and picked up one of the long bones. 'It happened so frequently in fact that sextons would keep a stout metal stave with a pointed end and a sledge hammer to hand in case they heard banging coming from the ground where a coffin had been recently buried. They would drive the stake down into the coffin, smashing a hole through the lid so as to get air down to the luckless victim and keep said victim alive, while they and any helpers they could find dug down to him or her. It was a race against time because they had to get down there before the build-up of carbon dioxide caused the victim to asphyxiate . . . but nowadays no one is buried alive because corpses are embalmed. But, occasionally, a person is pronounced life extinct when in fact they are still with us, alive, if not actually kicking, but that happens so rarely that it makes international news when it does.' Shaftoe ran his fingertip along the length of the bone. 'There was a case in the UK, quite recently, wherein an adult female had been pronounced dead

. . . no life signs at all . . . she even had the unmistakable clam-
miness of touch which fresh corpses have, and she was put in
a drawer at minus one degree Celsius to await embalming and
the coffin. And then a mortuary assistant, a bloke just like you,
Billy, opened her drawer and saw that a tear had formed in the
corner of her eye and he realized that that meant she was still
alive. He raised the alarm and the lady was revived and made
a complete recovery. It was just not her time. In Eastern Europe,
in the old days, they could not comprehend the notion of a coma
and they thought that a dead body which did not bloat was the
work of the devil, and so they either decapitated the person or
drove a stake through their heart.'

'Like Dracula?' Billy Button's voice shook.

'And as for the worms, Billy, well you can forget them. You
know –' Shaftoe swapped the skulls over – 'I just have a notion
that the skulls were wrongly placed. I think that is correct but
DNA will confirm it. You know, if I had a fiver for every person
that has said they want to be cremated or have their loved ones
cremated because they don't like the idea of worms chomping
away at their flesh, chomping away at their loved ones' remains
. . . well, I'd be a rich man.' Shaftoe paused. 'These two men
died terrible deaths, but you see, Billy, worms are subsurface
creatures, they never go lower than eighteen inches below the
surface, or half a metre in new speak. They don't go down as
far as the coffin.'

'Still, I'll be turned to ash just the same.'

'As you wish, Billy.' Shaftoe turned to consider the second
skeleton. 'Me, I want my bit of Merrie England to call my own
for eternity . . . or at least for a few hundred years or so. How
about you, Mr Vicary, a coffin or an urn? Have you decided?'

'Cardboard coffin for me,' Vicary raised his voice so that it
carried across the echoing laboratory which smelled strongly of
formaldehyde.

'A cardboard coffin?' Shaftoe looked puzzled.

'Yes, sir, my wife and I have talked about it and we have both
decided upon a green burial.'

'Well, good for you and your lady wife I say, good for you.'
Shaftoe beamed at him. 'I confess I have also given the notion
a little thought. How does it work?'

'They dig a vertical grave and lower the coffin of reinforced cardboard in head upwards, fill in and plant a tree over the coffin,' Vicary explained. 'Eventually you and the coffin will decay, leaving the tree to mark your final resting place. You can't choose the type of tree, though, because if they allowed that everyone would want an oak tree.'

'Don't know about that.' Shaftoe grinned. 'I think I'd like an apple tree, a Cox's Orange Pippin growing over me, or some other traditional English apple. 'So . . . Billy . . .' Shaftoe turned to Billy Button. 'Tell me about the bones, help me earn my crust . . . tell me what you see.'

'Male skulls, sir.'

'Yes. Good.'

'Most probably European . . . they seem too large to be Asian.'

'Again, good. Age . . . what sort of age were they when they died?'

'Twenty-five years plus, sir?' Button offered.

'Why do you say that?' Shaftoe smiled at him.

'The skulls have fully closed, sir.'

'Yes, but knitted, Billy,' Shaftoe explained, 'we use the term knitted . . . but, yes, they have fully knitted which happens at about the twenty-fifth year of life.'

'Knitted,' Button parroted, 'knitted, sir.'

Shaftoe stepped back from the table. 'Go for it, Billy, tell me more; tell me what you see.'

'Can I look into the mouths, sir?' Billy asked nervously.

'Yes, carry on; tell me what you see and what you then deduce from what you observe. The jaws move freely on both skulls.'

Harry Vicary became intrigued by Shaftoe's attitude towards Billy Button, noting especially how he empowered Button by including him in the post-mortem proceedings. Shaftoe was teaching him about leadership, about management of personnel. It was a wholly unexpected lesson, but also wholly welcome.

Button advanced on the first of the skeletons, took the skull and opened the mouth. He replaced it nervously and then examined the mouth of the second skull. 'There's hardly any teeth, sir,' he said, 'in either skull.'

'Yes . . .' Shaftoe spoke encouragingly, 'as if?'

'Well, as if they had all been knocked out.'

'My thoughts exactly.' Shaftoe smiled at Button. 'My thoughts exactly. It is in fact very unusual to see skulls with so few teeth, except where they have been deliberately knocked out as if in retribution for some gangland infraction of rules. So tell me about the bones?'

'The bones, sir, well, they are all dismembered, not attached to each other . . . even the spinal vertebrae have been separated.'

'Yes, I had to guess which bones went with the other bones when I was reassembling the skeletons but I think I got it right.'

'The femurs are intact, sir,' Button added.

'Yes. Why is that useful?'

'It helps determine the height of the person, sir.'

'Good. We have all four femurs, two significantly longer than the other two. In a person of normal build the femur length,' Shaftoe asked, 'is what approximate percentage of the overall height?'

'Thirty percent, sir.'

'Good man.' Shaftoe picked up a yellow retractable metal tape measure and measured one of the femurs of the other skeleton. 'We have one person here,' he announced, 'who, when he was alive, was five foot four inches tall, and his mate, when he was also with us, was five foot eleven. That is very approximate and possibly on the shorter side.'

'Understood.' Vicary continued to observe from the side of the pathology laboratory.

'So, well done, Billy.' Shaftoe smiled at Button who beamed with pride, like, Vicary thought, a rewarded child. Shaftoe pondered the skeletons. 'You know there are an awful lot of fractures here . . . an awful lot . . . no teeth to speak of but no damage to either of the skulls, and the scorching of the bones, that is widespread and has reached inside the fractures, so definitely peri-mortem, and yet, as I said, the skulls are intact.' He turned to Vicary. 'You know, Mr Vicary, this is like going back to pre-revolutionary France.'

'In what way, sir?' Vicary asked. 'Can't say that history was ever my strong point.'

'In the French Revolution in the eighteenth century, the revolutionaries had their cry of "Liberty, Equality and Fraternity".'

'Yes, I have heard that.'

'The request for equality,' Shaftoe continued, 'wasn't a request, or a demand for equality in the communist sense; what the revolutionaries wanted was equality before the law. They wanted one single penal code and one single set of laws. You see, in pre-revolutionary France there was quite literally one law for the rich and one for the poor.'

'Really!' Vicary smiled. 'I didn't know that.'

'Yes, it is quite true; to be specific there was one law for the aristocrats and one law for the commoners.' Shaftoe paused and examined a clavicle. 'Yes, like yourself I am no historian but I believe there were few crimes for which an aristocrat could be executed but many crimes for which a commoner could be put to death, and also there were different methods of execution depending upon your social status. So that whilst an aristocrat was guillotined, which was quite wrongly thought to be a pain-less and an instantaneous death—'

'Wrongly?' Vicary queried. 'I always thought . . .'

Shaftoe replaced the clavicle upon the stainless steel table. 'No, I assure you, death by Madame la Guillotine is very painful, but the condemned person does not make a sound because the vocal chords have been severed. There is also evidence that the executed person can remain conscious for up to fifteen minutes, more even, before succumbing to the injury.'

'That's interesting.' Vicary raised his eyebrows. 'Really very interesting; fascinating, in fact.'

'Isn't it?' Shaftoe drew a deep breath. 'It is . . . it was not at all quick and painless, but the point is that when the commoners were executed in pre-revolutionary France they were "broken on the wheel". That method of execution involved the condemned being tied to a large cartwheel which was positioned on the horizontal plane and then being beaten to death by the executioner, who used a heavy iron bar for the purpose, but during this the skull was not touched for fear of rendering the condemned unconscious or for fear of killing him too rapidly.'

'Strewth,' Vicary gasped, 'no wonder they had a revolution.'

'Indeed.' Shaftoe nodded. 'As you say, no wonder they had a revolution.'

'So you think, sir,' Vicary asked, 'that these two men were executed; that these bones are the remains of a slow execution?'

'Possibly, but don't rush me; don't rush your fences, Inspector.'

'Sorry,' Vicary mumbled.

'Let's just say that it could very well be that these two men were executed by being battered to death. It has a strong sense of premeditation about it and a strong sense of retribution. It was a slow, painful end for them, as if these two men upset the wrong geezer; as if they trod on the wrong set of toes, poor boys. The fact that the skulls are intact suggests the bones were separated to aid disposal, like I suggested earlier today. We can do a facial reconstruction with the skulls, obtain an accurate age at death from what teeth remain, and extract DNA . . . all that can be done and all that will be done.'

'Thank you, sir.'

'But as to cause of death, I am afraid that will be inconclusive. These injuries might amount to a cause of death in themselves . . . but . . . if they were hospitalized in time they could have recovered, and it was possibly occasioned in a remote place where the felons were not frightened of being disturbed, but that, as I said earlier, is also speculation.'

Penny Yewdall sat back in her chair with one knee raised, resting it on the edge of her desk as the wearing of her trouser suit permitted her to do. She leafed through the files which she had upon her desktop, occasionally taking a sip of coffee. Henry Vicary entered the CID room Yewdall shared with Ainsclough, who at that moment was tapping upon a computer keyboard. Vicary thought they looked busy and said so.

'Yes, boss.' Yewdall looked up with a ready smile. 'I'm trying to find a link, if there is one.'

'A link?' Vicary sank into the chair in front of Frankie Brunnie's desk.

'Yes, sir.' Yewdall sat forward. 'We have, we think, established that the note in the wall was written and left by one Desmond Holst who is also known—'

'Was,' Ainsclough corrected her, gently so.

'Yes, sorry, was . . . was also known as Ralph Payne.'

'Yes, I read your record in the file; Holst is his good guy name, Payne is his blagger's name.'

'Yes, sir,' Yewdall responded attentively, 'and here we have the file on Arnie Rainbird. He was charged with murder, but his plea of not guilty to murder but guilty to manslaughter was accepted by the Crown. He was sentenced to fifteen years and got out in ten. He was released seven years ago and has been quiet since then, by which I mean we haven't heard about him. He seems to be a career criminal so doubtless he'll be up to something.'

'Oh doubtless, as you say, doubtless.' Vicary pivoted Brunnie's chair to left and right. 'Doubtless.'

'We visited Des Holst's one-time long-time mate and fellow con, one Claude Bonner. He's a sad old blagger, totally burnt-out case, but he is the one who mentioned a house party up in Bedfordshire.'

'Yes, I read that also, something went on there. Is he a reliable witness?'

'Seems so.'

'Well . . . a pinch of salt.' Ainsclough tapped the top of the computer screen. The computer was down for updating this morning so we had to get Claude Bonner's address by phoning Wandsworth Prison.'

'Yes?'

'Claude reckons he was sent down after only his second appearance before the magistrates.'

'A bit harsh,' Vicary commented.

'So we thought, but the computer's back up now . . . I have his record here, he actually went down for the first time on his tenth appearance . . . so . . . he's untruthful and more than a little prone to self-pity.'

'I see.' Vicary grinned. 'But we can't dismiss what he told us.'

'No, sir.'

'So there was a week long party to celebrate Arnie Rainbird's release, with a bus load of girls from King's Cross, rounded up on the pavement with the lure of two hundred pounds for a night's work. Then a week later they are returned to London, given a quarter of that and not one of them complains. Something terrified them.'

'Seems so, sir.' Yewdall absent-mindedly chewed the tip of

her ballpoint. 'And Ralph or Desmond saw nothing; he was kept out of the way, slept in the bus for the whole week and had his meals brought out to him.'

'That is a very low form of gang member.' Vicary glanced out of the window. 'I didn't read that in your records.'

'No, sir, it was hearsay. I didn't think it was relevant . . .' Penny Yewdall's voice trailed off as Vicary gave her a despairing look and raised his right eyebrow. 'Yes, sir . . . sorry, sir . . . everything goes in the pot. I'll add it directly.'

'Yes, if you would. So tell me about Arnie Rainbird?'

'He's fifty-five years of age now, sir.' Penny Yewdall put the file she was reading down and picked up another from the pile on her desk and opened it. 'As I said, he has had no convictions since getting out of prison, which, as we agree, doesn't mean anything . . . anything except he's probably very good at keeping himself off the radar. He went down for stabbing a youth in a public house. Despite the guilty plea and the reduced charge they kept him on the move all right; Parkhurst, Strangeways, Full Sutton, Durham, Wakefield . . .'

'So do we know why he was considered an escape risk?' Vicary ran his hand through his hair.

'No, we don't, but nonetheless he was paroled after ten years.' Yewdall read the file.

'What do you read into that, Penny?'

'I think he knew how to play the game, boss, he knew how to work his ticket . . . a model inmate from day one, polite, cooperative, joined the Christian Union and always the first to volunteer when the showers needed scrubbing down. Never any bother at all. Any risk in respect to him seems to have come from the outside, someone trying to spring him, hence the frequent moves. But you can't deny a con parole for that; it seems to be a case of "spring me if you can but if you can't I'll work towards an early parole" sort of situation.' Yewdall shrugged. 'That number.'

'I see.' Vicary clasped his hands behind his head. 'You're right, can't deny him early parole for what his mates might do. Who are his mates, do we know?'

'He has one previous for armed robbery – collected five years for that – and he was one of a gang of four, which probably means a gang of ten or twelve.'

'Yes.' Vicary nodded. 'Chiefs above them and gofers below them.'

'Yes, sir.' Yewdall continued to read the file. 'All four of them went down at Southwark Crown Court.' She reached for other files on her desk. 'The three others were Fergus McAlpine—'

'A Scotsman?'

Penny Yewdall grinned broadly. 'You'd think so, wouldn't you, boss? I mean, with a name like that you'd think he had come from north of the border, but in fact, according to this file, he was born in Dartford.'

Vicary laughed. 'Probably has Scottish parents, dare say I should have seen that coming, though.'

'The second man in the gang was one Clive Allison, also born in Dartford.'

'School chums?' Vicary proposed.

'Possibly, boss, no indication of that here, but they were all very good at keeping their heads below the parapet. Nothing since they came out after five years in the slammer. And the third geezer, he's the exception, he's a bloke called Charlie Magg; he alone of the gang of four is presently a guest of Her Majesty.'

'He is?' Vicary beamed.

'Brixton, sir, on remand, he's awaiting trial for Grievous Bodily Harm and he has much previous for East End sort of villainy – burglary, car theft, a few GBHs – so he seems to be a bit of a hard man; then he teamed up with Arnie Rainbird's mob and also managed to keep his head down after his release, but only until a couple of months ago when he was arrested and remanded.' Yewdall put the file down on her desktop.

'And you think that they all might have been at the house party?' Vicary asked.

'It seems likely, sir,' Yewdall agreed, 'they seem to be good mates. They'd be wanting to throw a party for Rainbird's release, and what a party it seems to have been. Whatever happened shook up Desmond Holst quite badly, to the extent that five or so years after the party he was still shaken by it.'

'The bodies were in some mess,' Vicary spoke slowly, 'I haven't got Mr Shaftoe's report yet, too early to expect it and there are still tests to be done, but he said it was like the two men had been broken on the wheel.'

'What does that mean, sir?' Yewdall asked.

Vicary explained what was meant by being 'broken on the wheel' and watched the colour drain from Yewdall's face as he did so. 'All he could say was that the injuries and the scorching of the bones were peri-mortem, and that he could not identify a conclusive cause of death.'

'The old "Mile End Road Retribution Foxtrot", you think, sir?' Yewdall asked.

'Possibly . . . and we also don't know whether the murder of the two men happened at the week long party given for Rainbird's release or whether it was another unconnected incident that traumatized Desmond Holst, and terrified twenty plus streetwise women into silence.' Vicary paused. 'You know if we can find just one of those women, just one, then one will lead to two and two to three, and if one, just one, will talk . . . Do we know any of their names?'

'Not yet, sir.' Yewdall's voice had a strong note of determination. 'Not yet.'

'Good for you, Penny, good for you. And the next step, apart from tracking down as many of those girls as you can, is . . .?'

'We – me and Tom here – are going to pay a call on Charlie Magg in Brixton.'

'For?'

'Just a chat, sir, just to take the measure of him. If he's on remand he'll be looking at going back to prison for a while . . . See what response we get.'

'Very well.' Vicary nodded his agreement. 'Tom? Anything to add?'

'We also thought we would contact all the prisons Arnie Rainbird has been in; see if he had any consistent visitors in those ten years.'

'Good.' Vicary stood. 'That'll keep you two busy tomorrow, but of those tasks, identifying as many of the girls as you can, that is the most important; that and the identity of the woman who controlled them.'

An observer would have seen a short, rotund man dressed in a lightweight summer jacket with baggy corduroy trousers. The man would be carrying a khaki-coloured canvas knapsack over his right shoulder. The man would have been observed leaving the Royal London Hospital by a small door in the side of the building and then walking away with head down, shuffling gait, keeping himself closer to the walls of the buildings than to the road, and always, always being the one to move to one side when another foot passenger approached him. The observer would watch as the man halted outside the entrance to the public bar of a public house as if pondering whether to call in for a beer or two, and then, as if thinking the better of it, continued to shuffle along the pavement. By now the observer would think he was looking at a working man, unskilled or perhaps semi-skilled, who was making his way home after a day's work. In fact, the observer would be looking at John Shaftoe, MD MRCP FRCPath.

Shaftoe took the tube from Aldgate East to King's Cross St Pancras and from there he took the overground suburban service to Brookmans Park. From Brookmans Park he walked from the railway station, over the railway bridge, passed the Brookman Pub and Restaurant on his left-hand side, a 1930s red brick roadhouse with a parade of shops to his right. He ambled into Bradmore Green and the beginning of leafy suburbia and put himself at the steady climb to take him into Brookmans Avenue, which was lined with detached houses, often with twin garages, and wide U-shaped 'in-and-out' driveways. He continued walking up the road noticing again how the homeowners' cars, the Rolls-Royces, the Mercedes-Benzes, Porsches and Audis, were parked in the driveways of the houses and the more lowly cars of the domestic help, the Toyotas and the small Fords, were parked in the roadway. It was just not done for a home help to park their car in their employer's driveway, but this was Brookmans Park, where even the domestics travel to work by car. Shaftoe followed the road as it bent round to the right and walked until he was near the top of the lane, whereupon he turned into a gravel-surfaced U-shaped driveway and let himself through the front door of the house. He was warmly greeted by his wife who told him she had prepared a cold supper for him, given the weather, to which he replied, 'Champion, pet, just champion.'

After a supper taken in the early evening, as was the custom in the north of England, John and Linda Shaftoe, both from Thurnscoe, pronounced, 'Thurns-ku', near Barnsley, and both children of Yorkshire coal miners, and both uncomfortable in well-set Hertfordshire, settled down for a quiet evening at home, enjoying each other's warm company and speaking only to plan their next 'base-touching trip'.

'Londoners are requested to make only essential use of water.' The mantra, repeated frequently on the radio, ran through Penny Yewdall's mind as she stood in the street outside her house cleaning her car; her small, red Vauxhall which she often said was 'good enough for London but not any further'. She cleaned the lights and the windscreen, windows and the outside mirrors, but allowed the bodywork to remain unwashed. She stood back from the car as the sun settled and looked up and down Tusker Road and noted with pleasure that all the other motor cars parked in the street had the same badge of good citizenship displayed by their owners, not one being sparkling clean. She carried the soapy water back into her house and poured it on the small lawn at the rear of the building. Plants, she knew, did not like soapy water, but it was better than no water at all.

THREE

The two-tone grey phone on Harry Vicary's desk warbled softly. He glanced out of his office window and the summer sky over London that morning as he let the phone ring twice before he picked it up leisurely.

'Detective Inspector Vicary, Murder and Serious Crime Unit,' he said in a calm voice.

'Lady on the phone for you, sir; lady member of the public.' The voice of the switchboard operator had a nervous tone to it, and Vicary thought he was probably newly appointed. 'She is responding to the E-fits printed in today's *Standard*. She says that she thinks she knows the two men.'

'I see.' Vicary reached instinctively for his notepad and pen. 'Put her through, please.'

The line clicked and a querulous female voice said, 'Hello?'

'DI Vicary.'

'I may know the men in today's paper, in the *Standard*.'

'Oh, yes?'

'Yes. Would one of them have a scar on his cheek? He said he was attacked when he was in prison, you see.'

Vicary smiled to himself. 'Well, madam, the prints, the images in the paper, are E-fits; they are only an impression of what they might have looked like. So one may indeed have had a scar but we don't know that, not for sure.'

'Well, if it is the one I think it is he had a scar on his cheek . . . he did . . . on his right cheek.' The voice seemed to grow in confidence as Vicary identified an East London accent. 'And it said one was short and the other was tall?'

'Yes, there is a distinct height difference.'

'That's what the paper said, and they went missing five years ago?'

'More than five,' Vicary corrected her, 'we don't know how much more than five though.'

'Sounds like those two . . . only they left a lot of their stuff behind you see.'

'I understand,' Vicary replied. 'They were lodgers?'

'Lodgers, yes, they were lodgers in the basement. I let out rooms, do you see? I've been letting out rooms since my old man went before; he's in a better place anyway, God rest his old soul. He was an awkward old geezer but God rest him just the same . . . but he was an awkward old man at the end.'

'Yes, madam.'

'But I don't like doing it, renting out. I don't like having strangers in my house but I can't make ends meet no other way.'

'Yes, madam. So, madam, you are where?'

'Stepney, darling. I'm in Stepney, good old, sunny Stepney.'

'Can I please take your name, madam?' Vicary asked.

'Me, darling, I am old Violet . . . old Violet they call me. Violet Mayfield is my name.'

'Violet Mayfield.' Vicary wrote the name on his notepad. 'What's your address in Stepney, Mrs Mayfield?'

'Ninety-four Matlock Street, darling,' the woman replied, 'top end, near White Horse Road. If you're coming by tube you need to get off at Stepney East.'

'Stepney East,' Vicary echoed, though he knew his officers would be making the journey by car.

'Yes, darling, short walk after that.'

'Yes. Will you be at home for the rest of the morning, Mrs Mayfield?' Vicary asked.

'Rest of the old day, more like it,' Violet Mayfield replied, 'I have no need to go out anywhere until bingo at seven o'clock this evening, darling.'

'Good, good.' Vicary ran his hands through his hair. 'I will send two of my officers round to see you,' he advised. 'They will be with you later this morning.'

'Two?' Violet Mayfield allowed a note of surprise to enter her voice. 'You need two?'

Vicary smiled. 'Oh, yes. We like to go in pairs in case we get lost.'

'Oh . . . really?' Violet Mayfield sounded surprised. 'Well I never. That's a good idea. What happens if you do get lost?'

'We ask a policeman.' Vicary grinned, though he spoke without a trace of humour in his voice. 'But thank you for phoning us, Mrs Mayfield, we do appreciate it.' He replaced the telephone handset, gently so.

Harry Vicary stood, tearing off the top page from his notepad as he did so, and strode down the CID corridor to the office occupied by DS Victor Swannell. He stood in the doorway of Swannell's office. 'Busy, Victor?'

Victor Swannell looked up at Vicary and then indicated the mass of paper on his desktop, 'Me, sir? Always busy, that's me, boss. Never enough hours in the day,' Swannell replied with a broad grin. 'But for you, boss, I am at your service, ready, willing and able.'

'Good man, Victor.' Vicary held up the sheet of paper he had torn from his notepad. 'Name and address of a lady who has just phoned, she seems to think that she might recognize the two E-fits in today's *Standard*.'

'The *Evening Standard* which comes out in the morning?' Swannell stood as Vicary approached his desk and handed him the sheet of paper.

'Yes, as you say,' Vicary replied, 'they don't hang about; they like to hit the street as soon as. But this lady sounds promising; she sounds very interesting indeed. If she is right, at least one of the bodies was that of a jailbird; he's got form, and one had a scar which will probably help aid identification. Anyway, Penny Yewdall and Tom Ainsclough are chasing up a lead; they're south of the river in Brixton Prison. Can you visit this address and talk to this lady, Mrs Mayfield? Take Frankie Brunnie with you.'

'Yes, boss.'

'See what you see.' Vicary smiled. 'Find what you find.'

'Yes, boss.' Swannell reached for his jacket. 'I'm on it.'

'You know that he's still on a life-support machine, Charlie. You know the sketch; breathing and gurgling into tubes, wired up to a monitor, his face still looking like a massive beetroot. You know, don't you?' Penny Yewdall spoke calmly but looked intently at Charlie Magg.

'And that, Charlie,' Tom Ainsclough added, 'is after ten weeks, still no improvement. It's touch and go, Charlie, touch and go, and you know very well what that means.' Charlie Magg remained steadfastly silent. His face and eyes were devoid of any emotion that either Ainsclough or Yewdall could detect. Charlie Magg eyed Ainsclough and Yewdall with cold, steely blue eyes. He had a narrow face, with long, golden hair combed back over his head down to the collar of the blue-and-white striped, prison issue shirt he wore. The sleeves of his shirt were rolled up neatly, cuff over cuff, thus revealing massively tattooed and powerfully muscular forearms. The back of his hands and his fingers were stained with clumsy, self-inflicted tattoos which spoke of borstal training before he was twenty-one years old, and before he graduated to adult prisons. He was strongly built and stood about six feet tall, so far as Ainsclough could estimate, and was not the sort of man anyone with any sense, he thought, would want to get into a rumble with. It was, Ainsclough pondered, little wonder that his victim, his latest known victim, was still in a coma, with his face looking like a large beetroot, two and a half months after Charlie Magg had 'given him a little slap for being out of order'.

'So, with that in mind, we thought we'd pay a call on you, Charlie,' Yewdall continued, 'see if we can work something out for you. You help us, we help you.'

Charlie Magg still remained silent. He smelled strongly of body odour, clearly indicating his weekly shower and change of clothing was due. He fixed Yewdall with expressionless eye contact. He wasn't going to give anything away.

'If the hospital . . . if the doctors switch off the life-support machine the Crown Prosecution Service will be charging you with murder, Charlie,' Ainsclough quietly explained, 'and I can tell you that they want to do that, they badly want to do that, they really want you put away for a very long time. Not just for this of course, but for other things they haven't been able to pin on you. The CPS want you away for twenty years . . . at least. If the life-support machine is unplugged . . . and your victim begins the big sleep . . .' Ainsclough shrugged. 'Well, that is a mandatory life sentence for you, Charlie. You won't get out for at least twenty years and no one can survive more than ten years in maximum security. After ten years in a Category A prison institutionalization sets in. After ten years of high security life you get more comfortable on the inside and you get frightened of the outside. But you don't need me to tell you that, Charlie, you've seen broken blaggers struggling to get by after ten or fifteen years inside; their way of calling everybody "sir" and wanting to be told which brand of toothpaste to buy.'

Still Magg remained silent. Both officers thought that his massive, brooding presence made the agent's room in Brixton Prison seem small, cramped and overcrowded. Then, just then, there was a brief flicker of Magg's eyelids; his defences were weakening; what Tom Ainsclough had just said appeared to have reached him.

'We are in a position to help you, Charlie.' Yewdall was quick to exploit the apparent evaporating of Charlie Magg's resolve. 'That's why we are here, like we said. You know, Charlie, looking at you I can see you're a manly man,' Yewdall continued, 'you like the ladies; you've got an eye for the ladies, I'll bet. I'll lay good money that you have got a good eye for all those young female joggers in tight pants that jog round the parks in fair London Town, all those slender young things that sun themselves in their bikinis on the beaches on the south coast . . . or in the London parks. Those decorative girls who can brighten any man's day. You think, Charlie, if they take your victim off life support, and not because he's recovering, but because he's in a persistent vegetative state, then there won't be any eye feasting for you for twenty years. You'll see females during visiting hours and they won't be young and fit and there'll be no touching . . . and the young cons you see in the showers, well they will begin to look inviting.'

Charlie Magg's head sagged slightly.

'That's not a clever prospect, Charlie,' Tom Ainsclough promptly added, 'that's not a clever prospect at all.' Ainsclough glanced round the agent's room: plaster over brick walls, painted in two shades of blue, light above dark. A massive lump of opaque glass set high in the wall provided the only source of natural light; the illumination of the room being that from a fila-ment bulb behind a Perspex cover attached to the ceiling. The white-painted metal door was fastened shut, but behind it, in the corridor, stood two prison officers, for whose presence both officers were deeply grateful, because Charlie Magg was known to be prone to 'kicking off' at any time.

'So . . .' Yewdall smiled and spoke softly. 'How does an easily survivable ten stretch for manslaughter sound? You'll be out in five if you keep your nose clean and behave yourself. You can do that on your back, Charlie.'

'Ten?' Charlie Magg spoke for the first time. 'You can fix that?' he growled. 'I mean, straight up. Ten, out in five?'

'We can't promise anything, Charlie,' Penny Yewdall replied, 'but we can put in a word to the CPS, in fact we already have. You see, Charlie, the guy you rolled, Terry "Stepney" Stevenson—'

'He had it coming, well overdue for a kicking he was . . . well overdue.' Magg spoke in a low, menacing voice. 'I mean, well overdue.'

'Yes, well that's as may be, Charlie, but the point in your favour,' Ainsclough explained, 'the big point in your favour is that Stevenson is no friend of the CPS either. They have wanted him inside for as long as they have wanted you inside, Charlie, and it is not causing a great deal of distress to the civil servants of the CPS that he is very possibly about to become life extinct.'

'Life extinct,' Magg echoed, 'that's a new one on me.'

'Not new, though,' Yewdall explained. 'The lawyers and medics use the term, but it's not as though your victim was a man of the cloth or a doctor on his rounds. For that sort of victim there would be no deals . . . no mercy.'

'Do me a favour.' Magg glared at Yewdall. 'I know the rules; I wouldn't roll anyone like that. I know the rules, all right. I mean, I practically wrote them, but Stevenson was a blagger, and he helped himself to money that wasn't his. He was skimming . . . very naughty . . . he should've known better.'

'Probably it didn't belong to the person he stole it from,' Yewdall commented, 'or else it was bent money, proceeds of crime.'

'Both really.' Magg shrugged. 'There was some trading in white stuff, all got fairly divvied up and then Stevenson goes and sticks his paw in the pot and helps himself to thirty large . . . he'd already been given twenty large but that wasn't enough for him. He reckoned he was owed the rest so he took it. So I was given five large to recover the thirty and give "Stepney" Stevenson a good hiding; a right good kicking so he'd learn.'

'You did that all right,' Ainsclough sighed. 'You earned your money that day.'

'They wanted me to learn him not to do it again,' Magg replied. 'So I earned my money. So what?'

'It's highly likely he won't be doing anything again.'

'So I've got five thousand pounds in the Post Office to come out to.'

'Which brings us very neatly back to why we are here, Charlie,' Yewdall leaned back in her chair. 'Are you going to spend it in twenty years' time or in five years' time?'

Magg looked at Yewdall. 'Five years?'

'It's possible.' Yewdall nodded. 'It's on the table as a possibility.'

'But no guarantees,' Ainsclough emphasized. 'If you put your hand up to involuntary manslaughter, collect ten years, play the game, you could be out in five . . . and that's if we put in a good word for you; tell the CPS how cooperative you were with a major investigation. The CPS will inform the judge and request leniency, so a ten stretch with the possibility of parole is a real possibility.'

Magg relaxed his posture, also leaned back in his chair, folded his arms and said, 'So what is it you want to know about?'

'Tell us about Arnie Rainbird, Charlie,' Yewdall asked. 'We know a little about him but we sense there is much, much more we don't know. He seems a bit of a shadowy figure, iceberg-like, most of him is hidden from view, but his bulk is massive.'

Charlie Magg drew a deep breath.

'Do you have problems with that, Charlie?' Tom Ainsclough leaned forward. 'Do you have problems telling us about Arnie Rainbird?'

Charlie Magg nodded. 'Too right I do, I reckon that I'm a bit of a "life's worth" when it comes to grassing up Arnie Rainbird; too right I am worried.'

'More than your life is worth, you mean?' Again Penny Yewdall absent-mindedly chewed the plastic cover of the tip of her ball-point pen.

'Yes.' Charlie Magg raised his head. 'That's exactly what I mean. Arnie Rainbird is heap bad medicine and he has long, long tentacles, I won't be safe anywhere. He has eyes and ears everywhere.'

'Witness protection, Charlie.' Yewdall placed her pen on her notepad. 'It's a possibility, new life, new ID. It works and the offer is there.'

'Won't work for me.' Charlie Magg raised his eyebrows. 'It won't work for me if Arnie Rainbird is after me. I haven't seen Arnie in years but he knows me, I know him. I don't work for him any more, not on a permanent basis, but he can still use me for jobs.'

'Like turning "Stepney" Stevenson's face into a pulp?'

Magg shrugged. 'Maybe . . . occasional work like that.'

'A lot of blaggers find the thought of a new life appealing, Charlie,' Ainsclough prompted. 'Surprised you don't.'

Charlie Magg remained silent.

'We've talked about a twenty stretch being reduced to ten and out in five. The whole lot could be made to go away . . . all of it,' Penny Yewdall pressed, 'all of it, if you'll sign a statement and clamber into the witness box.'

'It's not so simple.' Charlie Magg smiled. 'I mean, I wish it was, I really wish I could sign a statement and climb into the witness box but Arnie Rainbird . . . he's part Italian despite his English name, got family in Italy . . . Milan, I think, and by family I don't mean regular Italians, I mean *Cosa Nostra*.'

'The Mafia!' Ainsclough gasped.

'You got it right, the Italian Mafia; so he's connected, but it's not just that, it's also that he cut his teeth in Italy. He learned a few things, like if you want to take revenge you ice the target's family, not the target.'

'Oh . . .' Penny Yewdall put her hand to her mouth.

'You see my problem?' Charlie Magg appealed to the two officers. 'I have three brothers and a sister, both my parents had six brothers and sisters, all of them married, and each had two or three children; I have about thirty cousins and one will be iced if I grass on Rainbird and go into witness protection and if not iced, then ruined in some other way.' Charlie Magg paused. 'I mean, my little sister, she works in a bank believe it or not, she doesn't know what I got up to. She suspects but she doesn't know. If I grass on Arnie Rainbird he'll have her tongue cut out to learn me for grassing him up, that's Arnie Rainbird. So if you offer me witness protection you have to offer it to an entire tribe and that's if they'll all agree to it.'

'Fair enough, Charlie,' Ainsclough replied softly, 'I see your problem.'

'So, supposing I do help you, like off the record.' Charlie Magg laid his two massive, nicotine-stained paws on the highly polished table top. 'No statements, just talk within these four walls; could you still help me? I mean, look at me, I am fifty years old, I'll be seventy when I get out.'

'It's a possibility,' Penny Yewdall replied, 'basic physics: for every action there is an equal and opposite reaction. The more you help us, the more we can help you.'

'Yes . . . yes . . . I understand that and, at my age, you wonder how much time you've got left.' Charlie Magg shook his head. 'I can't spend the last years of my life on the inside; I should be making the most of it down the boozer, playing darts, spending the occasional day in Ramsgate, getting some sea air into my bellows.'

'That's the ticket, Charlie.' Ainsclough smiled. 'Now you're starting to use your loaf. So, Arnie Rainbird, he's been very quiet, what's his game? What's he into?'

'Into?'

'Where's his money coming from?' Yewdall explained.

Magg glanced to his left and then leaned forward. 'Practically everything and anything if it makes money, but lately I hear he's moved into people smuggling. It's the latest business to be in, there is good money to be made and do-it-on-your-back sentences. He was into cocaine and heroin but moved out of that to smuggle people. The profits are the same as for smuggling white powder but the maximum sentence is just four years, though Arnie won't do any time as he never lets himself get close enough to the action. He was blackmailing teachers when he was at school, then ran protection rackets. He battered his way up but he also used his loaf.' Magg tapped the side of his head. 'He always used this.'

'Battered?'

'Yes, battered. Arnie Rainbird is well handy in a scuffle, keeps himself fit, got his own gym.'

'He was a minder?'

'He was,' Charlie Magg replied, seeming to the officers to be beginning to relax into a conversation once the rules had been set down. 'He was a casual heavy; he didn't just protect his boss.

If the boss wanted to put the old squeeze on a citizen, well, then he'd use Arnie Rainbird . . . Arnie was your man.'

'So he was a bit like you in that respect,' Tom Ainsclough said drily. 'I mean a bit like you put the squeeze on "Stepney" Stevenson?'

'A bit.' Magg shrugged. 'What can I say?'

'So who was Arnie Rainbird's boss?'

'"Legs" Connolly.'

Yewdall and Ainsclough glanced curiously at each other.

'It's OK.' Charlie Magg smiled. 'This goes way back; I mean so way back you wouldn't have heard of "Legs" Connolly. "Legs" Connolly was old when you were learning to use a knife and fork but he'll be in your files. So Arnie Rainbird was in "Legs" Connolly's firm. They did armed robbery in the main, that's where Arnie learned his skills when he came back from Italy. They did security vans, especially the collecting vans; the delivery vans carrying the wages, well, they always carry new notes in sequence; have to wash them before you can use them. That is a nuisance and it can be pricey, but the collecting vans, they just take till takings to the bank, all used notes, didn't need washing, still don't.' Charlie Magg paused. 'It could get a bit rough, it could get a bit like cowboys holding up stagecoaches in the Old West, but we were up for it and that's where I first met Arnie Rainbird. So, anyway, "Legs" Connolly disappeared, didn't he?'

'Don't know,' Penny Yewdall replied, 'did he?'

'You can bet your life he did.' Charlie Magg smiled. 'He was offed, iced; it's the way of it when top villains go missing, it's always because they have been chilled. Always. Any blagger really, but especially the top villains.'

'Seems so.' Penny Yewdall nodded her head gently. 'It does seem to be the case; a missing villain is a dead villain.'

'But by then Arnie Rainbird was a rising star. I was taking orders from him even though we started out together. By the time "Legs" Connolly vanished, Arnie Rainbird was getting a nice, well-earned reputation for being an evil swine of a villain. I mean, by then Arnie was collecting victims like they were going out of fashion; I mean, collecting them like there was no tomorrow. You know how it is in the other world.'

'The other world, Charlie?' Penny Yewdall asked. 'What other world?'

'The other world to your world, darling,' Charlie Magg whispered as though he feared a hidden microphone was in the agent's room. 'You don't get in and move up except in two ways: you do bird, you get some jail time under your belt, it's that what gives you street cred, it means you are not some cardboard cut-out. If you have no street cred you're just a cardboard cut-out and you never get to be anything but a gofer.'

'Fair enough.' Ainsclough nodded. 'I can understand that. So what's the second way?'

'The other way, the other way up.' Charlie Magg once again looked nervously to his left and right and lowered his voice as if fearing a hidden microphone. 'Well the other way up is the way Arnie Rainbird did it. You take a scalp, then you take another scalp . . . you take a few scalps.'

'You murder?' Penny Yewdall sought clarification. 'You take life . . . you kill?'

'Yes.' Charlie Magg once again glanced to his left and right. 'That's the second way, and that's how Arnie Rainbird got into "Legs" Connolly's firm and that's how he moved up the ladder. He was just very good with his fists and with his feet; handy in an argument, like I said. Well handy. He would be right in there with his fists, and putting the wellie well in; turn some old warrior's face to mush by stamping on him.'

'Again, not unlike you and your victim, Charlie.' Tom Ainsclough raised his eyebrows. 'Seems like you and Arnie Rainbird are like peas in a pod.'

'Oh yeah,' Charlie Magg sneered, 'so if that's the case what am I doing in here and he's out there living the good life? Naw, he rose, I didn't; he owns houses, yachts . . . and all I have got to show is five large in the Post Office. We are not so much alike, me and Arnie, not alike at all.' Magg sighed. 'You need to do more than I did if you want to move up. I mean, just put a Turk in hospital, even if you put him on a life-support machine for a week or two . . . that won't get you very far up.'

'A month or two,' Yewdall coldly corrected Maggs. 'He's been in a coma for ten weeks.'

'Still doesn't cut it,' Magg replied equally coldly. 'You have to take a scalp, deliberate like. If Stevenson dies it wasn't intentional on my part. You need to take a scalp intentionally, deliberately.'

'That's how Arnie Rainbird got started?'

'Yes.' Charlie Magg shifted position in his chair and once again looked around as he leaned forward and spoke in a near whisper. 'Yes, that's it. You have to take a scalp. Arnie Rainbird got noticed, so the story goes, when "Legs" Connolly wanted this geezer iced; he gave Arnie a chance to prove himself. So he sends Arnie and two blokes as his escort out to do the business. So this geezer is living in a flat in a council high-rise, isn't he, living with his old lady, just him and her, no kids to worry about making things untidy. So Arnie and a couple of boys went to this earthling's drum one night about midnight and they got through the front door like it wasn't there. The old lady starts to kick off, so Arnie Rainbird slaps her and she becomes very cooperative, most silent.'

'Because she's been knocked out?' Penny Yewdall commented drily. 'I know what sort of slap you mean.'

Charlie Magg shrugged. 'Then Arnie slaps the boy, but him, the boy, him he keeps awake, it's Arnie's way of doing things. Arnie Rainbird keeps his victims awake so they know what's happening to them, keeps them conscious right up to the end.'

'That's interesting.' Yewdall turned to Ainsclough. 'The skulls . . . they were not damaged.' Then she turned to Charlie Magg. 'Sorry, Charlie, carry on, you are doing well for yourself.'

'All right.' Charlie Magg seemed to focus his thoughts and continued. 'So . . . well . . . Arnie Rainbird and the two escorts truss this soldier up, I mean truss him well up, very neatly using cable ties to keep his wrists fastened behind his back and then push both ankles under the wrists. Can't get out of that, the ankles pull against the cable ties. No one can free themselves from that little old number. Then they wait . . . real calm like, watch a bit of late-night television. Then, at about two in the morning, they give the old lady another slap because she has woken up and is starting to make noises, but before that Arnie Rainbird gives a little advice about what will happen to her if she identifies anyone in a police line up.' Magg paused. 'Then they wait a bit more, and then they drag out the geezer, who is well out of luck, and by this time he knows it, I mean, he has messed himself something rotten and is making many pleading sounds, until Arnie puts some sticky tape across his north and south, thereafter he is most silent.'

'So you were told, Charlie.' Yewdall clasped her hands together and rested them on the table top. 'I mean you were definitely not one of the two redcoats who were provided as Arnie Rainbird's escort?'

Charlie Magg smiled and winked at Yewdall.

'Just get on with the story, Charlie,' Tom Ainsclough prompted, 'you're doing well.'

'All right . . . all right, so after two of the clock in the forenoon and once the late film is over, Arnie Rainbird and the escorts drag this old geezer out of his flat and along the corridor to the lift shaft, and the poor old shaking, quivering sod is bunged into the lift and up they go to the top floor, twelve storeys.'

'High enough,' Yewdall commented.

'It's the way Arnie wanted it. So on the top floor there is a steel ladder going up the wall to a trap door and the roof, and the trap door is always kept padlocked. No problem because Arnie did a recce the night before and has with him a very handy pair of bolt cutters, and then the padlock is no more. So they put a rope round the geezer's neck, haul him up to the roof and carry him to the edge of the roof, where below him is all of London Town very like a Christmas tree with many lights shining. So Arnie props the boy up and lets him have a last look at all the lovely lights and the buses and cars on the road, then the boys step back and leave it to Arnie Rainbird. The boys are there to help and to witness but the last bit is down to Arnie Rainbird if he wants to make a name for himself, if he wants to rise then he's on his Jack Jones for the last bit. It's just the rule of the game.'

'OK,' Tom Ainsclough said, 'understood.'

'So Arnie Rainbird pushes the boy to the edge, so by this time he's lying on his side facing outwards and Arnie leaves him like that for a few minutes, then he gently rolls him over the edge and the geezer is well topped. Very well topped indeed. That was Arnie Rainbird's first scalp.'

'You're being very informative.' Penny Yewdall smiled. 'You can't be frightened of Mr Rainbird.'

'Hey.' Charlie Magg held up his huge, fleshy hand. 'We agreed, I sign nothing. Anything I tell you is just between you and me. I'm helping myself as much as I can short of grassing Arnie Rainbird up. I am not giving evidence.'

'Just carry on,' Yewdall sighed, 'but I can tell you that if you and the other escort stepped back and let Arnie Rainbird push your victim to his death, you are all equally guilty of murder in the eyes of the law.'

'It wasn't the eyes of the law we were worried about,' Magg said with a grin, 'it was the eyes of "Legs" Connolly that concerned us.'

'All right,' Yewdall repeated, 'just carry on.'

'Do you remember the name and the address of the victim, Charlie?' Ainsclough asked before Charlie Magg could 'carry on'.

Charlie Magg shook his head. 'It's one of many, governor, and a long time ago now.'

'Just thought I'd ask, Charlie. Sounds like an unsolved crime to me.'

'It'll remain unsolved because I won't be signing anything.'

'All right, Charlie, in your own time,' Ainsclough said, 'we're all ears.'

'All ears,' Yewdall repeated.

'All right.' Charlie Magg paused once again and after looking to his left and right he continued. 'So "Legs" Connolly is well impressed. I mean, he is well impressed, or, is he well impressed . . . I mean, is he well impressed or not?'

'I would guess he was well impressed,' Yewdall replied.

'Too right he is well impressed, so "Legs" Connolly puts the word out that Arnie Rainbird is "all right" and the next time "Legs" Connolly wants another slime offed he puts Arnie Rainbird on the case, and Arnie is well keen to show how creative he can be. So, once the second geezer is overpowered he puts him in the back of a van and he and the escort run him out of London and out into Essex to the railway line where the Harwich to London trains run.'

'Fast trains,' Yewdall commented, 'very fast trains.'

'Very fast. Have you stood next to a railway line when a fast train is approaching?' Magg glanced at Penny Yewdall.

'Yes,' Yewdall replied. 'I think I can see where you are going, Charlie.'

'So you know what I mean?' Charlie Magg grinned menacingly.

'The rails sing,' Yewdall guessed, 'a high-pitched ringing sound?'

'Yes, miss.' Magg grinned. 'They sing, a really high-pitched noise; add a little vibration and if a geezer is tied across the line, he knows his number is up. I mean that train had that geezer's name on it. The slime is pulled tight across the line with ropes fastened to heavy objects, like cars, so he cannot pull himself clear, and his neck is on the line and his ankles are on the other line, and it is not long before the train comes and the rails begin to sing and ring, and the geezer is not happy and is saying so very loudly and the rails are also singing louder and louder and then . . . wham!' Charlie Magg made a low whistling sound. 'When the train had gone the geezer was in six bits; his two arms and his head was on one side of the rails, his two feet on the other side of the rails and the middle bit of him is between the rails and the claret . . . claret is everywhere and "Legs" Connolly is well impressed at Arnie Rainbird's creativity.' Charlie Magg took a deep breath. 'Then one day "Legs" Connolly is not there, not in his drum, not nowhere . . . thin air number, total vanishing act. No rumours before or after . . . no noise . . . no body is found, nothing, and Arnie Rainbird steps up and sits in "Legs'" chair and nobody makes even the slightest hiss of objection. Nobody will go up against Arnie Rainbird, not by then, because by this time Arnie Rainbird is mucho feared. Mucho feared indeed.'

'That, Charlie –' Penny Yewdall pursed her lips – 'that is very interesting, very interesting indeed.'

'Certainly is,' Ainsclough added, 'it tells us an awful lot about the man we are trying to get to know.'

'So . . .' Charlie Magg continued, 'Arnie Rainbird, now he is using his loaf and he says no more armed robbery, no more bringing in white powder, Arnie Rainbird says the firm is moving into people smuggling, that's when he says the money is the same but the penalties are a joke. So we start by smuggling them inside containers on the back of lorries, but the customs people have a nifty gadget for checking them now. They can detect human breath, clever old boys they are, so Arnie's firm switches

to fast boats at night. They wade in from the shore and they get
packed in like sardines right under the noses of the French, who
don't care. I mean why do you think the Frogs built that refugee
camp so close to the ferry terminal, so close to the entrance of
the Channel Tunnel? They did that to help get the refugees and
illegals out of France and into the UK. There's never been any
love lost between the French and the English and the location
of the refugee camp is proof. If the French wanted to help the
UK Border Agency they would put the camp a hundred miles
inland, but the camp makes things easier for Arnie Rainbird's
firm. So he takes 'em on board, crams them in like sardines in
a can, and at night they tuck their boat in behind a cross channel
ferry to keep it off the radar. Just as they are approaching
Ramsgate or Dover they turn north and put 'em ashore near
Margate. Once they are onshore they are on their own. Some
make it to London and make a good contribution to the black
economy, others get picked up and claim political asylum, and
that takes years to sort out. So job done, and like Arnie Rainbird
says, hardly any bird to worry about; few years max instead of
twenty for smuggling H. I mean, use your loaf . . . but this is
helping me, right? I mean I am beginning to look at an involuntary manslaughter charge?'

'Beginning,' Yewdall replied, 'you are beginning to look at
reduced charges. But we need more. So, you've still got a little
way to go yet, Charlie.'

Again the man looked at the hut in the adjacent field, his eyes
being drawn to it with some dread fascination. If he had had his
way he would have burnt the thing to the ground, burnt it and
buried the blackened timbers and all the ashes with it. Buried it
all in a deep hole and covered it up with soil and let the grass
grow green over it. That, he thought, that would be the only sure
way but the boss had said 'no'; the boss said that to burn it would
only look suspicious, so clean it, scrub it out on the inside with
bleach solution . . . the roof, the walls, the door . . . thoroughly
clean it, wash away all trace, but leave the hut standing.

The man stood – that day he was dressed in jeans cut off
above the knee, yellow T-shirt and blue sports shoes – and
walked outside his office. He had nothing to do, nothing but

answering the phone about twice each day and fielding the occasional callers. But the police calling like they had . . . they seemed to have gone away happy, but they had still called. After that the boss was especially insistent that the hut be left as it was. To burn it after the law had called, then that really would be inviting them to return, so said the boss. The man walked slowly across the rock-hard soil and parched grass, feeling the pleasant warmth of the sun upon his face, arms and calves and delighting in the birdsong. He walked to the hut and opened the door and stood back as the hot, stale air within escaped. He waited for a few moments and then stepped into the old building feeling the floorboards give under his weight and hearing the loud creaking as they did so. The man scanned the inside of the hut, the roof, the sides, the back of the door. He had done his job, it was clean, sanitized, thoroughly scrubbed. He wouldn't be going for a swim in the river one night, or going for an excursion in the boss's motor boat out to the edge of the estuary where the river meets the sea, also at night, with an engine block chained to one of his ankles. He always thought that to be a horrible death. The crew on the boat do their job, none of them feel anything; but the bursting of the victim's lungs as he is pulled downwards . . . and conscious, all the time conscious, that's the way the boss deals with any of his soldiers who mess up or give him any grief. The man knew that the boss likes it neat, not a trace left behind. He took one last look round the inside of the hut. He felt he was safe. He had done his job. He was safe.

He ambled back to his office in the first field and he thought his lot wasn't such a bad number really. He was just a gofer but he liked the solitude. He found he could cope with that and the greenery and the birdsong. A man can get tired of the city, of living on the manor, and he felt he could get used to this life. His eye was caught by a hawk hovering above the next field. Yes . . . yes, he thought, he could well get used to country living.

His was not a bad little number at all. As jobs for gofers go, his was not a bad little number.

But the hut, he turned to glance at it; the hut should have gone up in smoke a long time ago. A very long time ago.

* * *

'So.' Penny Yewdall scratched the itch on the back of her left hand. 'Did you know Arnie Rainbird when he got out of prison?'

'Yes.' Charlie Magg hunched his shoulders then relaxed them. 'Yes, I was still in his firm at that time, I still had my uses. That was about . . . what . . . five years ago now?'

'Seven,' Tom Ainsclough corrected him. 'It was seven years ago, last Easter.'

'Cor, time flies, eh?' Charlie Magg grinned.

'Only if you are on the outside, Charlie.' Yewdall held eye contact with Charlie Magg. 'On the inside it drags, but you don't need me to tell you that, Charlie.'

Charlie Magg glared at her. 'So what else can I tell you? You said there were two things?'

'Yes,' Tom Ainsclough leaned forward. 'What you told us about Arnie Rainbird was very interesting; now we want to know about the party.'

'The party?'

'The party, Charlie.' Yewdall also leaned forward. 'The week long house party up in Bedfordshire someone threw to celebrate Arnie Rainbird's release from prison; that party where the girls were supplied and then kept against their will.'

Charlie Magg sank backwards and folded his arms, looking at the floor. 'It was more like a garden party really; most of the action was in the garden . . . plenty in the house but mainly in the garden.'

'Garden party, house party, whatever,' Tom Ainsclough pressed, 'tell us about it.'

'Tell us about it, Charlie,' Yewdall added. 'It reached you, didn't it? The question reached you, the way you sat back, folded your arms, looking down instead of at us. You clearly know why we want to know about that party Charlie, so keep working for yourself.'

Outside the agent's room the rattle of keys echoed in the long corridor and a metal door slammed shut, followed by a second rattle of keys. Charlie Magg looked at the door in response to the sound.

'You could be out in five years, Charlie.' Yewdall read Charlie Magg's thoughts. 'Or in for twenty. It all depends on you, Charlie. Manslaughter or murder, because we all know the life-support machine is going to be switched off. After ten weeks and no improvement, it's going to be pull the plug time any day now.'

Charlie Magg's head sagged forward. 'Yes . . . don't you think I realize that?'

'So help yourself; tell us about the party,' Yewdall pressed.

'You're on dangerous ground.' Magg took a deep breath. 'You're on very dangerous ground there and you are taking me on with you.'

'We're not asking you to grass anybody up, Charlie.' Ainsclough spoke reassuringly.

'And I won't.' Charlie Magg glanced up at Ainsclough. 'I told you . . . no names, no pack drill, no signing of any statements and definitely no climbing into any witness box . . . no way, is that clear?'

'Clear . . . clear as a bell, Charlie,' Yewdall replied slowly. 'Crystal . . . I mean crystal. So, again, why the fear?'

'I'm in deep trouble if Arnie Rainbird finds out I'm even talking to you about him. I'll get carved in here, I won't be safe. I'll go back to the association area and say you're talking about Stevenson, that'll keep me safe. But if you start investigating that party, well, then Arnie's spies will know, they'll put two and two together.'

'We'll be discreet,' Ainsclough said, quietly. 'Tell us, is Arnie Rainbird still active?'

'He's active all right . . . you make him sound like a volcano . . . No, he's active all right, just ace at keeping off the old police radar but he's worth a gander, he's well worth a gander.'

'We'll give him a look but we need to know about that party, Charlie, we need to know.' Yewdall continued to press Magg.

'You're like a dog with a bone.' Magg glanced at her. 'You don't ever give up, do you?'

'Not easily, Charlie,' Penny Yewdall replied, icily, 'and especially not when I'm hungry, and right now, Charlie, right now, I need feeding. I am very hungry indeed. So feed me.'

Again Charlie Magg's head sagged. 'What to do . . . what to do,' he said to himself, 'what to do for the best.'

'The best is whatever is good for you, Charlie,' Tom Ainsclough encouraged. 'We can keep repeating it like a parrot in a cage, cop for ten, out in five or do the full twenty. You'll be seventy when you get out, like you said, or you could still be a youthful fifty-five.'

'Don't you think I know that?' Charlie Magg once again looked to his right and then his left. 'So what can I tell you?'

'All about the party, Charlie, what happened to make twenty or thirty women keep silent after being cheated like that? Promised two hundred pounds for a night's work then get bunged fifty for eight days' work. Something happened there. What was it?'

'What do you think?' Charlie Magg sneered. 'Use your old loaf if you've got one.'

'Serious crime?' Yewdall replied.

'Very serious.' Magg sat back in his chair. 'Like the most serious.'

'Like murder?'

Charlie Magg nodded. 'Like murder.'

'So,' Yewdall clarified, 'some person was murdered at the party up in Bedfordshire, specifically at the party seven years ago, which was thrown to celebrate Arnie Rainbird's release from prison?'

'Yes, that party.' Magg nodded. 'Maybe.'

'Maybe?'

'Don't want to be truthful. I mean, Arnie has spies, he has spies everywhere, so I'll just say, yes, maybe it was that party.'

'Fair enough,' Ainsclough replied, 'and maybe someone got topped at that party?'

Magg smiled. 'Yes, maybe . . . just maybe someone got cooled.'

'And in fact maybe more than one person got topped? Maybe two geezers got chilled,' Ainsclough continued, 'one tall, tooth-less geezer and one short, toothless geezer, maybe?'

'Yes,' Magg continued, 'maybe it was two what got topped, but you'll really need to quiz somebody on the outside.'

'On the outside?' Ainsclough queried.

'On the outside of these walls, mate,' Charlie Magg replied with a suddenly serious edge to his voice. 'Not just outside of these walls but on the outside of my world, outside the blaggers' world. You need to talk to someone who would get picked for jury duty . . . that sort of outside.'

'Like who,' Yewdall asked, 'like who do you suggest?'

'Like one of the girls.'

'The coach load of girls!' Yewdall sighed. 'They were rounded up at King's Cross, they were hard-edged street girls. OK, they'll have convictions for something, soliciting, shoplifting, possession of a controlled substance. They won't get picked for jury service. There's not a brass who isn't known to the police for something, but we need names and even then they're unlikely to want to help.'

Magg paused. 'They wasn't all brasses,' he replied softly, 'not all of them. A few were good girls . . . university girls.'

'University students!' Tom Ainsclough sat bolt upright. 'You are kidding?'

'Nope . . . I was a Boy Scout once –' Magg gave the Scout salute – 'Scout's honour. Some were good girls, they never did the other bit, standing on the street looking into passing cars, but what they were, were classy girls, classy call girls . . . or they were mistresses to some East End villain. They came to the party as well.'

'Invited,' Yewdall asked, 'just to be clear?'

'Told more like,' Magg replied, 'told that they were going to a party up in Bedfordshire and arrived with their old man. Arnie Rainbird had something to hold over them, over the men that is, so they did what they were told and brought their classy girl-friends. Nice clean girls, educated, a bit nose in the air . . . a bit posh. I remember there were about five of them. None of them knew what was happening until it was too late and they were trapped for the whole week. The coach load of brasses arrived first then the flash cars arrived, carrying posh girls in the front passenger seat.'

'Can you remember the name of any of the "good girls"?' Tom Ainsclough asked drily, he not having met a street girl he disliked and having met many lady magistrates he did dislike.

'Names?' Magg smiled. 'No . . . no names. I'm not refusing to give you names, it's just that I never got to know any, but . . .' Magg paused, 'one girl I remember, I remember her well. People got to talking . . . they got to know each other. That's how the five good girls met; they sort of found each other. They realized that they were not brasses and got to talking to each other.'

'Relationships developed,' Yewdall suggested, 'is that what you mean, Charlie?'

'Yes.' Charlie Magg nodded. 'That's a good way of putting it. You have a good way with words, darling. I never was good like that, but the girl I am thinking of, I really took to her but she was well outside my league, well out of my old class. She was a school teacher, a really nice girl, so well spoken, really shocked by what she was seeing but a very nice girl . . . tall, actress good looks, long pins. She knew it. She knew she had got what it takes but didn't put on the dog about it. She kicked up a fuss when she realized she wasn't going home after the first night and she was available to any man who wanted her . . . all the girls were and so Arnie Rainbird had her slapped. He didn't do it himself, he never does things himself . . . hardly ever, doesn't like to get his old hands dirty. But there was an older woman at the party, brought in to keep the girls in line and she was told to make an example of this girl, the school teacher, so she was well slapped in front of the other girls and then she was given to the Baptist for a bit of twenty ten.'

'The Baptist?' Yewdall queried. 'Twenty ten?'

'The Baptist, he's one of Arnie Rainbird's soldiers but he's not like Arnie. The Baptist doesn't like claret but Arnie Rainbird doesn't object to it.'

'The outlaw on the railway line,' Tom Ainsclough suggested, 'like him? When his head was cut off by the wheels of the express train a few pints of the stuff would spout from his neck at the next beat of his heart with such force that it would carry ten or fifteen feet from his body, that sort of claret?'

'Yes, like that, that was mucho claret, Arnie Rainbird style, but the Baptist, he doesn't like blood. He's not soft about it, he just doesn't like mess. He gets results but keeps it neat. So he uses water. He drowns them. Folk that Arnie wants iced get drowned because he uses the Baptist these days, or part drowned if they need a change in the old attitude department. So after this dark-haired teacher girl gets a right good slap, while she's still dazed, the old Baptist takes her to the swimming pool, dragging her by the hair with all the girls still looking on, and gives her his special bad attitude treatment.'

'Being the twenty ten?' Ainsclough anticipated.

'Right, governor, shoves her head under the water for twenty seconds, takes it out for ten, under for twenty, out for ten, and he keeps that up for fifteen minutes, possibly longer. Well that teacher girl she never showed no lemon after that and none of the other girls did either. Well, that was on the Saturday, the first Saturday. Arnie Rainbird had one girl made an example of and after that there was peace, but by the Tuesday or the Wednesday I was chatting to her. She was meek and mild by then with her boat race still bruised from the slap; looking like a black eye. She was just sitting there shivering even though it was in the middle of summer, but it was in the morning so possibly it was still a bit nippy and she had no clothes on, not a stitch – that's how they kept them in the house; took all their kit, clothing and shoes. Anyway, we just got to talking, we were in the kitchen and I made her a cup of tea and by then a little niceness went a long way with her.'

'That I can understand,' Yewdall said dryly.

'So after that,' Charlie Magg continued, 'after that we talked when we could, when she could, when things were quiet. I never forced myself on her. I could have done and she couldn't have refused. That was the party game, a few men had their way with her because the rule was anything goes to celebrate Arnic Rainbird getting out, and I mean anything.'

'But you didn't, Charlie?' Yewdall asked.

'On my honour, darling, there's stuff you do and there's stuff you don't do. There's a code among villains and I loved me old mum. Thank the Lord she isn't here to see this, but she set me on the right path when it comes to women. If a girl needs a slap that's one thing, but never take advantage. Only take what's on offer. I got this belief. If a mother doesn't want her sons to grow up to batter their old ladies, she doesn't batter the sons. Simple.'

'There's a lot of truth in that, Charlie.' Yewdall nodded. 'I think that's fair comment.'

'You think so, darling?' Charlie Magg's eyes gleamed.

'Yes . . . yes, I think there is. You see I used to work in the Female and Child Unit,' Yewdall explained, 'and I never met a man who had a down on women who didn't also have some issue with his mother. But anyway . . . carry on with your story. You're doing well, Charlie.'

'All right.' Magg paused, then continued, 'So, me and this girl
. . . Sandra!' Magg's face lit up. 'I remember now, Sandra, her
name was Sandra. It's coming back to me now. I haven't thought
of her in years . . . years. So anyway we became pals, me and
Sandra.'

'Do you remember her surname?' Ainsclough held his pen
poised over his pad.

'She never told me. I never asked.'

'What can you remember about her?' Yewdall asked.

'She was British but she had grown up in South Africa, in
Cape Town, and she had a strong South African accent. So when
the party happened she was not long back from there. She taught
in a primary school in the East End.'

'Big place?' Yewdall probed.

'Yes, can't remember which borough, but her parents lived in
the north country, in the North of England.'

'Another big place,' Ainsclough added.

Charlie Magg glanced around. 'Her parents lived in a town
with a church which had a twisted spire, so she said, but she
didn't say "twisted", she used another word.'

'Crooked?' Ainsclough suggested. 'A crooked spire?'

'Yeah.' Magg jabbed a finger in Ainsclough's direction. 'Yes
that was the word she used, a crooked spire. Why? Do you know
the town, governor?'

'Chesterfield.' Ainsclough smiled.

'You know the town, governor?'

'Can't say that I know it, Charlie,' Ainsclough replied, 'but I
have seen the crooked spire often enough. You can see it from
the train, really close. It's a famous north of England landmark.
Either it became twisted by a fire, or by subsidence, but it's safe
and still stands without needing any shoring up, and it's strong
enough to hold the bells which peel loudly when they need to
be rung. So I know the crooked spire and where it is but I've
never set foot in Chesterfield itself.'

'Well, Chesterfield it is then,' Charlie Magg replied. 'She,
Sandra, said she just wanted to look up at the crooked spire,
that's all she wanted to do. She just wanted to go home to her
old mum and dad. She told me she left home to go and live in
London; she wanted to see a bit of life. Reckon she did that all

right. By the time the party was halfway through all she wanted to do was get back up north and look at the church spire in her parents' town.'

'That's useful, Charlie.' Yewdall smiled. 'Very useful. If you remember anything else about her, you'll tell us?'

'Yes.' Charlie Magg reclined in his chair. 'I don't mind telling you about her, she's not a blagger.'

'So tell us about the house where the party was held. We believe it was up in Bedfordshire?' Ainsclough asked.

Charlie Magg seemed to the two officers to become more relaxed. 'Well, I am happy to tell you about the house, all I can really, because I don't know much. That's not going to harm anyone.'

'Fair enough.' Yewdall nodded in agreement. 'So does the house have a name? Can it be identified by some distinctive feature like a clock tower or a stable block, or a landscaped garden . . . a date in the wall, a tall tree . . . anything like that?'

'Ah.' Charlie Magg held up a stubby, nicotine-stained finger. 'You have the wrong idea there, darling, totally barking up the wrong tree there, governor. Not just the wrong tree, you're in the wrong part of the forest, so to speak.'

'We are?' Yewdall was intrigued. 'So what was it?'

'It wasn't an old mansion like you seem to think, governor.' Magg grinned. 'No, not a two-hundred-year-old stately home; the house is only about twenty years old, brand new as buildings go. Brick built, just two storeys, ground floor and first floor, angled roof because flat roofs don't work, not modern ones anyway. A veranda on the level of the first floor, shallow roof, so no attic space to speak of, but I went up there anyway; just couldn't resist a poke around. Honestly, it looks like something out of *Gone with the Wind* the house does, only it's made of brick and is practically brand new. It doesn't have a cellar either, just a crawl space beneath the floorboards on the ground floor. It's all "what you see is what you get".'

'Can it be seen from the road?' Tom Ainsclough asked.

'Yes, yes, it can, but it's at the end of a long, and I mean long, drive which goes between two fields, then there's a bit of a gravel area in front of the house. The gate at the bottom of the drive is kept locked. The post is delivered to a mailbox which is set in the gate, so no one really needs to call at the house. Each day someone walks down the drive to collect the mail from the letterbox bolted to the gate. I did it once; it took me twenty minutes there and back.'

'So a drive about half a mile long?' Yewdall estimated.

'Dunno, darling.' Magg shrugged. 'Can't say I ever measured it.'

'Well, if the average walking pace is four miles an hour, that's one mile every fifteen minutes, which makes the drive about half a mile long, possibly a little more . . . about three quarters of a mile long . . . a twenty minute walk there and back.'

'If you say so, darling.' Magg glanced to his left. 'If you say so.'

'Did you ever see anyone looking at the house from the road?' Yewdall asked.

'No, I never did and you can't anyway,' Magg explained, 'you can see just the top of the roof from the road; it's like the land hides the house from view of the road. I mean, if the roof was just two feet lower you couldn't see anything of the house. So you're looking across green fields full of cattle, then there's a thin line of red tiles, then greenery beyond the line of red tiles. The driveway is well fenced off and they have dogs in front of the house, but the dogs can't wander round the back of the house.'

'Alsatians? Dobermanns?' Ainsclough asked.

'Staffordshires,' Magg replied, 'well they were Staffies back then, six of them. They'd see any intruder off. May have different dogs now. During the party there was always a couple of minders watching the front of the house, and they had to be introduced to the dogs.'

'I see.' Yewdall spoke thoughtfully. 'So what is at the sides of the house and the back?'

'Some land at either side, but fenced off so you can't walk from the drive down the side of the house to the garden at the rear,' Magg explained. 'The only way to the garden at the back of the house is through the house and then out again through the back door.' Magg shook his head. 'The garden is as big as a football pitch. It is surrounded by a high fence of interlacing wire and within the fence they planted those fast growing plants that all the fuss is about . . . look like trees.'

'Leylandii?'

'If that's the name. Grew fast with massive roots. You can't get past the wire, can't see through those Ley . . . whatever,' Magg explained. 'Very private.'

'Leylandii,' Yewdall said. 'What's in the garden?'

Charlie Magg exhaled. 'Not much as I recall. A swimming pool close to the house – that's where the Baptist did his party piece with Sandra, the school teacher – that was on your left as you leave the house by the back door. On the right was a barbecue, brick built and a permanent construction.'

'I know the type.' Ainsclough nodded.

'After that not much, just a flat lawn.'

'Who owns the house?'

'Mate of Arnie Rainbird's.' Magg sniffed. 'A geezer by the name of Snakebite.'

'Snakebite?' Ainsclough wrote the name on his notepad.

'Snakebite,' Charlie Magg repeated, 'Johnny "Snakebite" Herron. Usually he just gets called Snakebite. He's another active geezer who keeps his head down. He can keep himself well off the Old Bill's radar. Don't know what Snakebite's game is; probably people smuggling like Arnie Rainbird.'

Yewdall and Ainsclough glanced at each other, and Ainsclough said, 'Well, that about wraps it up, Charlie. Thanks, we'll put that word in for you.'

'Thanks, governor.' Charlie Magg stood. 'Tower Hamlets.'

'Tower Hamlets?' Ainsclough also stood, as did Penny Yewdall.

'Yes, I just remembered that's the manor where she worked,' Charlie Magg said enthusiastically. 'Sandra, the dark-haired school teacher from . . . what's that town?'

'Chesterfield?'

'Yes . . . her . . . she worked in a primary school in Tower Hamlets; that's the manor she worked for, the local authority.'

'Tower Hamlets.' Yewdall smiled. 'Thank you, Charlie.'

'Yes.' Tom Ainsclough also smiled. 'Thanks, Charlie, it's been very useful, very useful indeed.'

'They was here for a good while they was, both of them, for a good while, that's why I remember them, I expect. Yes, I expect that's why. Find I tend to forget things, but I can remember those two.' Violet Mayfield revealed herself to be a red-faced, short-haired, plump woman with noticeably puffy ankles, so Frank Brunnie observed. This was caused, so his present lover, a nurse, had told him, by a weak heart. Violet Mayfield's heart had evidently weakened with age and was not by then able to pump her blood efficiently round her body, and so a proportion of it fell according to gravity and collected round her ankles. Brunnie thought Violet Mayfield to be in her late fifties, quite young, he felt, for someone to fail the 'puffy ankle test'; too young for a weak heart, but then that's life, he pondered; it is essentially unfair. It deals different hands to different people. Some women who were born on the same day as Violet Mayfield would still be slender, still swinging golf clubs gracefully, while dressed in slacks, or thinking it nothing to go on a ten or fifteen mile hike carrying a loaded rucksack, and equally, equally still, others would be bedridden, unable to rise without assistance. There is, Brunnie had found, just no rhyme nor reason to it all. Violet Mayfield's home was a terraced house on Matlock Street in Stepney. Brunnie and Swannell both found it cramped and cluttered, and smelling heavily of damp. Matlock Street was, it transpired, a short, narrow road, perfectly straight, lined on either side with mid to late Victorian era, flat-roofed terraced houses which abutted the pavement and comprised a basement, a ground floor and an upper floor. As they drove slowly along the road looking for Violet Mayfield's house, both Brunnie and Swannell noted how valued the houses seemed; many were lovingly painted in bright colours, or had carefully varnished doors. It was clearly an area of the East End which was becoming fashionable and was being gentrified. Violet Mayfield's house was close to the corner of White Horse Road and had, by contrast, a scruffy, uncared-for appearance. Within, Brunnie and Ainsclough met the clutter and the musty, damp smell, and both yearned for an open window and a modicum of breathable air.

'But is it the two men we are interested in who you remember?' Swannell clarified. He handed a print of the E-fits which had appeared in that day's early edition of the *Evening Standard*.

'Oh yes . . . yes, I don't need to see the photographs again.

It was those two.' Violet Mayfield took hold of the prints of the E-fits anyway and studied them closely. 'Yes, same two men. Definitely. One tall, one short. I mean there was nothing like what you might call strange about them, just two blokes who shared the basement room. Two single beds, mind. I don't allow any of that nonsense in my house. No, my old man would turn in his urn if he knew that was going on; yes, he would turn in his urn. But I had no complaints about them; they came and went and paid their rent on time. They was as good as gold, really, as good as gold. Then they were not here . . . just gone. Seems like they just left.'

'You mean they did a moonlight flit?'

'No . . . no, they couldn't have done because I take my rent in advance, always have done; two weeks in advance for that reason. They left all their kit behind, all their stuff – clothes, dole signing card – things they'd need they left behind, yes, they did, all of it, all of it 'cept what they stood up in, I suppose. I suppose they took that. I mean they had to do that, didn't they?'

'What were their names?' Swannell asked. 'Can you remember?'

'Leonard Convers and Sydney Tyrell. Tyrell was the tall one, yes, he was; Tyrell the tall . . . so Convers was the short one.'

'You have a very good memory.' Frankie Brunnie smiled warmly.

Violet Mayfield returned the smile. 'Wish I could say that but I can't, darling. Like I told you, I forget things easily these days. No, it's their rent books with their names on the front. I kept them didn't I? But I do like to keep my brain alive, what's left of it. I write figures down and add them up or subtract them from each other, and multiply and divide as well. My old man went demented in the end. I don't want to be like that, not at all. I knew he was going demented when he put his underpants on his head one day.'

'Yes.' Brunnie nodded. 'I have heard that this is often one of the early symptoms.'

'Really?' Swannell turned to Brunnie.

'Yes,' Brunnie addressed Swannell, 'as is forgetting a word just before you are about to use it and having some sense that it's going away from you, as if it is being lifted out of your head and then disappears up into space.'

'Yes –' Violet Mayfield looked up at the ceiling – 'my Albert was like that. He forgot words, then he put his underpants on his head, then he got to thinking that he was a little boy. Eventually they took him to hospital and he didn't come back, poor old soul. So I exercise my brain for half an hour each and every day, so I do.'

'Good for you.' Swannell smiled. 'Keep it up.'

'Well, it's for my own sake isn't it? I mean, as much as anything it's for my own sake.'

'So, the two men, Convers and Tyrell . . .' Swannell refocussed the discussion and beside him he noticed Frankie Brunnie take out his notepad and his ballpoint pen.

'Yes, those two.' Violet Mayfield handed the E-fit back to Swannell. 'Convers and Tyrell, well, they left seven years since. I have their rent books; I still got them. I keep them all. It helps me to put a face to a name.' She stood slowly, awkwardly, levering herself up out of the armchair in which she sat, struggling to her feet and then she walked unsteadily to the sideboard which stood against the wall adjacent to the fireplace and pulled open a drawer. Extracting two small brown-coloured rent books from the drawer, she turned and handed them to Swannell, returned to her chair and sat in it, heavily so.

'Seven years ago.' Swannell nodded slightly as he opened the books and read the last entry in each. He handed the rent books to Brunnie who also glanced at the last entry in each and then gave them back to Violet Mayfield. 'Did they leave anything?'

'Yes, like I said, they left everything, everything they were not wearing when they left my house for the last time; clothes, shoes, all their knick-knacks. They didn't have much, so not a lot was left.' Violet Mayfield breathed with clear difficulty.

'What did you do with it?' Brunnie asked.

'Put it all in plastic bags, kept it for a couple of months and when it seemed plain they were not going to come back for it I left it in the doorway of the nearest charity shop. Yes, I did.'

'Fair enough.' Swannell glanced round the room; he found it neat and well ordered. 'Can you remember anything about them, the two men, Convers and Tyrell?'

'Not a lot. They didn't say much . . . they came, they went, but they were definitely iffy; a right iffy pair of toerags if you ask me.' Violet Mayfield breathed shallowly then took a single deep breath.

'You thought so?' Brunnie asked. 'You thought they were dodgy?'

'Well, it's the way of it.' Violet Mayfield seemed to relax once again. 'You get a nose for it, don't you? It must be the same in your old line of work; get a nose for the bad ones. But they were low-down iffies, well low-down; not high-up iffies. I mean, what high-up villain would live in my basement?'

Swannell thought that Violet Mayfield had made a valid point. Her basement, he thought, would be the sort of accommodation sought by bottom feeders in London's underworld, the very lowest in the food chain.

'They didn't work,' Violet Mayfield added, 'they didn't have no proper job. Claimed dole and did a bit here and there. They had more spare cash than most doleys, enough to go down the boozer for the hour before last orders is called, so they had that bit of extra spending money coming in. So they were duckin' and divin'. Then they left as if going somewhere and never came back, no they didn't, never came back. Not at all.'

'Did they have any visitors?' Brunnie asked. 'Any that you remember?'

'None.' Violet Mayfield shook her head vigorously. 'I wouldn't ever allow visitors, not ever.'

'Do you think that we were a little unfair there?' Penny Yewdall squinted against the glare of the sun as she and Tom Ainsclough walked casually away from the castle-like edifice of Brixton Prison towards Brixton Hill Road. 'A bit out of order? Misleading him perhaps?'

Tom Ainsclough half glanced at her. 'You mean that we let him believe that he could negotiate commuting a plea of guilty to involuntary manslaughter in return for a reduced sentence when we both knew such was never going to happen? I mean, not after the mess he made of "Stepney" Stevenson's face and head?'

'Yes, that's what I mean.'

'No, I think we greased the wheels of the interview and nothing more.' Tom Ainsclough's eye was caught by the blue-shirted bus driver of a red double-decker bus as it whirred along Brixton

Hill. There was, he thought, something East European in the man's appearance, as though the man was Polish or Czech, something he could not put his finger on as he received the image for a second or two. He was, Ainsclough thought, less relaxed-looking and more serious-minded than is usual for drivers of buses in London, as if more eager to please. Neater also, with a perfectly ironed shirt, a sober-minded manner which betrayed no sense of humour; definitely, Ainsclough felt, not a home-grown bus driver. 'I wouldn't worry,' he continued, 'Charlie Magg has been round the block often enough to know how the CPS works. He knows he won't be able to negotiate anything at all unless he signs a statement or two and then climbs into the witness box. He's got to sign and climb and he knows it. What we did, if anything, was to take him on a little journey into cloud cuckoo land and I think he allowed us to take him there.'

'Signs and climbs,' Penny Yewdall echoed.

'And frankly,' Tom Ainsclough continued, 'after what he did to "Stepney" Stevenson, turning him into a vegetable for five thousand pounds, prior to the plug being pulled on the wretched man's life-support system, and then implicating himself in the murder of another man by pushing him off a twelve storey block of flats, and being party to tying another felon across a railway line . . .'

'You think he was there?' Penny Yewdall looked at Tom Ainsclough.

'Certain of it,' Ainsclough replied. 'The details were too numerous, too precise . . . the sound of the rails singing and the man pleading. He was there all right. So that is two cold cases we can warm up. We can cross-reference them to this inquiry, especially if those two blokes were murdered on Arnie Rainbird's behest.' Ainsclough paused. 'No, we didn't do anything back there to compromise ourselves. No way, no way at all . . . Charlie Magg is going where he belongs and he is going there for a long, long time. I promise you, you and I will be pensioners before he walks into a pub for a pint of beer again. If ever.'

'If ever . . .' Penny Yewdall opened her handbag and rummaged for her car keys.

Harry Vicary sat behind his desk and leaned slowly backwards in his chair. Frankie Brunnie, Penny Yewdall, Tom Ainsclough and Vic Swannell sat silently in a semicircle in front of Vicary's desk.

'So what do we know about Convers and Tyrell?' Vicary glanced out of his office window at the buildings of central London and the expanse of blue sky above. 'Anything?'

'Petty crooks, sir.' Swannell consulted a computer printout. 'Very petty. Enough to get accepted by organized crime as gofers. They both appear to have living relatives so we should be able to get a DNA match on the bones very speedily, but I think we can assume that the bones are those of Convers and Tyrell.'

'Yes, it seems a safe assumption, but it remains an assumption. We must try and link them to Arnie Rainbird.' Vicary paused. 'Now, that party up in Bedfordshire . . . some seven years ago . . . you say.'

'Yes, sir,' Penny Yewdall responded in an alert manner, 'seven years ago this summer.'

'That sounds interesting. We really need to know more about that party. It seems that it was Desmond Holst who wrote the note and drove the bus load of girls up from London on the pretext of good money for one evening's work . . . and Convers and Tyrell disappeared before the party?'

'Yes, sir.' Swannell again consulted the computer printout. 'A few weeks prior to the party.'

'All right . . . all right . . . So what do we know about the house?'

'New build property, sir,' Yewdall responded, 'fairly remote. According to Charlie Magg it is guarded like the Tower of London, at least it was when he was running with Arnie Rainbird's team. He seems to have fallen out of favour but he remains loyal. He gave enough information but nothing specific.'

'More background information really,' Tom Ainsclough added. 'He wasn't interested in going into witness protection but he gave a clear indication that something very heavy went down at that party.'

'Again, interesting, and people who guard their homes like that always intrigue me. Do we know who owns the house?'

'Johnny "Snakebite" Herron, he's got form for armed robbery but is also a known associate of Arnie Rainbird,' Penny Yewdall explained. 'Like Arnie Rainbird, he's adept at keeping himself off the radar, but Charlie Magg told us he was very likely to be making his money through a people-smuggling racket. It's very appealing to the likes of Arnie Rainbird, apparently, good profits to be made and penalties they laugh at.'

'Especially if they don't get their hands dirty,' Tom Ainsclough added, 'which they allegedly do not.'

'All right.' Vicary reached for his pen and notepad. 'Let's see if we can draw up a timeline. So, seventeen years ago Arnie Rainbird goes down for twenty years and comes out after doing ten. About the time he comes out, Convers and Tyrell go missing. Then a few weeks after he comes out, as if waiting for the summer weather, a party is thrown to celebrate his release, wherein something of interest happens, enough to intimidate a bus load of cheated but hard-nosed women into silence. Then some years after the party a geezer who appeared to have been a gofer for Arnie Rainbird's mob leaves a note in a wall he is rebuilding, which he knows will be found some day; it would probably still be hidden had it not been for a drunken driver who rammed and demolished said wall with his motor vehicle.' Vicary tapped his pen on his notepad. 'There's an awful lot of smoke here. We need to find the fire.' He paused. 'So, what's for action?'

'We need to know about Arnie Rainbird, sir,' Swannell offered, 'why he went down for twenty years. We need to know where he is now . . . what he's up to.'

'Yes.' Vicary nodded in agreement. 'We must pay a call on him, set the cat among the pigeons; let him know we are developing a keen interest in him.'

'We have to find the house in Bedfordshire, sir,' Frankie Brunnie suggested.

'Yes, we'll contact the Bedfordshire Constabulary; a little local knowledge will be useful. They probably know of the house if "Snakebite" Herron has a record, which he does have. So, Frankie and Victor, I'd like you two to stay teamed up together. Call on Arnie Rainbird and say hello from the Metropolitan Police, then find out all you can about the house in Bedfordshire and all about "Snakebite" Herron.'

'Got it, sir,' Frankie Brunnie replied.

'Penny.'

'Sir?'

'Find out all you can about the school teacher Charlie Magg mentioned, then take a trip up to Chesterfield. That's a one-hander, no need to partner up for that.'

'Yes, sir.'

'That leaves you with the task of confirming the ID of Convers and Tyrell, Tom. OK with you?'

'OK with me.' Tom Ainsclough nodded. 'OK with me.'

Harry Vicary took the tube to Leytonstone. From Leytonstone Underground Station he walked casually up Church Lane, which was lined with small shops and which had flats above them. When at the top of the lane, outside the church itself, he chose to extend his walk by turning down Leytonstone High Street, despite always finding it fume filled, being too narrow in his view to accommodate the volume of traffic which it now carried. He looked calmly into the shops as he walked past them and, crossing the road, he walked up Michael Road and thus into suburbia. He crossed over Mornington Road, being a quiet street of owner-occupied housing, and then joined Bushwood, and thus enjoyed the expanse of green that was Wanstead Flats, and which, he believed, allowed Leytonstone to breathe. Without the Flats or the park beyond the Flats, he reasoned, there would be little breathable air in the borough. He turned left into Hartley Road, being a neat terrace of late nineteenth-century terraced housing, with small gardens in front of the houses to separate them slightly from the pavement and larger gardens to the rear. As he opened the front door his wife stepped forward and embraced him warmly.

Later that evening, after he and his wife had shared a perfectly cooked shepherd's pie, helped down by a jug of chilled water, they walked out arm in arm, both by then clothed in casual wear. They walked to the centre of Leytonstone and entered the Assembly Rooms, wherein they sat with a number of other people, a few of whom they recognized and acknowledged in a quiet, friendly manner. At the appointed time the visiting speaker stood and addressed the group, saying, 'Hello, I am Mary Jane and I am an alcoholic,' whereupon Harry and Kathleen Vicary, along with all the other persons in the room, replied, 'Hello, Mary Jane.'

After the conclusion of that evening meeting, Harry and

Kathleen Vicary walked into a pub and each had a glass of fruit juice and nibbled their way through a packet of dry roasted peanuts. Just because one is an alcoholic, they would often explain, does not mean that one cannot continue to enjoy pub culture, such as quiz nights, and use pubs to escape from the house once in a while. Later still, they folded into each other's arms and both slept a nourishing, trouble-free sleep.

FOUR

'It really wasn't so very difficult.' Penny Yewdall sipped the very welcome cup of tea which had been warmly pressed into her hand by Sandra Barnes. 'Not very difficult; quite easy in fact. We just had to follow procedure and be . . . well, a bit persuasive, but I must say the Department of Education of Tower Hamlets, London Borough of, were most fiercely protective of you and of your forwarding address. We had to go right up the top of the management mountain, encountering obstacles as we progressed. It was like climbing Mount Everest by the most difficult route, and when we did get to the top they insisted on phoning us back with the information to ensure that they really were talking to the Metropolitan Police. If they had still refused to let us have your address we would have had to obtain a court order and that would have been quite time-consuming. Even then they could only provide us with your parents' address and phone number.'

'Yes.' Sandra Barnes showed herself to be the raven-haired woman who had been described, accurately so, thought Penny Yewdall, by Charlie Magg in the agent's room at Brixton Prison. Sandra Barnes had aged little and was still a slender-figured woman of pleasing appearance whose South African accent had not completely vanished. 'Yes, my mother phoned me this morning and I phoned you immediately. I must say that you have made good time.'

'I jumped straight on a train; underground to St Pancras, then to Chesterfield . . . taxi here, to your door. I don't think the taxi driver was particularly impressed; it wasn't a long journey.'

'I can imagine. My husband was a taxi driver before he joined the fire service . . . it was one among the many jobs he had before he settled, and he told me that taxi owners make the good money only on the long journeys. Your driver must have been an owner-operator. An employed driver wouldn't be bothered about the length of any journey; he lifts the same money at the end of the week, no matter what.'

'Dare say that's true.' Penny Yewdall glanced round Sandra Barnes' home. It was, she noted, a new-build detached house, with three bedrooms overlooking Eastwood Park in Chesterfield, Derbyshire. Within, the house was kept in a neat and tidy and clean manner, though children's toys were heaped in a corner and children's drawings had been attached to the wall. Light was allowed into the living room courtesy of a large front window, and the sense of airiness was heightened by the Barneses clearly favouring light colours for their wallpaper and furnishings. A compact hi-fi system stood on a low table beside the fireplace, upon which stood a small, bronze carriage clock. On the other side of the fireplace stood a modestly sized television set. The room itself smelled of air freshener.

'So, tell me, I am burning up with curiosity.' Sandra Barnes raised her eyebrows. 'Why me? What can I do to help the Metropolitan Police?'

'Well . . .' Penny Yewdall sat forward and placed the cup and saucer she was holding on her lap. 'How can I explain this? I think they sent me because I am a woman. At least I was when I was under the shower this morning,' Yewdall added with forced good humour.

'You certainly seem to be one . . . lucky you.' Sandra Barnes smiled. 'I wouldn't want to be a man and I am so pleased I've got girls, though my husband aches for a son. Being a firefighter he's a very manly man and wants a son to go to rugby matches and cricket matches with. He wants a son to take to the National Railway Museum, the very mention of which makes the girls go "yuk"! So you seem to be the real deal. Mind you, I have met some men who can make a passable woman in a dim light, and I can't help but feel sorry for them. The effort that must go into the disguise, even training their voice, but that's what goes on in those nightclubs in London; heavens, they'd be lynched if they got dressed up like that round here! This part of England can be very intolerant of that sort of thing.'

'North, Midlands, South . . . small towns are all the same in my experience. Intolerant as you say, but . . .' Penny Yewdall relaxed backwards into the sofa on which she sat. 'I'm pleased you see me as another woman. I am the genuine article.'

'So.' Sandra Barnes also relaxed in the armchair which she

occupied, 'So, this is girl talk, is that what you're saying to me?'

'Probably.' Penny Yewdall once again glanced discreetly round the room. 'But it's probably more grown-woman talk . . . but, yes, that's what I am saying, and you are not under suspicion, because if you were then there would be two of us, but, yes, it's woman to woman time . . . if you don't mind.'

'Do you know, I think that I know why you are here. I think that I can guess why you have travelled such a distance to see me, and have done so out of the blue like this.' Sandra Barnes looked up at her ceiling.

'Oh?' Penny Yewdall queried. 'Being what?'

'The garden party,' Sandra Barnes replied after a pause, 'it can only be about that, about a garden party once held in a fairly isolated part of rural Bedfordshire; it has to be about that. Is it?' Sandra Barnes lowered her eyes and looked at Penny Yewdall. 'Is it about that so-called party?'

'Yes.' Penny Yewdall nodded her head slowly. 'Yes, it's about that . . . as you say, the "so-called" garden party. It did not sound to be much of a party.'

'I knew people would start talking, eventually, and I knew it would return to haunt me. I just knew it wouldn't go away and stay away. I mean, it couldn't. How could it stay buried?' Sandra Barnes leaned forward and placed her cup of tea on the glass top of the coffee table which stood in front of the chairs and settee. 'That sort of thing just cannot remain buried.'

'So, tell me about the party,' Penny Yewdall pressed gently. 'I have to tell you that it's important that you tell me, Sandra. I can call you Sandra?'

'Yes.' Sandra Barnes nodded and smiled. 'Please do.'

'I am Penny.'

'Penny . . . nice name.'

'Penelope on my birth certificate, but I have been Penny for so long that Penelope would seem strange.' She paused. 'But you have to tell me. I cannot lead you by my questions.'

'I see. I dare say you must not, cannot put words in my mouth.'

'And I will not do so,' Yewdall added. 'So, Sandra, in your own time . . .'

'How to begin . . .' Sandra Barnes seemed to scan the

cream-coloured carpet for the answer. 'Well, what I can say in the first instance is that it wasn't what I would call a party, not a garden party in the real sense of the term. If my daughters ever come home and say that they have been invited to a garden party, I promise you that I will feel very uneasy; the term has that resonance with me now. I dare say it always will.'

'Interesting that you call it a garden party. It wasn't a house party?'

'It was in and out of the house, but being the summer of that year and a hot summer at that, it was mostly outside, and what you will be interested in happened on the lawn and in the swimming pool. So I have come to think of it as the garden party.'

'Fair enough, the garden party it is.'

'The men ate out mostly, as well, by the barbecue area . . . and drank outside.'

'Again, fair enough.'

Sandra Barnes paused as if thinking, as if mustering courage, then she said, 'Look, Penny, one woman to another, I value my house . . . my home, nothing immoral has ever happened in this house. It's a family home. It's a sanctuary . . . it's akin to a sacred place for me.'

'I fully understand,' Penny Yewdall replied, 'fully understand.'

'I don't ever want to talk about the garden party in this house. Even just talking about that week would seem to contaminate my house; it would seem to violate it.'

'So can you suggest where we should go?' Penny Yewdall asked.

'The park –' Sandra Barnes pointed in the direction of the front of her house – 'it's just across the road. We can walk in the park; it's a lovely day.'

'Yes.' Penny Yewdall beamed. 'A day like this; a walk in the park . . . and walking is good for talking. You know, I have noticed that for some reason two people talk more freely when they are walking than when they are sitting together in a room. So, yes, admirable suggestion.' She stood.

Eastwood Park in Chesterfield, Penny Yewdall found, was a modest park, a flat area of grass with football and cricket pitches and a gaily painted swing park for the amusement of infants. It was surrounded by green-painted, round-topped railings and a concrete path wound round the inside perimeter. Nineteenth-century housing surrounded the park on three sides; the fourth side was occupied by twentieth-century houses, one of which was the home of Sandra Barnes. As Penny Yewdall and Sandra Barnes entered the park by a gate adjacent to Sandra Barnes' house, they saw, to their relief, it being midweek, that the park was sparsely occupied.

'So, what can I tell you?' Sandra Barnes fell into step with Penny Yewdall and walked sufficiently close to her that occasionally their shoulders touched.

Yewdall glanced around her noting the red-bricked houses under black-tiled rooves of northern England. 'As I said, Sandra, in your own words and time.'

'Ah, yes.' Sandra Barnes nodded. 'You can't lead me with your questions. Well, we were all duped, all cheated, all of us. All the women that is; all except one older woman who knew what was going on. She was there to keep us in line, but at least we lived to tell the tale, at least there is that to be thankful for. At least we survived with nothing more than emotional scarring.'

'Survived?' Penny Yewdall echoed. 'Others didn't?'

'No . . . I'll tell you,' Sandra Barnes replied, 'you see, I was what you would call a mistress. I was a rich man's plaything. I dare say that I sold my body but I never stood on a street corner, though most of the women at the garden party were street girls . . . but you can't live in London on a primary school teacher's salary, so you have to do something other than teaching if you are going to survive. It's difficult for unmarried schoolmistresses to survive up here where the cost of living is less, but in London it's impossible. So I allowed myself to be bought and I am not proud of it. It is a regret. I have to live with it and I do regret it. But I went with another girl to a club, she was a poorly paid low-grade civil servant I knew who had a sugar daddy, and the club is where sugar babies and sugar daddies went to meet each other, to check each other out, looking for a "click". I went a few times and eventually I got a proposition which I found interesting. He was decorative and wasn't posh, working-class background the same as me, but he'd made something of himself in the world of finance . . . so he said.'

'So he said.' Penny Yewdall smiled.

'Yes, so he said,' Sandra Barnes sighed. 'Well, I did say that we were duped and for me that was the beginning. Anyway, arrangements differ from couple to couple but my "daddy" installed me in a flat he owned in Earl's Court. I mean, no wonder it's called "kangaroo canyon".'

'So I believe.'

'I mean,' Sandra Barnes continued, 'all those young Australians taking a gap year to visit the mother country and all they wanted to do was stick together and drink Foster's lager. I mean, what's the point of them travelling to the other side of the planet just to be with each other all the time and drink Australian beer?'

'Search me.' Penny Yewdall grinned. 'But they're born upside down so they probably don't think logically.'

Sandra Barnes laughed. 'I wish I had thought like that at the time, it would have helped me to make sense of it all.' She paused for a few seconds. 'So there I was paying a peppercorn rent of just one pound a month.'

Yewdall gasped. 'That is peppercorn, for London that is peppercorn.'

'I know, but he was clever . . . shrewd, shrewd is the word I think I would use to describe him. By paying a rent, no matter how small, and recording it in a rent book, and by getting me to sign a rental agreement he ensured that my status in the eyes of the law was always that of tenant.'

'Shrewd, as you say,' Yewdall said.

'Yes,' Sandra Barnes replied, 'you see, he told me once of a story; a true story. A man owned a second home, unknown to his wife, and he installed a mistress in the second home whom he'd visit when he felt the need for a little horizontal relaxation, all unknown by his wife.'

'Of course.' Penny Yewdall's eye was caught by a youth of perhaps fourteen years walking slowly in the park. 'I mean the wife is always the last to find out anything.'

'Indeed. He also allowed the mistress to live in the house so as to sit it, as it were, keeping the burglars out, but no money was exchanged. She got rent-free living in exchange for her services and he got a house-sitting service for nothing, and this arrangement went on for some years,' Sandra Barnes explained. 'Like, a lot of years.'

'I think I know where this is going.' Penny Yewdall returned her attention to Sandra Barnes.

'Yes. So it came to pass that one day the man, the owner of the house, wanted to sell the house so he gave his bit of stuff her marching orders, but said bit of stuff had more about her than the man thought and she said that after all those years, in excess of ten, I believe, she had some moral claim to the property. So it went to court and the jury found in her favour and she became the outright owner of the house.'

'Nice.' Penny Yewdall pursed her lips. 'Very nice.'

'Yes, good for her, I thought,' Sandra Barnes replied. 'I can well imagine the man being less than pleased, very less than pleased, but my sugar daddy said that the man was an idiot, all he had to have done was to get that woman to sign a rental agreement, give her a rent book and take even just one penny a month, but in the event she lived there permanently as her own and only home so . . .'

'Squatter's rights?' Yewdall anticipated.

'Yes, that's what decided that court case, an ancient legal right going back to medieval times. If you live in a property for seven years or more you can claim it as your own. But my sugar daddy was determined that that wasn't going to happen to him, so I got charged a nominal rent but I wasn't bothered; I wouldn't have stayed for seven years anyway. So I paid a quid a month for a lovely flat in Earl's Court, a sitting room, a bedroom, a dining kitchen and a bathroom. The whole building was once a large family home with servants' quarters. I was on the ground floor. All the other flats were occupied by yuppies, really high earners and my "daddy" said I could have a "Tom", by which he meant a boyfriend, but the "Tom" couldn't visit me there, I had to go to my boyfriend's flat, if I had one. I just had to keep myself available for my sugar daddy every Monday, Wednesday and Friday evening.'

'I see,' Penny Yewdall replied softly. 'You know, I can understand the attraction of that arrangement for a girl who does not want to get involved . . . clean, safe, comfortable.'

'Yes, and it was clean and comfortable, always clean, always comfortable and it was safe, safe until the garden party, then it was anything but safe.' Sandra Barnes shook her head slightly.

'Oh, and I got a three-week holiday in the Canary Islands and also a two-week Easter holiday in Cyprus, all part of the deal. I suppose I looked eye-catching in a bikini in those days. I was taken along to set him off on the beach and in the bar at night, either stretched topless on a beach towel or perched on a stool in a stupidly short skirt, with a bronze, suntanned body; his to show off to the world like a glittering trophy, but I wasn't unhappy; nothing came out of my salary. I was even able to save, not much, but when the time came I had money to return to Chesterfield with. Not bad for a primary school teacher in inner London.'

'Not bad.' Penny Yewdall glanced at Sandra Barnes with a slight, approving smile. 'Not bad at all.'

'And there were other compensations. My man was in his mid-fifties and so the physical demands were less. Sometimes me and Tony – that was his name – me and Tony would return from the restaurant,' Sandra Barnes explained, 'and clamber into bed, there'd be a little fumbling and groping and then he'd fall asleep. Only when he visited on Fridays did he stay in bed the following morning, or during the school holidays, but usually I was going out the door as prim Miss Barnes, in a very proper three-quarter length skirt, and going to teach infants basic literacy and numeracy, while he was still sleeping off the previous evening's red wine.'

'How long,' Penny Yewdall asked, 'were you his mistress?'

'About a year and a half . . . two Christmases and one and a half summers. We met approaching one Christmas, I remained his mistress until the next Christmas, then it all ended abruptly at the wretched garden party in the middle of the second summer . . . so, yes, about a year and a half.' Sandra Barnes paused. 'You know, I thought that being a rich man's mistress was the end of my innocence, but the actual end of that was the garden party.' Sandra paused as an elderly male dog walker approached them. The gentleman was dressed in short sleeves, white trousers and a panama hat and was being pulled along, it seemed to Penny Yewdall, by an eager corgi. As he approached, the man doffed his hat and said a cheery, 'Good afternoon, ladies'.

'Good afternoon,' Barnes and Yewdall replied simultaneously.

Sandra Barnes remained silent for a few moments until she was certain that the elderly dog walker was safely out of earshot. 'That day . . . it was a Friday in July, early July – he arrived at about six p.m. like he said he would, having told me that we were going to a party.'

'At six!' Penny Yewdall exclaimed.

'Yes,' Sandra Barnes replied, 'at six. I thought it strange, but I had learned by then that "her indoors" must not ask too many questions and because I had been told that we were going to a party I was well tarted up. I don't mean a ball gown but . . . how shall I put it . . .?'

'Elegant?' Penny Yewdall suggested.

'Yes –' Sandra Barnes held eye contact with Penny Yewdall and then looked ahead of her – 'that's the word, elegant; long skirt, nylons, heels, jewellery . . . all the jewellery I had, just a few cheap bangles really.'

'I get the image.'

'Usually,' Sandra Barnes carried on, 'Tony arrived dressed in the male equivalent, smart suit, highly polished shoes . . . reeking of aftershave. I mean, Tony would never be mistaken for a woman, like we were saying earlier. I mean, he was one hundred percent supercharged testosterone. Good gracious . . . no . . . Tony in drag . . . never. But anyway he arrived in a T-shirt and faded denims.'

'Dressed down?' Penny Yewdall asked. 'Would you say dressed down?'

'Yes.' Sandra Barnes nodded in agreement. 'That's a good way of putting it. You have that skill, Penny, but yes . . . so . . . I am dressed to kill because he's taking me to a party, wearing all the finery he bought for me, and he is dressed to sloth about the house on a Saturday morning. So I am told to get the fancy kit off and so I do, not happily, because I had dashed home from work and spent an hour getting arrayed for the fray . . . make-up, clothes . . . all that number.'

'Yes.'

'So it all came off. Had to wash all the war paint off, put the good clothes away, returned wearing a T-shirt and a pair of jeans I had cut down, quite savagely, into a pair of skimpy shorts, tennis shoes . . . no socks even, I left the socks off as a form of protest. So it's all getting a bit confusing by then . . . so we go out, lock the flat up and there's his blue Porsche, double-parked, and we get in . . . hood down and the first thing I notice is a suitcase behind the seats, so by then alarm bells are beginning to ring a bit softly . . . a bit in the distance, but ringing nonetheless.'

'I can bet they were,' Penny Yewdall replied.

'So.' Sandra Barnes took a deep breath. 'I am thinking what sort of party is this that we leave for it at six p.m.? Mind you, it was nearer seven by the time I had got changed, but so unusually early still, and dressed as we were dressed . . . for a party? Then the suitcase in the back of the Porsche, a change of clothing for him, none for me . . . I mean, just how long is this party going to last?'

'Indeed.'

'So this was Tony Sudbury flying his true colours,' Sandra Barnes continued. 'He had told me he was in the world of finance, so I thought a stockbroker or someone in insurance in the City, but he was flying his true colours that week. He really showed his true self.'

'It is always the case, eventually,' Penny Yewdall replied, but continued to speak minimally, giving just short responses. It was, she knew, so, so important not to lead Sandra Barnes, though she did allow herself to say, 'You're going to tell me he was in the criminal sort of financial world?'

'Yes,' Sandra Barnes replied, 'in a word, yes. And how. I mean East End organized crime, the whole heavy number, where even he with his convertible Porsche, his properties, and him in his fifties, even then he had to call people "boss" and do what he was told. My eyes were well opened at the party.'

'Tony Sudbury, you say?' Penny Yewdall made a mental note of the name.

'Yes, like the area of London, Sudbury-on-Thames.'

'I know it, or rather know of it, driven through it a few times, quite a pleasant area,' Penny Yewdall commented.

'I'll take your word for it,' Sandra Barnes replied drily, 'but that was his name, Tony Sudbury, "Flash" Tony Sudbury. I suppose I should have seen that as an early warning sign but I didn't, I just didn't.'

'Seen what?' Yewdall queried.

'His whole Flash Harry attitude . . . loved hard cash, wallet bulging with the stuff. I mean what stockbroker does that? They use credit cards or cheques but Tony used to flash a wad of readies about whenever he could. He even once did that stupid stunt of lighting a cigar with a burning twenty pound note, but very occasionally he did write a cheque and that's how I know his real name was Tony Sudbury. Usually he'd give me cash if I needed something, but once he wrote a cheque for five hundred pounds, told me to buy a watch with it. He thought I needed a watch you see. At least a better watch than the watch I had at the time.' Sandra Barnes paused and looked away from Penny Yewdall.

'Something bothers you?' Penny Yewdall enquired gently.

'Yes . . .' Sandra Barnes replied slowly, 'can I tell you something, Penny?'

'Of course.'

'I stole from him. I felt so guilty and I still feel so guilty . . . but now what could have happened to me haunts me.'

Penny Yewdall remained silent.

'That cheque he gave me to buy a watch. I cashed it . . . I paid it into my bank account. You see, despite the lifestyle, the flat in Earl's Court, the dinners, a man with a Porsche, I didn't have a lot of money behind me. So I bought a nice-looking watch from a charity shop, and bought a new strap for it just hoping he wouldn't want to see the presentation case or look at the guarantee.'

'Oh . . .' Penny Yewdall raised her eyebrows.

'"Oh" is right,' Sandra Barnes breathed deeply. 'The worst I thought could happen is that he'd give me the heave-ho and trade me in for another sugar baby, but at the time I thought he was a man in the field of city finance, not a villain in the world of gangster finance. You don't steal from an East End blagger and get away with it. If I lived at all it would be with broken arms and legs . . . the risk . . . I was skating over thin ice there. I realize now that the Tony I was dealing with would have cut up rough, so the guilt is now compounded with the fear of what I could easily have invited on myself. A sense of my life being spared . . .'

'Yes, many of us have those experiences, the scythe of the Grim Reaper passing within a hair's breadth of one's life. It leaves you hearing an echo saying, "I'll get you next time, don't worry . . . I'll get you on the way back",' Penny Yewdall commented as a male jogger in a tracksuit jogged up from behind them and passed them.

'Yes, it feels like that, like a fatal car crash that didn't happen by dint of a split second or a fraction of an inch . . . but the memory stays and haunts you.'

The two women fell silent for a few moments then Sandra Barnes continued. 'So we're in the Porsche driving through central London. We drive north and Tony, he's done this journey before, I could tell; he knew where we were going all right. So we leave London on the A1, the Great North Road, as it is sometimes called.'

'Yes, I know the road,' Penny Yewdall replied.

'So we drive up the A1 and we turn off at Biggleswade, the Biggleswade exit. I remember that was the turning because the name has always amused me, such a funny-sounding name and it also reminded me of the Biggles books for boys written by Captain W. E. Johns . . . *Flying Officer Biggles* and titles like that. My older brother used to read them and leave them lying about the house, much to my father's annoyance, because he was ex navy, my father, he liked good order, everything in its place.'

'I can imagine his annoyance.' Penny Yewdall smiled.

'So we came off at the Biggleswade exit and followed the signs for Bedford, but we never got as far as Bedford because we turned off the main road and drove along country lanes for a while.'

'Good. This will help us.'

'It will?'

'Yes,' Penny Yewdall explained, 'we must locate the house in question, it's essential that we do that.'

'I see.' Sandra Barnes looked down at the pathway upon which she and Penny Yewdall walked.

'I don't think that I can help you there, not the precise location,' Sandra Barnes was apologetic. 'I doubt I could find it again especially because I now think that Tony drove a deliberately complicated long way round from the main road to the house as

if to get me disorientated. When we left the house the return
journey to the main road seemed to take only a few minutes. So
getting me lost was clearly all part of the plan, along with a
change of clothes for him but not for me.'

'I see. We'll find the house. We knew it was in Bedfordshire
and we have contacted the Beds. Constabulary,' Penny Yewdall
explained. 'We'll pick their brains. It certainly sounds like the
sort of house they'll know about. It was a new build we understand with a roof of red tile?'

'Oh, it was a real nest of vipers, the police will know about
it, all right.' A note of anger crept into Sandra Barnes' voice and
was clearly noted by Penny Yewdall. 'And, yes, that is a good
description . . . new build, red tiles, set back, well set back from
the road. There were not a lot of grounds in front of the house
but at the back it was huge, mainly lawn, but there was a swimming pool and a barbecue area with tables and seats round the
burner. Dare say the swimming pool was a bit optimistic for the
UK but that was a hot summer, like I said, and so it got used
that week . . . in more ways than one. There was a second pool
inside the house, that was more sensible, a heated pool and you
could swim in there when there's two feet of snow on the other
side of a pane of glass.'

'Good, all part of building the picture,' Penny Yewdall replied.

'So we arrived. Tony parked the car in front of the house next
to another car and off to one side of the car parking area was a
single-decker bus, or rather a coach, I should say. Then it was
"Get your kit off, girl".'

'Just like that!' Penny Yewdall felt shocked.

'More or less.' Sandra Barnes spoke quietly. 'Sorry, but this
is where it gets a bit difficult.'

'OK, Sandra, take your time,' Penny Yewdall replied comfortingly. 'But it's vital we know what happened at that party; we
need as much detail as possible.'

'Yes, I realize it is important . . . believe me, I know why you
have travelled all the way up from London.'

'Thank you for saying that, we appreciate your cooperation.'

'I stepped into the house, behind Tony. Usually it was me first,
him second, but this time it felt like I was being led into the
house . . . and . . .' Sandra Barnes shook her head. 'I confess I

don't think I have seen so many naked girls since I was in the showers at school . . . and they all looked frightened. It was then that I was told to take my kit off, "Take your kit off girl, all of it, or we'll take it off for you".'

'"We'll",' Penny Yewdall queried, '"we'll take it off for you"?'

'Yes. It was a woman who said that. She was past her prime, well past it; middle-aged, short but very muscular . . . and she gave some serious grief to any girl who stepped out of line. The other girls were all holding a black plastic bag and a bag like that was pushed into my hands by the older woman and she repeated what she had said, "Everything off and put it all in the bag". So by then I was thinking, what have I got myself into?, but I peeled it off anyway. It was all I could do. By this time Tony had walked off leaving me at the mercy of the older woman. So it all went in . . . shoes, clothing, jewellery, watch, handbag and all the contents of the handbag. Then she opened a small room off the main vestibule and we were told to dump our plastic bags in there, which we did, and the door was locked and the woman pocketed the key.'

'You were trapped,' Penny Yewdall observed.

'Yes, yes we were,' Sandra Barnes replied, 'and we knew it; none of us were going anywhere in a hurry.'

'No telephone?'

'Well, any mobile phones were in the plastic bags among the clothes behind a locked door.' Sandra Barnes forced a smile. 'The one landline was in the entrance hall which I found later was fixed so it could only take incoming calls. So, we were trapped, as you said. Outside the door were some lowlife geezers like minders and then there were dogs which were left out at night, and we had a walk over a rough surface on bare feet to the road down a long, very long drive. The back of the house was fenced off with a twenty foot high wire fence beyond a line of Leylandii, with fields beyond that. So, yes, we were trapped all right, and I soon realized that if I was going to survive this so-called party I was going to have to cooperate. The girls were then herded, and that is the only word, herded like cattle through the house into the rear where men were standing drinking beer and eating hamburgers. All they did was give us a casual glance and that just made us feel even more vulnerable. I learned the whole thing was to celebrate a fella called Arnie Rainbird coming out of prison after a long time inside. It was then that all doubts about who Tony Sudbury was just vanished, totally evaporated. It was then that I realized that this party was for top-end villainy, organized crime. No wonder he'd flash his money around like he did. Never found out what sort of crime though; drugs, I assume.'

'Used to be,' Penny Yewdall said, 'they were moving out of drugs by then and getting into people smuggling.'

'People smuggling?' Sandra Barnes repeated in astonishment.

'So we believe.' Penny Yewdall glanced at Sandra Barnes. 'Huge profits to be made with only puny penalties to fear.'

'I did wonder. Thank you for telling me that.' Sandra Barnes nodded her head gently. 'I did wonder what their line of crime was. It's not the sort of thing you can ask.'

'Certainly isn't,' Penny Yewdall replied, 'not if you don't want to disappear.'

'Yes, yes, I realized then that they were that sort of crew. So, the party . . .'

'For want of a better word,' Penny Yewdall said.

'Yes, if you can call it a party.' Sandra Barnes looked to her left. 'If you can call it that. Well, the evening began, drink flowed and there was a buffet, but we learned quickly that the buffet was a man-only affair. One girl helped herself to a slice of cold pizza and got a good smack across her face for doing so by one of the men, and then it was anything goes, for the men that is. Once the men were fuelled up the women began to get used, with myself and the other "good" girls finding ourselves to be quite popular and much in demand. We were told that "Arnie's been inside for ten years, he's got a lot of catching up to do", and he caught up all right, him and his mates.'

'I'm sorry.' Penny Yewdall grimaced. 'I really am sorry. We understand it went on for a week . . . longer in fact.'

'Yes.' Sandra Barnes drew breath between her teeth. 'You understand correctly. On the Saturday morning, the morning after the first night, we, the girls that is, had been given breakfast . . . a bowl of cereal each. One of the girls asked if she could have her two hundred pounds and a ride back to London. Apparently a lot of the girls were street girls, they'd been hired . . .'

'Yes.' Penny Yewdall once again glanced at Sandra Barnes. 'The offer was two hundred pounds for a night's work.'

'Yes, for them. There were four other girls like me, sugar babies whose "daddies" had decided that they were "time served" and thus expendable. We were each just told we were going to a party. The older woman said, "No, darling, not one night, it's going on for a little longer than that", and the men who were loafing about started to laugh.'

'Oh . . .' Penny Yewdall groaned, 'I wondered how you had found out.'

'It was then we found out, breakfast time on Saturday, and silly me, silly me who had told herself that cooperation and passivity was the only way to survive started to mouth off, "You can't keep us here against our will, that's false imprison-ment . . ." and all the rest of it. The older woman, the only female who kept her clothes on, she just strides over to me and slaps me, just once, but it sent me reeling. I saw stars and fell over. I've never been slapped so hard . . . ever. I was told later that it knocked me off my feet, that for a split second my entire body was in the air and my cheek felt like someone had put a hot iron against it. Then she picks me up by my hair and drags me outside, telling the other women to follow her. Then . . .' Sandra Barnes' voice trailed off. 'Sorry, the next bit is a bit difficult.'

'It's all right,' Penny Yewdall said quietly, 'you don't have to tell me. We know what happened to you then.'

'You do?' A note of surprise crept into Sandra Barnes' voice.

'Yes, we do, we got a fair summary from Charlie Magg,' Penny Yewdall explained. 'He remembers you well. He seemed to take quite a shine to you.'

'Charlie!' Sandra Barnes smiled. 'Oh, Charlie, he looked after me. He couldn't rescue me but he was a source of comfort. How is he?'

'He's in Brixton Prison probably facing a murder charge.'

Sandra Barnes sighed. 'I am sorry to hear that.'

'Yes, he'll be going down for a long time.'

'Brixton Prison?'

'Yes.'

'I will write to him.'

'He would appreciate that,' Penny Yewdall replied, 'but don't let him have your address.'

'Don't worry.' Sandra Barnes forced a grin. 'I am not that stupid.'

'Good.'

'So you know what happened then, after I got slapped like that?'

'Yes, you were half-drowned . . . they made an example of you.'

'Didn't they just. I thought I was going to die. All the girls standing round the edge of the swimming pool. I was told it went on for about fifteen minutes but it felt a lot longer.' Sandra Barnes paused. 'But it worked; after that we were all so meek and mild. The party continued and it was anything goes because the women were trapped there, and trapped by a load of heavy geezers . . . it really was survival time.'

'It sounds like it,' Penny Yewdall replied. 'It certainly sounds like it.'

'There was one guy, a little rat-faced geezer, who had a real downer on women. One day he played football with one girl's head, on another day he used a second girl as a punchbag. He had to be pulled off both times and both times it was Charlie Magg that pulled him off.' Sandra Barnes paused. 'Strange bloke was Charlie, he never seemed to take advantage of the women, any of us, but by heavens could he get violent with men. So it really doesn't surprise me that he is looking at a murder charge.'

'So,' Penny Yewdall asked, 'I am just curious, what were the sleeping and eating arrangements?'

'Sleep!' Sandra Barnes snorted with derision. 'I dare say the answer to that is in a man's bed if so summoned, until you were kicked out, but otherwise one stretched out on a sofa, curled up in an armchair if one was small enough . . . in the corner of a room, really anywhere you could put your head down when things got quiet, usually after about one or two o'clock each morning. We'd eat in the kitchen, just a little food each morning so we were always hungry. We were put on a dishwashing rota and that became popular because we were always well away from male attention then and we could also pilfer leftover food. We had the use of one particular bathroom near the kitchen but

they had taken the door off. No escape at all, you see, none
at all.'

'They had thought of everything,' Penny Yewdall snorted
sourly.

'Hadn't they just?' Sandra Barnes continued. 'Apart from what
happened to me and the other twenty plus women. I suppose you
really want to know about the two men who were murdered?'

Surprised at the offer of information, Penny Yewdall fought
to contain her excitement. She was able to hold the pause and
then said, 'Yes, yes we do. We know their names but that's about
all we know.'

'I can't tell you from beginning to end because I was one of
the ones who fainted,' Sandra Barnes apologized.

'You fainted?'

'Nearly all of us, all the women did, apart from the mighty
atom that was meant to keep us in line, I don't think she fainted.
She was a hard, hard woman.' Sandra Barnes looked skyward.
'You know, even now it doesn't seem real.'

'Oh that,' Penny Yewdall replied, 'that I can well understand.
Believe me.'

'So . . . the bloodletting . . . the murders.' Sandra Barnes
steeled herself. 'This is another difficult bit . . .'

'As I said before, Sandra,' Penny Yewdall replied calmly, 'in
your own time.'

'In my own time,' Sandra Barnes repeated, as she and Penny
Yewdall strolled slowly along the pathway, 'dare say I have plenty
of that. Well . . . it was about halfway through the so-called party,
on the Wednesday or the Thursday, that two wretched men were
brought to the house. But the sight they presented, they looked
like shipwrecked sailors . . . long hair, straggly beards, frail,
emaciated, toothless . . . human skeletons. It was certain that
they had been kept against their will and kept alive on a starvation diet. One was short and the other was tall and there was
fear in their eyes; their eyes were bulging with fear as they were
pushed to the ground in front of the party boy and said, "We
didn't say nothing, Mr Rainbird, we didn't grass you up", stuff
like that.'

'I see,' Penny Yewdall said, 'that explains the motive behind
it, gangland retribution.'

'So . . . we . . . all the women, naked as the day we were born except the older woman who wore her nice blue tracksuit and tennis shoes, we all got told to stand in line, then one of Arnie Rainbird's lieutenants said to us "Watch and remember", and the two shipwrecked sailors were pleading for their lives. Then two of the men – one was the rat-faced bloke – he and Charlie Magg appeared carrying golf clubs, I mean a golf club each, the heavy ones . . .' Sandra Barnes cupped her hands – 'those with a club on the end, not the ones like you get to use on a putting green, the heavy ones used to hit a ball off the tee . . .'

'Drivers?' suggested Penny Yewdall. 'They're called drivers.'

'If you say so . . . but the heavy ended ones,' Sandra Barnes continued, 'they had one of those each and Charlie Magg felled the first geezer with a blow to the back of his legs, then he and the rat-faced one started to pound him with the drivers on his chest, arms, legs, but never his head. They didn't want to kill him, they kept him conscious. He was screaming and the women . . . they started fainting. He was howling and then the woman who wore the tracksuit and who was also watching started to grin.'

'Grin!' Penny Yewdall was incredulous.

'I kid you not, a wide grin and a gleam in her eye. She said, "Wind him, he's too noisy", and the rat-faced geezer brings his golf club down on the man's stomach. After that he was quieter, but they kept raining blows, and Arnie Rainbird is watching all this while he's sipping a glass of wine. I tried to look away, tried to close my eyes but you just can't help looking . . . and the sound of the clubs on this poor man's body . . . I just can't describe it. After a while he stays still, I reckon it was because he couldn't move his arms or legs any more . . . then they stop. I never heard anyone tell them to stop but they both stopped at the same time. Then the guy who had half-drowned me, he picks the wretched man up by his hair and drags him across the lawn to the swimming pool and does his thing, immerses his head and holds it there, then brings it out . . . then puts it under again . . . in and out . . . in and out . . . and then after a while he doesn't bring it out. The poor man can't struggle of course because every bone in his body is broken, but the guy called "The Baptist", he holds his head there for ten minutes, probably longer. While this was happening I noticed two other blokes piling up firewood as if making a bonfire at the very bottom of the garden. The Baptist pulls the bloke from the pool and two other guys carry the body to the bottom of the garden. He was dead . . . I . . . we had just seen a man murdered and the other bloke was just kneeling and making a wailing sound . . . trembling with fear. Then Charlie Magg and the rat-faced bloke pull the other hairy shipwrecked survivor to the centre of the lawn, and then I join the other girls lying in the grass . . .'

'Sorry?' Penny Yewdall asked.

'I mean, I fainted. I was one of the last to faint but eventually I felt light-headed and I blacked out.' Sandra Barnes once again looked skywards. 'I must have been out for quite a long time because I woke up feeling cold, the sun was setting, and the swimming pool had been emptied and four girls had been set to scrubbing the sides and the bottom of it with stiff brushes and a bleach solution . . . like they do in public swimming baths . . . if someone drowns, they empty the pool and clean it and then refill it.'

'Yes.' Penny Yewdall nodded. 'That is the policy.'

'I don't think they were really being sensitive, though,' Sandra Barnes explained. 'I think it was because the water was contaminated with blood so it was a matter of hygiene, not sensitivity.'

'I see,' Penny Yewdall replied, 'that makes sense. They may also have wanted to get rid of evidence.'

'And those women in the pool were being well supervised by my man, my ex, Tony Sudbury, "Scrub it well or I'll scrub it with your head", shouting like a sergeant in the army. Then he turned to another member of Arnie Rainbird's team and said, "Scrubbers scrubbing a pool" and they both laughed.' She fell silent. 'I don't know whether I want to write to Charlie Magg after all. He was so protective to the women yet he could do that to another man.'

'It probably wouldn't be a good idea, really, but it's your call,' Penny Yewdall replied, as a young mother, beaming with pride, approached from the opposite direction pushing a pram. She and Sandra Barnes smiled warmly at the woman who returned their smiles.

'At night they burnt the two bodies.' Sandra Barnes carried

on with her story, seemingly, thought Penny Yewdall, finding it easier to talk after her initial reluctance. 'That smell . . . so sickly sweet . . . I'll never forget it; the smell that burning flesh makes is horrible . . . the way the bodies twisted in the flames.'

'You saw that!'

'They made us watch it, all in a line. They made us line up to watch the murders and they made us line up to watch the cremation. Some of the girls fainted at the cremation as well. I didn't; I kept telling myself that at least they're dead, not feeling anything. And the following day . . .' Sandra Barnes added, 'they did it all again.'

'More victims?'

'No, no, I mean that they built another fire and a guy they called "The Butcher", he cut the charred bodies with a saw and a machete and put the bits on the second fire. They used coal to build the second fire for some reason, probably because it produces more heat than wood produces. But in the morning after the second fire there were just bones in the ash, no flesh at all, and the bones were put in a big cardboard box and given to a gofer, and The Butcher said, "You know what to do with them?" and the gofer says, "Yes, Mr Harley."'

'Mr Harley?' Penny Yewdall queried.

'Yes,' Sandra Barnes replied confidently. 'It was "Yes, Mr Harley." I had, I still have a friend with that surname so I remembered it, it registered, "Yes, Mr Harley."'

'Mr Harley,' Penny Yewdall repeated. 'So The Butcher was called Harley. That is very useful. Did you get to know any of the other girls?'

'Chatted to a few, but really only got to know one; she was a hard street girl on the outside but lovely on the inside. She had been brought there with the other street girls on the coach with the promise of two hundred pounds for one night's work.'

'Do you remember her name?'

'Elizabeth Petty. She was known as "Long Liz". We came to be quite pally, but just for the duration of the party. A really tall girl, over six feet, and she was a bit of a history lesson,' Sandra Barnes added.

'Oh?'

'Well you see one of Jack the Ripper's victims was also called Long Liz.'

'Yes, I seem to remember that, "Long Liz" Stride, wasn't it?'

'Yes.' Sandra Barnes nodded. '"Long Liz" Stride and she was all of five feet seven inches tall. Poor diet, no sun getting through the smoke over East London in the 1880s meant that the people were short, so short that someone who stood five feet seven inches tall was called Long Liz because of her height. But in the early twenty-first century a girl from the East End has to stand in excess of six feet to earn a nickname like Long Liz, so we are larger and taller and healthier.'

'A history lesson, as you say,' Penny Yewdall agreed, smiling. 'We learn something every day.'

'Indeed, Long Liz was a tall East End girl with no qualifications, she took a few wrong turns, accumulated a few petty convictions . . . so she ended up on the street; just a basically good girl trying to survive.'

'"Long Liz" Petty,' Penny Yewdall repeated, committing the name to memory. 'Interesting name.'

'So . . .' Sandra Barnes once again looked down at the pathway upon which she and Penny Yewdall were walking; it consisted of plain black asphalt mixed with grit to create a harder-wearing surface. 'So, the party continued but the men were flagging by then and the two murders had put a real damper on things.'

'I'll bet.' Penny Yewdall sighed.

'Yes, I think by then that the men just wanted to get back to their manor and get up to the pub. A weekend of it would have been sufficient for most of the men, if not all,' Sandra Barnes added, 'but a week, a whole week of readily available young females . . . all those naked bodies, it just stopped getting exciting for them and started to get tedious; but Snakebite was adamant that it was Arnie Rainbird's coming out party, like he was a debutante or something, and so it was going to last the long week, including two weekends. He wanted it his way and he always got it his way, and so it went on until the second Sunday afternoon when the old woman unlocked the room where all our kit was stored and handed out the plastic bags, and we passed them round amongst us until we found the bag with our own clothes in it. When we were all good and presentable we were told to get back on the bus. I sat with Long Liz on the journey back but we didn't talk, no one did; the journey was undertaken in utter silence. I mean utter and complete silence. It was as if we were all dazed. Anyway . . .' Sandra Barnes paused, 'getting to the end of the tale now.'

'You've done very well,' Penny Yewdall replied warmly, 'very well indeed.'

'Thanks. It's not been easy but it's been good to talk about it. Sometimes you have to talk about things . . . Well –' Sandra Barnes looked down, took a deep breath, and paused before she continued to relate her experience at the garden party – 'we were dropped off at High Barnet tube station and all the street girls and also the five play babes were given an envelope each . . . containing fifty pounds, but written on the front of the envelope was the name and address of each one of us. I mean, they called out the name on each envelope and when a girl put her hand up the old woman handed the envelope to her. You see, at some point during the week the older woman must have been through the plastic bags containing our clothing and handbags and had noted the identity of each of us, including our address, and my envelope had my parents' address up here in Chesterfield, not the address that Tony Sudbury had installed me in as his plaything.'

'Oh . . .' Penny Yewdall groaned, 'oh my. So they were telling you that they knew your identity and address?'

'Yes.' Sandra Barnes took another deep breath. 'Just telling us, all of us, not to go to the police, and no one complained because just then life had become very, very precious. Very precious indeed.'

'I know that emotion,' Penny Yewdall replied.

'Do you?'

'Yes,' Penny Yewdall said firmly, 'yes, I do . . . but that's another story.'

'So there we were in a bus outside High Barnet Underground Station receiving fifty quid in really cheap brown envelopes and nobody made any kind of complaint or comment. We had seen two men murdered in a horrible way, been made to watch the way their bodies had been disposed of, two women had been battered half to death – I still had a black eye from the slap the older woman gave me a week earlier. We had all been used in every way that a man can use a woman. After that the one hundred and fifty pounds we had, or the street girls had, been short-changed by was like a penny on the pavement – it just wasn't worth stopping to pick it up. Even before we got to High Barnet I was thinking, did it really happen? At the tube station we just wanted to get off the bus; life, like I said, had just become so very, very precious.' Sandra Barnes walked a few paces before continuing. 'When we got off the bus, the girls just went either of two ways: about half went down the inclined path to the tube station and the rest, me being one, waited for the next London Transport bus to take us into the city. Liz, Long Liz, went down the path to the tube station and that was the last I saw of her. No one talked while we were waiting for the bus and we stood well apart from each other. When the double-decker number 134 came we did the same, just sat well apart from each other.'

'I can understand that,' Penny Yewdall replied. 'I mean, you represented a reminder of a horrible event for each other, didn't you? What did you do then?'

'Returned to the flat in Earl's Court, I did that journey in the T-shirt, cut-down jeans and shoes with no socks, and spent just one more night there, packed my bags, posted my resignation of my job, got a train north. I buried the memory of the garden party for a year or two and then it returned piecemeal; sometimes when I can't sleep the memory floods into my mind, like a film which just keeps repeating itself over and over and over again.'

'Would you make a statement?' Penny Yewdall asked.

'No. No. No . . .' Sandra Barnes shook her head vigorously. 'No statement. I'll help all I can, off the record, but these people have my parents' address, and so they can find me easily enough. I can't go into witness protection; my husband is well settled in his career. I am now Mrs Sandra Wynstanley. I like my name, it has a certain ring to it . . . and my daughters are well settled in their school. So, sorry. No written and signed statement. No verbal evidence in the witness box.'

'Police!' Big-boned, bearded Frankie Brunnie spoke authoritatively into the intercom which was attached to the solid wooden gate which stood at the bottom of the driveway separating Johnnie 'Snakebite' Herron's house from the public highway.

'What's it about this time?' The replying voice was gruff, moaning, hostile. 'You're harassing me. You got nothing better to do?'

'Just a few questions, Mr Herron,' Brunnie replied in a deliberately calm, though still very seriously toned voice. 'It's nothing to be alarmed about, just a routine visit.' He stood upright and he and Victor Swannell surveyed the scene about them. It was indeed as Penny Yewdall had said Charlie Magg had described it: a long, straight, roughly surfaced – almost cratered in places – driveway ran between two fields used for grazing cattle and was strongly fenced at either side. At the top of the ground a long, wide mound of soil, grass covered, went from left to right; behind it were to be seen the bright red tiles of a recently built house, though the house itself was hidden from view.

'Wait.' The voice leapt out of the intercom. 'I'll get the dogs in . . . just a couple of minutes.'

Frankie Brunnie bent down so his mouth was close to the intercom. 'We can wait, we are not going anywhere.' He stood upright again and he and Swannell waited in silence, both men enjoying the escape from inner London, both savouring the vast expanse of green, the rural smells and scents, the birdsong and the occasional fluttering butterfly. It was, they both found, a pleasant excursion to the house of Herron in Bedfordshire. For famed London Town is, they had both learnt to accept, overcrowded, dirty and malodorous. Presently the male voice once again leapt from the intercom. 'All right,' he said with a clear note of resignation. 'You can come in now; the gate will open and close by itself.' The gate then clicked open upon being released from its locked position and swung wide silently. Brunnie and Swannell returned to their car and then drove through the gateway and up the unevenly surfaced driveway. As he drove, Swannell saw in the rear-view mirror that the gate was closing behind them, clearly responding to a timing mechanism. He drove slowly until he reached the top of the drive and turned left into a forecourt, which was indeed large enough to accommodate a coach and a number of other cars, in front of a two storey house, which appeared to be about twenty years old. Swannell parked the police car beside a blood-red Ferrari, beyond which was a black two-seater Audi. The front door of the house was open as the officers arrived and in the doorway stood a tall, well-built man. He had long, silver hair which he wore in a ponytail; he was clean-shaven with a pinched face and cold, piercing eyes. He had, thought both Brunnie and Swannell, 'criminal' written all the way through him like a stick of Clacton rock. A small King Charles spaniel sat at his feet, then, upon the approach of the officers' car, stood and barked aggressively.

'Not the sort of dog or dogs we were expecting,' Swannell remarked as he and Brunnie got out of their car, though he did so with a smile.

'The Dobermanns are in the cage,' the man replied aggressively. 'He does for the house. The Dobermanns are for the grounds. So what do you want?'

'Just a chat and a little information,' Frankie Brunnie replied as he and Swannell approached the man. 'You are Mr John Herron?'

'Yes,' the man snarled, 'that's me.'

'The owner of this property?'

'Yes.' Herron hissed his reply through clenched teeth. 'So what is it you want?'

'A few answers to a few questions,' Swannell replied, still smiling. 'Questions about yourself, this house, the goings on in this house and in the garden at the back of the house.'

'Goings on?' Herron seemed alarmed. 'There's no goings on in this house.'

'Nothing to worry about then is there?' Swannell approached Herron. 'Do you chat here on the front step, or inside?'

'Here,' Herron replied, then pushed the spaniel with his foot and said, 'Quiet!' He turned to Swannell. 'It's a good day. Here will do.'

'You know, Johnnie,' Brunnie said. 'You don't mind if we call you Johnnie . . .? You know, Johnnie, folks who don't invite us into their homes make us suspicious because we always think it means they have got something to hide.'

'It makes us want to come back mob-handed, search warrants and all. And we like doing that.' Swannell added.

'We open every cupboard, open every drawer, pull up the

carpets . . . all that number,' Brunnie added. 'But you know that, you've been served a search warrant before now.'

Herron breathed deeply, clearly fighting to contain his anger. 'You'll have done your checks.'

'All criminal records checks done, mate,' Swannell replied. 'The Bedfordshire Police know you . . . in fact, they are very interested in you . . . and also the Metropolitan Police.'

'That's us,' Brunnie smiled.

'You're from the Met?' Herron spoke sharply with a clear note of alarm in his voice.

'Yes, all the way from New Scotland Yard via the Bedfordshire Police in Luton, just to see you.' Swannell stood square on to Herron. 'Nice day for it.'

'So you'll know I am not wanted for anything.' Herron's breath smelled of mouthwash. 'I've done no crookin' for years.'

'That we know of,' Swannell replied. 'So what have you been doing in order to be able to afford a pile of bricks like this?'

'This and that.' Herron avoided eye contact with both officers. 'Mostly that.' Then he stepped aside. 'You'd better come in; I can do without a revisit. Hope you'll see and hear what you want and leave me in peace. I just want a quiet life.'

Swannell and Brunnie stepped over the threshold and into the entrance hall of the house which they saw was wide, well illuminated with natural light, and spacious. A slender, auburn-haired woman, dressed in a T-shirt and jeans and much younger than Herron, appeared from a corridor to the right of the foyer and upon receiving a glare from Herron, turned and went back the way she had come, rapidly so.

'That was the trouble and strife,' Herron announced dismissively. 'The third.' Swannell watched the woman leave the entrance hall noting how frightened she seemed.

Herron glanced at Swannell in the exact manner he had glared at his wife. Then he said, 'This way, please.' He led Swannell and Brunnie into a vast, to their eyes, and garishly decorated, to their taste, living room. The floor was covered by a yellow carpet neatly fitted to each wall, the walls were papered in yellow patterned wallpaper, the ceiling was painted a light shade of blue. The furniture was a matching set of white settees and armchairs. A glass-covered coffee table interrupted the floor space. The wide window looked out on to the back lawn of the house; a huge lawn surrounded by Leylandii reaching upwards for perhaps twenty-five feet. An outdoor swimming pool and barbecue area were also noted by the officers. 'So you have questions?' Herron sat on a chair but kept Swannell and Brunnie standing.

'It's about Arnie Rainbird,' Swannell announced. 'You know Arnie Rainbird?'

'Arnie? Yes, I know Arnie, haven't seen him for years, but yes, I know Arnie, course I know Arnie; we go back a long, long way. He's retired, just an old blagger put out to grass same as me; we both enjoy the quiet life now so a visit from the Old Bill puzzles me.'

'I dare say it would,' Swannell smiled. He, like Brunnie, was tall but he was of a slighter, thinner build and smartly dressed, an observer might think, in a lightweight summer suit. 'It's actually not just about Arnie Rainbird, Johnnie, it's also about a felon called Sydney Tyrell. Remember him, Johnnie; tall, old geezer?'

'And it's also about a short geezer called Leonard Convers,' Brunnie added.

'Tyrell, Convers.' Herron pursed his lips and shook his head. 'Can't say I know them . . . now or ever.'

'Really? You see we think you might know them,' Swannell pressed forward. 'You'll have read about the bones?'

'The bones?'

'Found in a wood up in Ilford. It made the news, we got good press coverage. They were buried in a wood.'

'Yes . . . that . . .' Johnnie 'Snakebite' Herron pointed to a plasma TV screen mounted on the wall opposite the window. 'Yes, I did catch that item, didn't pay it much attention though.'

'Shame, because those were the bones of Tyrell and Convers, they were their earthly remains.'

Herron's jaw slackened, his eyes dilated, slightly but nonetheless noticeably. It was, thought Brunnie and Swannell, an interesting and noteworthy reaction. 'So what has that got to do with me and Arnie Rainbird?'

'Ah.' Swannell smiled. 'That is the question; we are here in order to ask you to help us to answer just that question. You see, you and Arnie were in the same firm at about the time that Convers and Tyrell got chilled . . . then heated up in a sense.'

'We were?'

'Yes,' Brunnie replied, 'and Tyrell and Convers, we don't know how they fitted in, if they fitted in at all, but we do believe they were gofers, a pair of low grades.'

'Well that explains it.' Herron smiled. 'Always a lot of gofers, always a lot of them, can't be expected to know them all.'

'Anyway, Arnie Rainbird got himself banged up.'

'Yes, someone grassed on him.'

'Who would do that,' Brunnie asked, 'to a nice bloke like Arnie?'

'Dunno.' Herron sat back in the chair. 'Don't think anyone ever knew.'

'Well, we'll leave that on one side but when Arnie came out – served only ten of his twenty stretch – you threw a party for him here . . . in this house . . . and out there in the garden.'

'I did?'

'Yes,' Swannell replied coldly. 'You did.'

'All right, so I did.' Herron shrugged. 'So what? When a top blagger is released he always gets a party thrown for him. It's the way of it. I swear I never knew that was against the law.'

'We have only just heard about the party,' Swannell explained, 'seven years ago this summer. Word has just reached our little shell-likes and what we heard in our little shell-likes doth interest us.'

'Muchly,' Brunnie added. 'It doth muchly, muchly interest us.'

'Oh yes?' Herron replied, defensively.

'Yes,' Swannell continued, 'because it was about that time that Convers and Tyrell disappeared. They went missing a few weeks beforehand.'

'Coincidence.'

'Possibly.' Swannell smiled. 'Possibly.'

'Has to be,' Herron persisted.

'I wouldn't be so sure,' Victor Swannell replied. 'You see, the clever old medics can tell us a thing or two. And in the case of Convers and Tyrell they can tell us that those two boys were well smashed up. All the bones were broken, some maybe before death, some after. They were definitely sawn in places but that would have been after death to make them fit neatly into a container, I would think, but all were charred.'

'Charred?' Herron queried.

'Burnt,' Brunnie explained. 'They had been burnt on a fire. Did you have a bonfire at the party you threw for Arnie Rainbird seven years ago, here in this house and in the garden out there?'

'Just a barbecue.' Herron nodded to the barbecue area.

'So no big bonfire at all?' Swannell clarified.

'No.'

'And you'll give us a statement, a signed statement to that effect?' Swannell asked.

'Possibly. I'm a bit wary of giving statements. I'll need my solicitor present before I do that, so I won't be signing anything today.'

'OK, but you're certain there was no fire during the party, just a barbecue?' Swannell asked.

'Certain,' Herron replied with finality. 'Definitely no other fire.'

'All right, we'll see what Arnie Rainbird says.'

'You'll be visiting him?' Herron seemed alarmed.

'Yes, of course.' Swannell glanced round the room, so very garish, he thought. 'If it was his party he'll know what went down.'

'He'll say the same as me,' Herron insisted.

'Possibly.' Brunnie nodded gently. 'But see it from our point of view, Johnnie, two gofers got well served up right about the time that Arnie Rainbird gets out after a ten year stretch, they were battered and their bones were burnt.'

'Not here they weren't.'

'Well, you say that.' Victor Swannell shifted his feet a little. 'But we have people who say different.'

'Who?'

'Ah . . .' Swannell smiled. 'That is something we have to keep quiet about.'

'But people,' Brunnie added, also smiling, 'note the plural, more than one person . . . we mean people . . . two or more.'

Herron scowled at Brunnie.

'Do you live here alone, Johnnie?' Victor Swannell asked. 'I mean just you and the trouble and strife?'

'Yes,' Herron replied in a muted manner, 'just me and her.'

'Your wife is much younger than you?' Brunnie studied Herron's facial expressions. He had to concede that the man wasn't giving much away, but he was displaying a little emotion and what he did display was, thought Brunnie, very interesting.

'Yes, she's younger. I like it that way,' Herron explained. 'It makes me feel young. None of us get any younger and I like slowing that bit up if I can. But technically speaking we are not married. I only married once, technically speaking.'

'So we understand.' Swannell smiled. 'I told you we paid a courtesy call on the Bedfordshire force in Luton. They have a keen interest in you, Johnnie, a very keen interest.'

'They have?' Herron growled. 'I don't ever see much evidence of them.'

'Yes, they're still interested in the whereabouts of wife one and wife two.'

Herron remained silent.

'They disappeared, apparently,' Brunnie added.

'Yes, people do . . . always tragic.'

'Agreed, but ninety-five percent are located one way or another within twenty-four hours. But when the wife of a wealthy man disappears and is not found, that is a little suspicious. And when wife number two of that selfsame man also vanishes, that becomes very iffy and –' Swannell held up his index finger – 'when the man is known to the police as a career criminal then, well, then we understand the interest the Bedfordshire boys and girls have in you, we understand it very well.'

'They've had me in for questioning a few times but they've always let me go, and it's been a few years since I was last questioned.' Herron shrugged. 'I reckon we have to wait until they turn up, then we'll see what they have to say for themselves after walking out on me like that.'

'Unless . . . unless . . . you know it is possible for there to be murder convictions without a corpse.'

Herron shrugged. 'So the Bedfordshire Police told me but they could only tell me of two such convictions.'

'But it can happen.' Brunnie glanced out of the window at the vast flat lawn at the rear of Herron's house. 'Nice and convenient,' he added, turning to Herron.

'What is?'

'Wife number one and wife number two disappearing like they did,' Brunnie explained. 'I mean, with a house like this, a divorce would be very costly . . . but I dare say that is a matter for the Bedfordshire Police.'

'I'm glad you see it that way.' Herron braved a wink at Brunnie.

'So tell us a bit more about the party,' Victor Swannell asked.

'More? Thought you'd got off that and were on to my missing wife and girlfriend.' Herron let a note of alarm creep into his voice.

'Hardly started,' Brunnie smiled. 'Hardly started.'

'Nothing more to tell. We all had a good time when Arnie came out.'

'Are you still in touch with the guests?' Swannell asked.

'One or two . . . a card at Christmas, you know how it is.' Again Herron shrugged.

'What about the girls?' Brunnie probed.

'What about them?'

'Still in touch with them?'

'Naw.' Herron smirked.

'They were promised two hundred smackers for a night's work. They got fifty quid for nine days' work.'

'They wouldn't have come otherwise, but I don't know the details; I just allowed my house to be used. The catering was done by someone else and the girls came under catering.' Herron smirked.

'So who did the catering?' Swannell snarled.

'Do you know, I can't remember. It's been a long time and anyway none of them complained.'

'No, they didn't; that's because they were terrified into silence.'

'That's a shame,' Herron leered.

'We are hearing reports, Johnnie; something really very heavy went down at that party, something which terrified a bus load of streetwise women.'

'So sorry to hear that.'

'But that's a real weakness, Johnnie, it has a flaw.'

'A flaw?'

'Yes,' Swannell explained, 'time, Johnnie, that's the flaw. It's like that saying about fooling people, "You can fool some of the people all of the time, and you can fool all of the people some of the time, but you can't fool all of the people all of the time". Abraham Lincoln said that.'

'Yeah.' Herron looked at Swannell. 'I heard that somewhere.'

'So, it's just like that. You can scare some of the people all of the time, and you can scare all of the people some of the time, but you can't scare all of the people all of the time.'

'So those working girls, those brasses, they were well scared after the party.' Brunnie held eye contact with Herron. 'But that was seven years ago.'

'And in those seven years their circumstances change,' Swannell explained. 'They can get so they are not frightened any more, not frightened at all.'

'That's right,' Brunnie added as he watched colour begin to drain from Herron's pinched face. 'I'll tell you a story, Johnnie,' Brunnie continued. 'There was once an old blagger who was dying, and he knew he was dying – not old, only in his fifties, but he was definitely on the way out – he only walks into a police station and provides information and details about a murder that took place years earlier. He was part of the team that did it and he wanted peace of mind when he was dying. We dig up the body, and his two partners, who also did the business on their victim, well they're still in good health and they go down for life. And the first boy, he gives evidence in court; he lives just long enough to do that.'

'So people's circumstances change,' Swannell added. 'They can sometimes lose their fear, you see, and you somehow put the frighteners on about thirty women, but that was just a short-term solution which could backfire on you because it's also given us thirty potential witnesses. We just need two or three to give evidence.'

Herron remained silent but he could not conceal the worried look in his eyes.

'And we are tracing them,' Brunnie added. 'We have officers tracking them down now, and if they're brasses they'll very likely be on the PNC database.'

'PNC?'

'The Police National Computer,' Swannell explained, 'recorded by their real names and any alias or nickname, and these girls network, remember, they know each other. We trace one, we'll get the name of another and we trace her . . . we'll get the name of another and quite soon we'll have the names of all the girls who were at Arnie Rainbird's coming home party.'

'That's how it works, Johnnie,' Brunnie said. 'The law can reach a long way back in time to get information to convict somebody in the present, and right now one of our colleagues is chasing up a girl, a girl who was at the party.'

'Which one?' Herron was clearly alarmed.

Swannell tapped the side of his nose with his finger. 'You know better than to ask that question, Johnnie, but take it from me, that girl will be chatting to one of our colleagues right now.'

'And you know the real encouragement we can offer, Johnnie?' Brunnie added with a smile.

'What?'

'Witness protection, Johnnie.' Brunnie continued to smile. 'Witness protection.'

'That's it.' Swannell nodded gently. 'That's the big invitation. Some people can't go into witness protection because of their wider circumstances: children in school, need to be close to a relative, in a good, well-paid job and other such considerations.'

'For others,' Brunnie added, 'it comes like a Godsend; it comes to them like a mother. Their lives are in such a mess that they can only dream about starting a new life with a new identity, new National Insurance Number, a new address, a new town, a whole clean slate, and helped with a little learning from past mistakes. People used to do it all the time in Victorian times, Johnnie, sneak out of the house with the family silver, pawn it and buy a railway ticket to a new life. Can't do that today, not now we are all on some computer or other, but . . . but . . .' Brunnie paused, 'if one or two or three of those thirty girls are now in such a mess that the offer of witness protection would be like manna from heaven to them . . .'

Herron continued to pale.

'It's often the way of if, Johnnie.' Swannell shrugged. 'You see some people will agree to go into witness protection because they want to see justice done, but others, well others don't care much about justice, but they see witness protection as a way out of it all and a whole new start, and that can be a very powerful motivation. It's very inviting. And either reason suits us, so long as we get evidence.'

'We can trace people very easily, Johnnie,' Brunnie added. 'A name, a nickname, an approximate age and we can begin to knock on doors, and, like I said, we are already talking to one of the girls who was at the party. But if you're telling the truth and nothing heavy happened at the party in question, then you've got nothing to worry about, but if something did happen to interest the Murder and Serious Crime Squad . . .'

'That's us,' Swannell added with a smile.

'Then,' Brunnie continued, 'well, then we have up to thirty potential witnesses to tell us what happened, and it only needs just one or two to climb into the witness box in exchange for a new life somewhere. Don't get up, Johnnie.' Brunnie smiled gently. 'We'll see ourselves out.'

That evening Frankie Brunnie stood at the window of his flat overlooking Walthamstow High Street, staring with awe at the vast crimson sunset that was the sky over London Town. Below him the pedestrianized street was empty save for a few solitary foot passengers, the market traders who occupy the area during the working day having long departed for home. The shops also were locked and shuttered.

Frankie Brunnie's lover, the nurse, who had just a few days previously told him of the 'puffy ankle test', the failure of which being an indication of a weak heart, approached him from behind and placed his hand on Brunnie's shoulder. Frankie Brunnie smiled and placed his own hand upon that of his lover, and then turned and kissed him.

FIVE

Harry Vicary breathed deeply, slowly leaned forward, resting his elbows on his desktop, and clasped his hands together, interlocking his fingers as he did so. Sitting in front of his desk was his team, Victor Swannell, Frankie Brunnie, Penny Yewdall and Tom Ainsclough, all remaining silent, waiting for him to speak. Vicary glanced to his left and pondered the buildings on the south side of the river, which then, strong and solid, were glowing becomingly. He turned and addressed his team. 'A lot of smoke,' he said softly, 'in more ways than one, but nonetheless an awful lot of smoke without any fire, no substance. We seem to be edging closer to Arnie Rainbird; we're crowding him and his crew very nicely, very handsomely indeed. Herron we have visited, Charlie Magg is inside already looking at a murder charge if they pull the plug on his wretched victim. Do we know if he is still on life support? The victim, I mean.'

'We don't know, sir,' Tom Ainsclough replied promptly. 'It's not our investigation so we won't be notified as a matter of routine, but we can find out easily enough.'

'Do that will you, Tom? If Charlie Magg knows he's looking at a murder charge . . . looking at a conviction for murder, in fact, not just a charge of murder . . .' Vicary unlaced his fingers, 'then he might, just might, be willing to lubricate the machinery of justice and begin to work his way to an early parole. Even if he serves ten to fifteen years it means he is unlikely to die in prison and that can help persuade him to be of assistance to us.' Vicary paused. 'Did we find out anything about the two murders he mentioned when you two visited him?' he asked looking at Penny Yewdall and then at Tom Ainsclough. 'I mean the ones where he definitely wasn't present and it was all down to Arnie Rainbird trying to make the right sort of impression upon the right sort of person.'

'I tracked them both down, sir.' Penny Yewdall sat up in the chair. 'They are both cold cases but the murders were exactly as Charlie Magg described. He really had to have been there. One poor bloke trussed up and rolled off the roof of a block of flats, another tied across the railway line in front of the Harwich to London boat train express; both about twenty years ago when Rainbird was a rising star, a man in the ascendant. I have asked the collator to cross-reference both those cases to Charlie Magg and have Charlie Magg recorded as a principal/major suspect. I imagine he'll be visited by the Cold Case Review Team, once he is convicted, be it for manslaughter or murder, unless you wish . . .'

'No, no.' Vicary held up his hand. 'We won't muddy our waters, leave both cases to the CCRT, but ensure he is cross-referenced to this case –' Vicary patted the thickening file to the right-hand side of his desktop – 'the Convers and Tyrell murders.'

'Yes, sir.' Yewdall scribbled a note on her to-do list, which she drew up at the back of each notebook she kept, transferring any undone tasks to each new notebook.

'So, smoke, but, as I said, still short of an arrest.' Vicary leaned back in his chair. 'So, solutions team, ideas, suggestions . . .'

'I would like to trace Elizabeth Petty,' Yewdall said. 'It's . . . well, hers is the only other name we have for any of the women at the party, so-called, and she would have seen what happened. Sandra Barnes' description of her running down the inclined path to the platform at High Barnet tube station stays with me. She was clearly a very shaken girl. She might be willing to talk now. She sounds like she has a bit of previous, some small-scale stuff, so we'll have a record of her. I mean, if nothing else, she might be able to give other names of women who were at that . . . event, and one by one we might trace the women who were there, until we find one or two who will talk, sign a statement and get into the witness box.'

'Yes,' Vicary murmured, 'it won't be easy but it's worth a shot. Ideally we need at least two witnesses, but Elizabeth Petty sounds like a good place to start, in fact she sounds like the only place to start. Do you want someone with you on that, Penny?' Vicary scribbled on his notepad.

'I don't think so, sir, thank you.' Penny Yewdall smiled confidently. 'It's another one-hander. It sounds a bit like yesterday's trip to Chesterfield; sometimes it's just better to leave the girls alone to talk girl talk.'

Harry Vicary grinned broadly. 'Leave the girls to do what the girls do best . . . all right, that's your task, you talked yourself into a job there.'

'Yes, sir. I ought to be safe, just calling on a woman.'

'And sending a male officer with you might look a bit over the top and so be counterproductive.' Vicary paused. 'But you know the rules; you all know the rules.' He glanced at the officers sitting in front of his desk. 'Let this office know where you are at all times. Tom . . .'

'Yes, sir?' Ainsclough stiffened in his chair.

'It's time we knew more about Tyrell and Convers; somehow they linked to Arnie Rainbird and they did so in some way that led to their murder at the so-called garden party. Some way that caused great annoyance to some person or persons unknown, but most likely it was to Arnie Rainbird. They were reported as claiming that they didn't tell anybody anything before they were topped. It sounds like Arnie Rainbird believed they had grassed him up, rightly or wrongly. It also sounds like they were kept somewhere against their will, had their teeth knocked out, were starved and then brought to the garden party to answer to the East End sense of justice for informing on Arnie Rainbird. If we can prove that to have been the case, then Rainbird's going back inside.' Vicary wrote on his pad. 'That's a definite single-hander, just a lot of paperwork to wade through; a paper trail to follow. But please let me know if you have to leave the building.'

'Yes, sir,' Tom Ainsclough replied as he caught a whiff of Penny Yewdall's perfume, and as a telephone in an adjacent office was heard to ring twice before being answered.

'So.' Vicary looked at Swannell and Brunnie. 'It sounds like you two gentlemen work very well together when it comes to leaning on felons, especially those who believe that they are in quiet and comfortable retirement. You seem to have rattled "Snakebite" Herron's little cage and done so quite soundly, if not actually poked at him with a sharpened stick pushed between the bars of said cage, which is, of course, just what we wanted you to do. He'll be rattled now, very well rattled, and he will have made a few phone calls after you had left, one of which will have been to Arnie Rainbird. So how about you doing the same thing to him? Visit Arnie Rainbird just to let him know we are interested in him.'

'Love to, sir.' Brunnie smiled.

'Good . . . good.' Vicary turned again to Tom Ainsclough. 'Tom, can you also find out what we know about the villain who is known as "The Baptist"?'

'Yes, sir.'

'He sounds like the man who actually put an end to the sufferings of Convers and Tyrell, though we'll also be charging Charlie Magg and the rat-faced guy with their murders as well. If . . . if we can find someone to come forward and make a statement, and that's a big "if".'

'Yes, sir . . . "if", as you say.' Tom Ainsclough wrote on his notepad, 'The Baptist'.

'It would indeed be a very pleasing result of this inquiry if Herron, Rainbird, Magg, The Baptist and the rat-faced guy were to stand in the dock of the Central Criminal Court in a few months' time. But, as we agree, for that to happen we need evidence. It doesn't sound like we'll get any forensic evidence; the two golf clubs with blood from the victims and fingerprints of Charlie Magg and the rat-faced guy all over them will be long gone. The pool will have no trace of Convers' blood or Tyrell's blood after seven years and after it was scrubbed clean by the women under the sergeant major-like supervision of Sandra Barnes' ex sugar daddy.' Vicary paused. 'Any result in this case is going to be because of witness statements and that will be your job, Penny, at least in the first instance.'

'Understood, sir,' Penny Yewdall replied.

'You see, I can't picture any of Arnie Rainbird's crew coughing, not to the extent that we need, anyway. Even Charlie Magg won't cough to that sort of extent.' Vicary glanced at his desk top. 'So, it seems to me that the only possible witnesses will be numbered among those women who were lured to the garden party, which is why I think it will be your job to find them, Penny, as I said, at least in the first instance.'

'Fully understood, sir.' Penny Yewdall smiled and nodded. 'Fully understood.'

'So, Victor and Frankie, you know what you are doing, but

do any issues arise from your visit to "Snakebite" Herron yesterday? Any avenues to explore there?'

'Just the issue of the two previous wives who vanished, but the Bedfordshire boys are on to that and possibly the safety of the third wife. She seemed frightened of him.'

'Is she in danger?' Vicary asked.

'Yes, I think she is, but as to whether the danger is immediate or is a brooding threat we can't say,' Swannell replied. 'But I do think that the danger has lessened after our visit. We were able to remind Herron that contrary to popular belief there have been successful prosecutions for murder despite the absence of a corpse. It was pleasant to watch colour drain from his face when we said that, so wife number three is a lot safer now than she was last week.'

'Good . . . good.' Vicary nodded his head slightly. 'That's very reassuring. So, go and call on Rainbird, the man himself. Read his file before you leave. It reads like a soldier who got his good conduct badges because he wasn't found out, rather than because of actual good conduct. He acquired no record at all, not to speak of, just sufficient to get his street cred in the eyes of the underworld. Yet, he climbs to run a very heavy crew and then he gets his first major conviction when he is in his mid–thirties, and he has a list of criminal associates which reads like a felons' *Who's Who*. His victim was one Daniel Meed, just twenty years old when Rainbird filleted him with a butcher's knife. I'll go and talk to his family – Daniel Meed's family, I mean – seventeen years on. Had he lived, Daniel would now be assessing his life as he approached the big 4-0. His home address is in Chiswick, not many jailbirds there. OK, that's it. Let this office know where you are at all times.'

Elizabeth 'Long Liz' Petty's home was a ground floor conversion in a Victorian era terraced house in Waterloo Road, Canning Town. It offered, Yewdall saw, cramped accommodation and was kept in an untidy manner, with clothes strewn across the floor and empty vodka bottles littering the flat. The unmade bed was pushed into a corner beneath the window, which looked out on to the massively overgrown back garden. Two small armchairs were pushed close up to the small fire grate which at that moment was empty. A sink with a pile of unwashed dishes therein stood in the opposite corner of the room to the bed, and a small electric cooker sat on the chest of drawers beside the sink. The bathroom which Elizabeth Petty used was evidently elsewhere in the house, and likely shared with other tenants, but apart from that necessity of life, it was clear to Penny Yewdall that everything that Elizabeth Petty did when she was not out of doors, she did in this small room; she slept, cooked, ate and relaxed here. Liz Petty showed herself to be tall, blonde-haired, drawn about the face, and emaciated rather than slender. She had a small upper body and achieved her height by means of long, very long, thin – painfully thin, it seemed to Yewdall – legs.

'So now you can see why they call me "Long Liz".' Elizabeth Petty rolled a cigarette in a slow, deliberate manner. She patted her bony knees.

'Yes, I can see why.' Penny Yewdall smiled as she glanced around the flat. 'Lucky you, a lot of women would kill for a pair of pins like yours,' she added diplomatically.

'Possibly, but not if they had to take everything else that comes with them.' Petty indicated her flat. 'Some life I lead; I would chop six inches off my legs if I could be like some of the women you see round here – married, good husband, children – it's them who have it all, not me and my long legs.'

'Perhaps,' Yewdall replied as the dank smell of Liz Petty's flat reached her and she noticed the small television set and small hi-fi system located underneath the sink.

'So, Sandra Barnes did all right. I am pleased for her, she was a good girl. She will have made a nice woman. She never looked down on the brasses at that damn party . . . and here am I, still a brass and this is what you get for being one . . . and a few visits to the hospital – the odd broken rib or bust nose . . . all part of the risk you run. I still earn money but not as much as I used to earn. You age very quickly when you're on the game. I mean very quickly.'

'You don't fancy settling down with some form of employment?' Penny Yewdall asked. 'It might not pay well but it's safer than working the streets.'

'Ha!' Elizabeth Petty scoffed as she lit her roll-up with a flourish of a bright yellow disposable cigarette lighter, cupping her hand round the flame as if she was standing outside in a strong wind. 'I'm unemployable, darling, no qualifications, no time nor the inclination to apply myself to a course of study. I wouldn't be able to hold down a job stacking shelves, even if I was able to get a job like that. I was on the street early in life; just fifteen when I fetched up at King's Cross. I was tall enough to pass myself off for older; it was the only way I could survive.'

'Did you ever return home?'

'Naw.' Elizabeth Petty pulled deeply on the roll-up and exhaled the smoke through her nostrils. 'No, no intention of returning. For one thing, I can't be seen like this. I look used, worn out, my mother would be able to tell what I was doing the instant she set eyes on me and so would my old man, and he would say to my old mum, "See, you see that, you see what I told you? I told you she was going to be no good. She never was good. She isn't good and she never will be no good."'

'That's why you left home, that attitude on your father's part? It couldn't have been easy for you growing up with a parent like that.' Yewdall observed.

'Yes, that . . . being told I was "no good" all the time.' Elizabeth Petty took another deep drag on the roll-up. 'That and a few other things beside. Like my old man never being able to work out which was his bedroom and which was mine when he wandered home from the pub, and my old mum who didn't seem to care which bed he slept in.'

'I'm sorry.' Yewdall spoke softly.

'Well.' Petty shrugged. 'It happens. A lot of girls who are on the game have similar tales to tell. So that's me, all the way from beautiful Basingstoke to sunny Canning Town, E16. I didn't get very far, did I?'

'But you're still not but one-third of the way through your life,' Yewdall pleaded, 'there is more ahead of you than there is behind you.'

'I'm twenty-seven, darlin'.' Petty once more drew heavily on the cigarette. 'I look twice that age and I feel twice my age.'

'You certainly do not look twice your age,' Yewdall replied rapidly and a little angrily, 'I can tell you that. You are twenty-seven and you look twenty-seven, and I am not just saying that.'

Elizabeth Petty shrugged. 'Thanks, darling, that will keep me going for a whole month or until some fat old punter says, "How much? There's younger ones down the street knocking it out for half that", whichever comes first; probably the latter knowing my Donald Duck. But thanks anyway, and it's a fact that I am not far short of thirty; the first thirty years is all but behind me and that's the most important isn't it? The first thirty years dictate the rest. That's when you lay your foundations; that's when you marry well if you can, start your family.'

'You could hide your past, Liz,' Yewdall said encouragingly. 'I mean, if you stopped working the street you'd soon lose that used-up look about your face and you'd stop dressing like a tart, your good looks would re-emerge. Leave the Smoke and start again, a small town somewhere.'

'So what would I do for money?' Petty looked at Yewdall. 'And it will still be in the eyes, darling, it'll still be there. The face might soften but the hard, cold eyes of a street girl won't ever leave me, not for a likely time, anyway. So I'll be out again tonight in my heels and my short skirt, up at King's Cross, the old crossroads of the world, one of them anyway. London's other meat market; Smithfield for cattle and King's Cross for the sort of cattle that can walk upright.'

'Are you a clean girl?'

'I am now.' Petty drew deeply on the cigarette. 'I caught a dose once but the old penicillin did its job. Did you know venereal disease is getting resistant to penicillin?'

'I have heard that, yes.' Yewdall once again glanced round the cramped, damp bedsit.

'So the doctor told me. The amount of penicillin needed to cure a dose of syphilis is now one thousand times larger than the amount needed in the 1940s. Imagine that.'

'Aids? Herpes?'

'No . . . and no, clear of all that. Last time I had a check up I was, that was just a week or two ago.'

'Do you shoot up?'

'No.' Elizabeth Petty shook her head. 'Do you know I have never done that, never pumped heroin into myself.'

'Any children?'

'No.' She paused. 'Mind you, I did get a termination once,

but I have never gone full term and had it taken from me because I was an unfit mother.'

Yewdall smiled. 'Well, look at yourself, Elizabeth . . .'

'Liz, people call me Liz.'

'Liz. Look at yourself, Liz. I can't see any obstacles to you turning your life around.' Yewdall smiled again.

'I thought you was the Old Bill?' Petty eyed Yewdall with suspicion.

'I am.'

'Well you'd better be careful, darling, you're sounding like my probation officer or a social worker, even sounding like a lady magistrate in her twinset and pearls, smiling down from the bench, telling me I'm going to get a second chance, the whole new start calypso.' Petty put her hand up to her face for a moment. 'You know, it's not so easy, you have a lifestyle, you're known for who you are, things are expected of you, you have mates who you cling to.'

'I do understand, Liz, believe me I do.' Yewdall sat forward. 'And that's all the more reason to think about the whole new start calypso, all the more reason to move to a new town with a new name and start a clean life.'

'A new name?' Petty seemed intrigued.

'It's a very good way to start a new life, a new image . . . longer skirts and dresses, a more elegant ladylike appearance; three-quarter length skirts or even ankle length skirts, or dresses of the type that the hippy girls wear; you could carry those with your figure.'

'You think so?' Liz Petty held eye contact with Penny Yewdall.

'Yes, they look so comfortable, you'd really suit long dresses and every town has its library and its adult education classes, that's where you meet people, and also there will be hiking clubs, amateur dramatic societies, that sort of thing. Meet healthier minded people. All right, every town has its seedy side, just don't go there.'

'But my past will come out.'

'Only if you let it, and even if you don't hide your past it's still all right if you are making a break from it.'

'Yes.' Petty dogged her butt in a cheap tin ashtray which balanced on the arm of the chair in which she sat. 'Yes, since you put it like that, I'm fed up with feeling dirty all the time, dirty and used; you've helped me. I just needed someone to say that to me; I was just at that point.'

'Good.' Yewdall smiled warmly. 'Because the police assist as well as arrest people, you know. The police can be like probation officers or social workers or lady magistrates in their twinsets and pearls.'

'So I see.' Elizabeth Petty relaxed back in her chair, as if, Yewdall thought, already contemplating a fresh start in her life. 'So you'll want to know all about the garden party up in Bedfordshire seven or eight years ago?'

'Will I?' Yewdall grinned, gently.

'Well it's the only thing that Sandra Barnes and I have in common that the Old Bill would be interested in.' Liz Petty reached for her tobacco and then seemed to have a change of mind and retracted her hand.

'Fair deduction,' Yewdall replied.

'The only deduction.' Liz Petty looked up at the high ceiling of her flat. 'I knew it would come back to haunt me but I won't be giving evidence, I can tell you that now.'

'I was afraid you'd say that.' Yewdall relaxed back into her chair.

'Yes . . . yes, I bet you were, darling, but it's not your little body which will be fished out of the Old Father, is it? It's not your throat that will be slit from ear to ear before they dump you in the river, is it?' Petty paused. 'I will tell you all I know, I will tell you all I saw, but for that I need a drink.'

'How much?' Yewdall reached for her handbag.

Petty smiled 'No, I mean a *drink* drink, darling. I don't mean a drink as in a wedge of cash, I mean a drink as in a vodka and coke.'

'I see . . . I thought . . .'

'No, there are still things I won't charge money for.' Petty smiled. 'There are not many things, but I will give information for nothing, especially about that garden party. Have you ever stood just a few feet away from some poor geezer who's writhing on the ground, coughing blood, while two East End heavies beat his body to a pulp with golf clubs? The sound . . . and I don't mean the sound coming from his mouth . . .'

'Can't say I have,' Yewdall conceded in a quiet voice.

'Well I have, twice in one day, so for that I will give information. Can we go to the Vicky Arms? It's not the nearest battle cruiser to here but it's the most comfortable. All the other boozers round here are rough old dens, even at this time of day.'

Penny Yewdall stood and smiled. 'Of course we can, if you don't mind being seen with the Filth?'

'They won't know you're the Old Bill, darling, not in those plain clothes.' Petty also stood.

'Don't be so sure, sometimes I think I have "police" stamped on both cheeks.' Yewdall took a deep breath. 'It just seems that way, but if you're comfortable to be seen with me . . .'

'I'll take the risk and I need to talk the garden party out of me, and for that I need a drink. Let me get me jacket, darling.'

The front door of the house was opened slowly, but also in a rapid response to Harry Vicary's pressing of the front doorbell. Vicary removed his panama and said, 'Hello, Mr Meed, I am DI Vicary of the Murder and Serious Crime Squad of New Scotland Yard. We spoke on the phone.'

Donald Meed, frail and elderly, extended his hand. 'Thank you for the phone call, I appreciated the advance notice.' Donald Meed was a tall man and was dressed casually in summer clothes. He stepped sideways and invited Harry Vicary to enter his home. Vicary stepped into a neatly kept, clean-smelling hallway and was then shown into a spacious, airy lounge which was also neatly and cleanly kept, but given Mr Meed's frailty it seemed to Vicary to speak of a visiting housekeeper, rather than good housekeeping on the part of Mr Meed. The house itself was, thought Vicary, a late Victorian or early Edwardian building. Detached, it stood on Staveley Road, Chiswick, with a small, well-manicured front garden, with a stone path which led to the centrally placed front door. Once in the living room and seated, Vicary cast an eye round the room and found it all appropriate to Mr Meed's age and social position. It had a strong, immediate post World War Two feel, with sober-minded decoration. The rear garden, which could be seen from the sitting room, was, like the small front garden, lovingly tended and, like the interior of the Meed household, it also spoke of hired help.

'I am sorry to call at such short notice, sir; a phone call just thirty minutes prior to calling is not a good period of notice.'

'It was sufficient. I have a dicky ticker and sudden surprises could be dangerous but half an hour's notice, well, as I said, is sufficient. You said that you wished to call in respect of my son's murder?'

'Yes, sir, we believe that some new information has come to light.'

'Even though someone was successfully prosecuted?'

'Yes, sir, but information in respect of associated crimes.'

'I see . . . well, anything I can do to help. Confess we, that is my wife and I, were confused by the success the man had in having his conviction for murder quashed and replaced by a conviction for manslaughter because the original sentence of twenty years still stood. A little academic we thought. That's my wife, Dorothy.' Meed pointed to a framed photograph of a woman which stood on the mantelpiece, as he lowered himself into his armchair. 'But then we found out the manslaughter charge enabled him to apply for parole earlier than would be the case had the murder conviction remained.'

'Yes, sir, that is the case; that's the way of it,' Vicary replied.

'And now he's out. Seven years ago he was released. We were notified by a letter from the Home Office. He was still in prison when Dorothy passed on. That was a blessing because she would have found it difficult to know that he was out, a free man, while Daniel was in his grave. He picked up his life . . . our son didn't live to see his twenty-first birthday . . . it's so unfair.'

'Yes,' Vicary replied softly, 'the police often encounter such unfairness.'

'I am sure you do, Mr Vicary,' Meed sighed, 'I am sure you do, as you say, it is the way of it.'

'I am sorry if this is going over old ground but can you tell me,' Vicary asked, 'if your son had any previous connection with the man Rainbird?'

'Good Lord, no. Rainbird was a career criminal, a real villain; Daniel was an undergraduate at Liverpool University. He was studying law. We had no knowledge of any reason why he and his girlfriend should have been in a pub in the East End; we . . . I mean I . . . still don't.' Meed paused as if collecting his thoughts.

'You know, when the police called to tell us our son had been killed in a pub fight in the East End we refused to believe it. We said that they must have the wrong Daniel Meed, but they showed us his student union identity card which had his photograph on it, but even then we didn't believe it until we saw his body in the mortuary of the Royal London Hospital. He was apparently involved in a fight in a pub. He picked up a broken bottle to defend himself and then dropped it quickly and offered no resistance, so the witness said. So that made the murder charge stand, but on appeal Rainbird claimed he still felt under threat, or was reacting to the threat or some such argument, and that was accepted by the judges who heard his appeal. Rainbird fled the pub but one man was courageous enough to come forward and name him. Rainbird still had the clothes he was wearing at the time when the police caught up with him a few days later. He hadn't washed them and Daniel's blood was still on them, and he also had the knife. The pub's CCTV was out of action at the time . . .'

'I was going to ask,' Vicary commented. 'Ordinarily that would have been very useful.'

'So the issue wasn't who killed Danny, it was whether the crime in question was murder or manslaughter. Fella called Fretwell gave evidence against Rainbird. As he left the witness box Rainbird called out, "You can run but you can't hide, Fretwell".'

'Fretwell,' Vicary repeated.

'Yes, I remember the name because I thought it quite unusual.'

'Do you know of anyone who can shed any light on why on earth he would be drinking in a pub on the other side of London?'

'Only his girlfriend at the time Diana . . . Diana Wortley was her name, still is. I believe she lives with her parents, quite close to here, but sadly I hear she has gone down with a wasting disease. My son and her were the boy and girl next door; they seemed very happy together.'

'Wortley,' Vicary said, 'living in Chiswick. There won't be many Wortleys in Chiswick; it's not a very common name.'

'No, it's a town up in Yorkshire, I believe, so the name is probably more common in the north country, but that was her name, Diana Wortley. Nice girl.'

                              *   *   *

Penny Yewdall scanned the interior of the Victoria Arms in Canning Town. She saw its appeal. It had, she thought, a very solid yet welcoming interior. The roof was lower than the cavernous interior of The Neptune at Seven Kings, where a few days earlier she and Tom Ainsclough had made enquiries about one Desmond Holst. The windows of the Victoria Arms were of frosted glass, with the name of a long defunct brewery etched on them, and through which could be glimpsed the occasional red double-decker London bus as it whirred past. The bench seats and chairs in the pub were of upholstered maroon and the tables were solid metal supports topped by a thick, highly polished wooden surface. The carpet was of a darker maroon than the seats and chairs. The bar was of carved, and also similarly highly polished, wood. The television set was tuned in to a sports channel, but, mercifully in Yewdall's opinion, the sound was turned to mute. The only other customers in the Victoria Arms that morning were an elderly man who sat engrossed in the horse racing pages of a tabloid and a few feet beyond him an elderly woman, who in turn was engrossed in a schooner of port and who mumbled to herself intermittently. Yewdall and Liz Petty occupied a corner seat, as far from any overhearing ears as they could. 'Oh, well.' Liz Petty lifted her vodka and coke to her lips. 'It's five o'clock somewhere; your health, darling.'

'Cheers.' Yewdall raised her glass of orange juice. She noticed that the white-shirted barman was pointedly ignoring them, which, she felt, meant he was very, very interested in them. She hoped indeed that Elizabeth Petty was correct in her belief that she, Penny Yewdall, would not be recognized as a police officer.

'So, the garden party.' Liz Petty put her glass down on the polished table top. 'Well, we got recruited by the old woman . . . Pearl was her name. She went up and down the pavement picking out the youngest. I was twenty, I think . . . about that, and I was still naïve enough not to know that if something sounds too good to be true it usually is. Two hundred pounds just to be one of a few girls at a party for one night . . . and it sounded safe, a lot safer than you were, than you are, if you get into a car with a strange punter.'

'Yes, your occupation is the most dangerous of all.' Yewdall sipped her orange juice.

'Don't I know it, and who is bothered? A working girl gets murdered and no one cares. Sometimes doesn't even rate a mention in the newspaper. Yet when the interest rate goes up half a percent it makes the headlines. There's no justice.' Liz Petty shook her head.

'Unfair . . . you're right . . . but Pearl, was she a bodybuilder do you know?'

'Something like that, or a female wrestler. Why? Do you know her?'

'Yes, I think so.' Yewdall glanced at the barman, still not looking at them, but also still seeming to be very interested in the two women.

'So anyway, they laid on a coach – not a single-decker with hard seats, but a real charabanc luxury number – so it all seemed kosher. The girls were relaxing, chatting away . . . summer, light nights, nice evening, but the journey was longer than we had been led to believe and some girls got a bit nervous. So, anyway, we arrive at the house. Big it was, but not an old mansion. By then no one was talking; by then we were wondering just what we'd let ourselves in for, and we file off the bus and into the house. So Pearl says, "Right, girls, everything off . . . get your kit off" . . . and she hands round plastic bin liners. Some girls hesitate and Pearl says, "The only way back to London is on the coach and that doesn't leave until tomorrow, and you want your money, so you work . . . so kit off."' Liz Petty took another sip of her vodka. 'So Pearl collects the bin liners full of clothes and handbags and she locks them in a room, so then we were staying whether we liked it or not. So we just stood around and some girls began to sit on the floor. Then a little later a car arrived and that was the first time I saw Sandra Barnes and she saw us. I mean, the look of shock on her boat race . . . and her Tom just left her standing there. Walked past us, not a glance did he give us; just walked past us and Pearl says to Sandra, "So what? Did you think you'd be playing musical chairs?" You could tell she was frightened and you could tell she wasn't a brass; this was all new to her. We got to talking later and she told me she thought her Tom was a stockbroker in the city. That week she found he was a gangster and she was his moll. There were two or three others like her; girls who were mistresses. They arrived in flash cars but they all went back to London on the coach. Reckon their usefulness was over. Everything was taken from us, everything, not just our clothes and watches and jewellery and handbags but . . .' Elizabeth Petty tapped the side of her head, 'but in here as well. Everything was taken from us.'

'Your sense of self?' Yewdall held eye contact with Petty. 'Yes, I understand, believe me I do; your sense of self and your sense of self-worth; and Sandra's man walking past you without taking any notice of you, that was rehearsed.'

'You think so?' Petty sighed.

'I feel certain it was; all part of the plan.' Yewdall sipped her drink. 'Ignoring you, weakening your resistance.'

'It did that all right.'

'Sandra said she walked on to the back lawn and the men there looked at her and ignored her; went back to drinking beer and eating from the barbecue.'

'Yes.' Petty looked at the table top. 'That was how it was; twenty-five or thirty naked young women suddenly appear in front of a bunch of men and not one of them reacted, it was like we were invisible.'

'It was all planned, believe me, it was all part of the plan to make you feel you were not worth anything,' Yewdall explained. 'It was designed to make you feel that you were not important.'

'It worked. I just wanted to give up, not resist anything.' Long Liz Petty spoke with discomfort. 'It brought a lot of things back for me.'

'Yes. I am sorry.'

'Well, the party started that night as dusk was setting and we found out it was for a blagger who had been in the slammer for ten years. I won't go into any details.'

'It's all right,' Yewdall smiled. 'I can imagine.'

'So we gritted our teeth and each one of us was thinking about the two hundred pounds and a ride back to London in the morning. So the morning came; all the geezers were still snoring away. We asked when we were going back to London and Pearl says, "A week tomorrow, girls. This party is going on all week and none of you are going anywhere until I say so", and it was then that Sandra Barnes kicked off and started mouthing off, and Pearl . . . Pearl just took three long strides over to where Sandra was standing and slapped her. And I don't mean slap, I mean *slap*. I've seen girls slapped about but that slap was the hardest I've ever seen . . . just one slap.' Liz Petty drew a deep breath. 'But it knocked Sandra clean off her plates.'

'Plates?'

'Plates of meat, feet, darling,' Petty explained. 'It lifted her clean off her feet.'

'Of course, sorry.' Yewdall smiled. 'That was slow of me.'

'Sandra picked herself up and staggered away in a daze, holding her cheek, and she had a black eye for the rest of the week. You see, if you slap someone hard enough the blood goes into the eye socket and it looks like they've been punched.'

'I know.' Yewdall smiled. 'I've seen that quite often over the years.'

'Sorry, darling.' Petty reached for her drink. 'That's me teaching my grandma to suck eggs. So, the party; it settled down with the girls all getting used for what they were brought to the house to be used for. We didn't even get a proper meal, not once in the whole week were we fed. A little breakfast, but mainly we had to pilfer food to stay alive.'

'Yes.' Yewdall held up her hand. 'Sandra described all the arrangements quite well. I understood two girls got very badly assaulted?'

'Little rat-faced, ginger-haired guy called Fergus, he was dragged off each one by Charlie Magg, who said, "Come on Fergus we don't need the Filth investigating no murder."'

'Fergus?' Yewdall asked.

'Fergus McAlpine.' Petty nodded. 'Fergus McAlpine. The party went on all week and we heard things, we got to know who was who. I overheard Charlie Magg say to The Baptist . . . you know about The Baptist?'

'Yes,' Penny Yewdall said, 'we know a little about him but anything you can tell us will be useful.'

'Well, Charlie Magg was talking to The Baptist and The Baptist said, "Good job you were there, Charlie, McAlpine has a thing about women."'

'So that was Fergus McAlpine?' Yewdall clarified. 'The small ginger-haired, rat-faced, geezer who beat up the two women, that was Fergus McAlpine?'

'Seems it was.' Liz Petty drained her glass.

'Another drink?' Penny Yewdall asked, and stood and walked to the bar.

'So,' Penny Yewdall said as she sat back at the table with a vodka for Liz Petty and another orange juice for herself, 'Sandra told me about The Baptist.'

'Yes . . . thanks.' Liz Petty sipped her drink. 'Pearl told him Sandra had been lippy and, well, let's just say The Baptist took Sandra and showed us all how he got his nickname, and Sandra didn't give no more lip to anyone after that. No one did.'

'Yes, so then later in the week we understand something really bad happened?' Yewdall probed.

'Yes, the two straggly-haired geezers . . . can't tell you much.'

Penny Yewdall felt a pang of disappointment.

'I was one of the first ones to faint, darling.' Liz Petty shrugged her shoulders. 'I mean, I may have been on the street for five years by then, but I was still only twenty years old and I'd never seen anyone battered to death then drowned, just to make sure.'

'You saw that?' Yewdall asked.

'Not all of it; like I said, I fainted, little food for four or five days then watching that.'

'So what did you see?' Penny Yewdall noticed the barman standing closer to where she and Liz Petty sat, noticeably closer; not looking at them, but listening, intently so.

'Towards the end of the week it was, two geezers got pulled through the house and on to the back lawn . . . thin, wasted, long hair and beards, pleading for their lives; they were rabbiting on about not grassing on anyone, but the guy Arnie Rainbird wasn't having any of it. They took one guy and put him down and started working him over with golf clubs; that noise, a squelching sound, blood in his mouth, but they avoided hitting his head. I fainted so I didn't see much after that.'

'Who assaulted the victim?'

'Charlie Magg and Fergus McAlpine.'

'Sure?'

'Yes, definitely.' Liz Petty looked about her. 'I hate this smoking ban, I need a fag . . . but, definitely, I remember. Charlie was the guy who liked women. He never took advantage all week but he could give a geezer a fair slap, and Fergus McAlpine, well, he just took everything he could get and hated men and women equally, I remember thinking that before I passed out. So, yes, it was Charlie Magg and Fergus McAlpine who did the business with the golf clubs.'

'What was the next thing you remember?'

'I came to and people were just standing round, the men and the women. I stood up and for some reason I walked over to the swimming pool and saw the water was streaked with blood. I was told someone had stabbed him in the stomach after The Baptist had drowned him.' Liz Petty bit her fingernail. 'Can't think why anyone would do that. I mean, if the geezer was dead by then. I need a smoke.'

'To let the gas escape from the body,' Yewdall replied, 'that must have been the reason.' Yewdall took a sip of her drink. 'But if you didn't see that . . .?'

'No, I can't say I saw that, but I saw the body had been carried to the bottom of the garden and laid across a bonfire. The bonfire wasn't lit,' Petty explained.

'Yes, I understand,' Yewdall replied, 'it was ready to be lit.'

'Yes, then they did the same thing to the other poor toerag, calling him a grass. Pretty well as soon as they started on him I fainted again.' Petty spoke apologetically. 'I'm sorry.'

'I think I would have done the same,' Yewdall replied comfortingly, 'no reason to be sorry for anything. So then . . .?'

'Well, then I came to again and sat on the lawn for an hour or so, as did the other women and a few of the men. No one was saying anything, then it was Sandra Barnes' Tom, he seemed to be put in charge of the women. He came out of the house and said, "Right . . . on your feet", and we walked to the bottom of the garden and stood in a line and watched them burn the two corpses. The air just filled with a horrible sickly sweet smell, I'll never forget it, and again the women just started collapsing either side of me as the bodies burnt.'

'Fainting?'

'Yes . . . and they kept that fire going all that evening and into the night, with one bloke tending it and separating the bones from the rest, and he kept saying to us, "This is what happens if you grass."' Liz Petty paused. 'So that's why there's no old statements from this girl, darling, I don't want that end. I don't want my bones to be put in a cardboard box and given to Pearl's husband to be dropped in the river.'

'Her husband?' Yewdall queried.

Petty took another sip of her vodka. 'One evening, Pearl was having a real bitch with the guy, telling him what a wimp he was, "You really are, Des, you're a proper wimp. You turned out no good, you're just not up to it any more, no bottle at all", and how "Father" would have been ashamed of him. So, Pearl, the woman who slapped Sandra Barnes, was the wife of Des, who I also heard being called "Desmond" by another of the geezers.'

'That's interesting.' Penny Yewdall looked at Liz Petty. 'Very interesting. They were keeping it in the family.'

'Seems so. So, Des, or Desmond, the coach driver, was given the box of bones and told to tip them into the Old Father. He must have driven away in a motor because the coach didn't move. So he would have found a bridge and into the river they went, somewhere quiet,' Liz observed, 'can't see him tipping them off Tower Bridge, but upstream where the Thames is narrow and there's small footbridges. I'd have gone there if I was him.'

'Fair enough.' Penny Yewdall sat back into the bench seat which ran along the wall. 'That would make more sense.'

'So, the next old morning I was on swimming pool cleaning with Sandra Barnes' Tom . . . or her ex Tom, barking at us like he was a sergeant, "I want it scrubbed sparkling and I mean sparkling", throwing his voice, making it echo round the empty swimming pool, but not shouting.'

'Projection.' Penny Yewdall smiled. 'It's called projecting your voice.'

'Well, he projected it all right, "Any of you what don't give a hundred and ten percent just isn't going home. We've had one fire, we can have another" . . . Ah . . . yes.' Liz Petty put her glass down. 'He said, "It's a deep river, plenty of room for your bones as well", so that is when I knew where Des had tipped the bones, in the Old Father, but not exactly where.'

'All right.' Yewdall paused. 'So you remember Sandra Barnes. Do you remember any of the other women?'

'Just Davinia.'

'Davinia?'

'Yes, she wasn't a brass. She was like Sandra, a rich man's

mistress, and, like Sandra, she only found out where her old man got his dosh from the hard way.' Petty shrugged.

'Do you remember anything about her?'

'She was a bit posh. She had her rent paid for by her man in return for "benefits". She and I were washing up once – we liked washing up because there was food to be pilfered – and we talked about making a run for it, but we decided against it. The garden was fenced in with twenty foot high wire fencing and the front was guarded by dogs. We were barefoot; the only phone in the house was fixed to take incoming calls only and it never rung, not once. So we decided that we just had to stick it out. Probably a good job we did, because that was just before we saw those two guys murdered. They would have made a right example of us if we had run for it; four bodies on the fire, not two.' Liz Petty rolled a cigarette. 'So I'm here, still alive, still kicking. I survived.'

'Do you,' Penny Yewdall asked, 'recall anything about Davinia?'

'Full of regret, full of shame, full of guilt, blaming herself for being stupid. She kept saying, "I am so stupid, stupid, stupid. How could I have got caught up in all this?" I remember she came from Reading.' Liz Petty laid the roll-up on the table. 'Her father was a solicitor and her mother was a clergywoman, a curate, I think she said. I don't know what a curate is but it's something to do with the church.'

'It's all right.' Yewdall smiled briefly. 'We know; it's like the bottom rung of the hierarchy. You start as a curate and end as an archbishop . . . but that's helpful.'

'Interesting.'

'Yes, not many clergywomen in the Church of England in Reading with a daughter called Davinia and whose husband is a solicitor.' Penny Yewdall took out her notebook and wrote her telephone number on a blank page, and then added 'Penny' beneath it. 'That's my phone number.' She handed the notepaper to Liz Petty. 'The last number is actually a "one", but I wrote "seven", as you see. You have to remember it's a "one". That number could make things difficult for you if the wrong people find you in possession of it.'

'OK.' Liz Petty read the number then folded the piece of paper and put it in her handbag. 'Thanks. Oh, I remember that Pearl's brother was one of the gang.'

'Her brother?'

'The one man who she showed any time for, and just about the one man that had any time for her. They were like husband and wife, and after Pearl had that bitch against Desmond, the bus driver, she said, "At least I have a brother who's got the bottle it takes, if I haven't got a husband with it", and then she added, "He even calls you 'Mr Harley'; his own brother-in-law . . . he calls you 'Mr Harley'. That says it all . . . it says it all."'

'Again, how interesting that is.' Penny Yewdall smiled. 'How interesting. It really was all in the family, but listen, Liz . . .'

'Yes?'

'Just think about the offer of witness protection. We can use you in the witness box and you can use a fresh start. Arnie Rainbird can make people disappear but so can the police, though not in the same way, of course.' Penny Yewdall reached for her handbag. 'I promise, no one will find you.'

'You can really do that?'

'Yes, we really can.' Penny Yewdall stood. 'We both benefit. Can I buy you another drink before I go?'

'Yes, thank you. I'll go outside and smoke my fag, but another drink sounds good.' Liz Petty fumbled in her bag for her cigarette lighter. 'I've got some thinking to do. A new start, what street girl wouldn't want that?'

'It was all so, so silly, so very, very, silly . . . the waste . . . so silly.' Diana Wortley placed her aluminium walking stick to one side of her legs and looked down at the carpet. Beside her was a small table on top of which were plentiful bottles of tablets and bottles of medicine.

It was tragic. Vicary read the cluttered room. Here, he thought, was despondency and here was life's unfairness. 'It was not silly, Miss Wortley, it was a tragedy.'

'No . . . no.' Diana Wortley shook her head. 'It was silly, take it from me, Mr Vicary. It was very silly, very stupid youthful silliness which led to the tragedy, and without the silliness there would have been no tragedy.' Diana Wortley had a thin, wasted frame, her face was drawn, her eyes sunken. 'He was going to be a people's lawyer, so he said, not a rich man's lawyer; that was young idealist Daniel. He wanted to champion the underdog and because of that he felt he had to rub shoulders with the East Enders. How could he represent them, he would say, he would ask . . . how could he represent them if he didn't understand them? So he'd take me drinking in pubs down the Mile End Road, and in Stepney and Whitechapel. He was such a naïve idealist, poor Daniel. You know you don't have to know what someone smells like if they don't wash or change their clothes for three days in order to represent them. Lawyers argue points of law. They can prepare their case from documents and photographs. A lawyer need never even meet his client, but Daniel didn't see it that way. Anyway, he eventually got into a fight; looked at someone the wrong way or something.'

'Which you saw, I presume?' Vicary asked.

'No . . . well, apparently . . .'

'Sorry? I don't understand. "Apparently" you saw the fight?'

'Yes, apparently.' Diana Wortley forced a smile. 'I recall sitting in the pub; the next thing I remember is waking up in a hospital, shaking like a leaf, but even now I don't remember anything of the in-between. I had . . . I still have what I understand is called "Hysterical Island Amnesia", HIA for short. I sustained no injuries, no bang on the head – which can also cause island amnesia; no physiological reason for it, so it's all in the mind. I am the classic hysterical female. And then on top of that I go down with multiple sclerosis.'

'I am sorry.'

'That's life. You didn't have to look very hard to find me, did you? I was living with my parents when Danny was murdered and I am still living with my mother; Father died a few years ago.' Again she forced a smile. 'Some life, eh?'

'Again,' Vicary replied, 'I am sorry. I wish I could do something.'

'Thank you, anyway. So I was unable to tell the police anything and I still can't tell you anything. I attended the trial of Arnie Rainbird, I went each day with Daniel's parents and it all hinged on whether Danny had a weapon in the form of a broken bottle and was threatening Rainbird with it. The prosecution said that Danny had dropped the bottle and was offering no resistance.

And in a pub full of men, only one stepped forward and gave evidence against Rainbird, confirming that Danny had dropped the bottle well before Rainbird stabbed him. The jury found against Rainbird and he went down for life, for murder. He was a brave man . . . I mean the man who gave evidence. He was very brave. Arnie Rainbird's conviction was later overturned on appeal, but he was still convicted of the lesser charge of manslaughter. I believe he's out of prison now, only served ten years. The manslaughter charge meant he could apply for an earlier parole.'

'Yes,' Vicary replied, 'that's the way it works.'

'So, he's picking up the pieces of his life, he's rescuing what he can and Daniel is in the soil . . . it is so unfair.'

'You can't leave a man alone, can you?' The woman spat the words. She was short, with dark hair – clearly had a fiery temper.

'It's just a friendly chat,' Swannell replied in a calm, soothing voice.

'Very, very friendly,' Brunnie added. 'Just couldn't be more friendly.'

'And if he doesn't want to chat you'll be back with a warrant,' the woman snarled. 'I know how you work.'

'Yes, possibly,' Swannell continued to be calm. 'We could do that but we'd rather not.'

'Let's keep it unofficial,' Brunnie added.

Arnie Rainbird then appeared behind the woman and stood staring at the officers. He showed himself to be tall, well groomed, clean-shaven, with cold, piercing eyes, and wore blue jeans and a blue T-shirt. He was lean and muscular; his physique had benefited from prison life and he hadn't let liberty soften him. 'I was expecting you,' he announced speaking in an East London accent. 'Snakebite phoned me.'

'We thought he might,' Swannell replied.

'You knew he would, more like.' Rainbird stood in the doorway of his home, which the officers found was a solidly built Victorian house set in its own grounds in Hertfordshire, and they knew not a brick of it had been bought using honest money; all on the back of ruined lives; all purchased with the money used to purchase heroin before the present source of income derived from human trafficking. 'You're just putting the frighteners on me.'

'Sorry you feel like that, Arnie, but it's really just a social call. We just wanted to introduce ourselves.'

'We've been asking a lot of questions about you, Arnie,' Frankie Brunnie added, 'so we thought we'd come and meet you; put a face to a name and all that.'

'So you can go now,' Arnie Rainbird snarled, 'you've put a face to a name; you needn't stay here, you're wasting space.'

'Things might get a little more serious, Arnie. You have read about the bones being found in Ilford a few days ago?'

'Yes, so what?'

'They belonged to Convers and Tyrell, but Snakebite would have told you that so the "so what" doesn't cut much ice.'

Arnie Rainbird remained silent. He was stone-faced.

'The gofer who was supposed to drop the bones in the river,' Swannell explained, 'well, he had other plans didn't he?'

'In fairness, the bones were not intended to be found until we were all well into the next world, but a geezer got drunk and rammed his vehicle into a brick wall, and out popped a note telling us where the bones had been buried,' Brunnie explained. 'And here we are.'

'And here we are,' Swannell repeated. 'Very creative all round; getting battered, then drowned, then their bodies burnt to reduce them to bones. If they did go in the river they would never be found, but the gofer, he was creative as well, and like we said, here we are.'

'We are learning about the party to celebrate you getting out,' Swannell continued with a smile, 'a garden party . . .'

Arnie Rainbird continued to remain silent.

'Lots of lovely witnesses,' Swannell said, 'mainly brasses, but not all, scared into silence, but it's the old elephant in the room number.'

'What does that mean?'

'Well, if something is so huge, so monstrous, it is sometimes easier to ignore it, but the nature of elephants in rooms is that over time they get smaller. With every day that passes they get a little smaller, they pygmify, and they pygmify, until they get small enough to recognize, and then they get talked about, and after seven years the goings on at your coming home party are now small enough for folk to talk about them.'

'Like who, who's talking?' Arnie Rainbird's knuckles whitened as he gripped the front door of his house.

'Can't possibly tell you that, Arnie.' Swannell grinned. 'That would be telling, but there were a lot of girls there who were all free agents, not part of any crew. The fear you had them in is wearing off. Do you know where they still are? Girls move from drum to drum, get married, change their names; just move on in life and leave the street. We are investigating a double murder, Arnie, it won't be manslaughter; you won't be getting out in ten years, not this time. This time you're going back for life.'

'I was fitted up for that last charge, that boy in the pub.'

'You knifed him.'

'I may have . . . I may not have, but the rat who gave evidence against me, he wasn't even in the pub.'

'So how did he know what happened?' Brunnie asked. 'He had to be there.'

'He was primed, your lot primed him, told him what to say. We knew him, he was a blagger and he was looking at eight years for armed robbery so he gave evidence. The charges against him were dropped and he vanished . . . police witness protection.' Arnie Rainbird eyed Swannell and Brunnie coldly. 'You won't be doing that to me again. You won't be fitting me up again.'

The whirring machine which kept the lungs of Charlie Magg's latest and possibly last victim inhaling and exhaling and kept his stomach supplied with liquidized food was, in an atmosphere of sorrow and solemnity, switched off. The supervising physician said, 'All right, it's done. Somebody call it.'

'Eleven fifty-six in the forenoon.' Staff nurse Bridie O'Driscoll 'called it' in her thick Irish accent upon consulting her watch, which hung upside down on the left side of her tunic. She thought as she called it that the decision to switch off the machine and thus terminate the wretched man's life was a decision which was taken none too soon. It always had, in her opinion, been hopelessly optimistic to think that the patient could ever recover, and if he did regain consciousness he would never be anything more than a vegetable. The physician pulled the bed sheet over the man's face. 'I dare say that makes it a murder now. I'll notify the police.'

*   *   *

Tom Ainsclough tapped on the door frame of Harry Vicary's office. He held a manila file in his hand and, Vicary thought, he looked worried.

'Do you have something, Tom?' Vicary put his pen down and reclined in his chair. 'Come in . . . take a pew.'

'Yes . . . yes, sir. I've been following the paper trail like you asked me to, digging up what I could about who I could.'

'Yes?'

'Well, sir, I confess I am a bit worried.'

'I thought you looked troubled. Do sit, please.'

'It appears that there was once a crew called The Whitechapel Fleet.' Tom Ainsclough slid into a chair in front of Vicary's desk.

'Fleet?' Vicary smiled. 'As in a fleet of ships?'

'Yes, sir.'

'It's a good name for a gang,' Vicary commented.

'Yes, I thought so too, sir.' Tom Ainsclough also grinned briefly. 'But it's really the only thing that is amusing.'

'Oh?'

'The chief of The Whitechapel Fleet was a fella called Eddie Fretwell, aka "Slick" Eddie to his mates, and "Slimy" Eddie or "Slimy" Fretwell to his enemies. It seems that he was a sort of eye-on-the-main-chance individual, out for himself all the time and would sell anybody out to save his skin, hence "Slimy" Fretwell or "Eddie the Slime", another name he acquired.'

'I see.'

'Well, "The Fleet" cruised Whitechapel and were not on good terms with Arnie Rainbird's crew, and they each had recognized territory with The Fleet being the smaller of the two outfits.'

'OK . . . I follow.' Vicary picked up a ballpoint pen and began turning it over and over in his hands.

'They avoided all out war,' Ainsclough explained, 'because The Fleet were still in the middle of the twentieth century; strong arm boys blowing safes, stealing wages and bulldozing their way into jewellers' shops, whereas Rainbird's team had got into illegal substances and then into people smuggling. So they didn't like each other, but at the same time they didn't tread on each other's toes.'

'I'm with you,' Vicary replied, 'carry on.'

'It turns out that the prosecution's witness to the murder for which Rainbird was arrested was none other than Eddie "The Slime" Fretwell.'

'Rainbird's enemy!' Vicary sat forward. 'I see where you are going, and I don't like the sound of it.'

'It doesn't sound good, does it, sir?' Ainsclough replied. 'The two gangs were territorial; the murder took place in The Cross Keys just off the Mile End Road, right in the middle of Arnie Rainbird's territory, and not only that but it was his much favoured pub.'

'So Eddie Fretwell would not have been there?'

'No, sir. If Eddie Fretwell set foot in The Cross Keys he'd wake up in the Royal London Hospital, probably with his entire body encased in plaster.' Ainsclough raised his eyebrows. 'He would not have been present when the fight took place, as you say.'

'Who was the senior officer in the Daniel Meed murder?'

Tom Ainsclough consulted the file. 'One Detective Inspector Scaly.'

'Scaly?' Vicary smiled. 'As in scaly dragon?'

'That's what it says here, sir.'

'Is he still with us?'

'Yes, sir. He is now with the Anti Terrorist Squad.'

'Him,' Vicary said, 'him I would like to have a little chat with.'

Victor Swannell, feeling weary and drained, returned home to his modest terraced house on Warren Road in Neasden, where he, like the majority of householders, had concreted over their small front lawns to form a parking space for the family car. Warren Road was laid out before mass car ownership was the norm and was just not wide enough to permit the householders on both sides of the street to park their cars at the kerb. He entered the house by the front door and found his two teenage daughters sitting on the lounge floor, both deeply engrossed in an Australian soap opera which at that moment was being shown on television. They did both manage to say, ''Lo, Dad', but didn't take their eyes off the screen. He went into the back garden, which was filled with the sound of the incessant hum of traffic on the North Circular, where his wife was weeding the rose bed.

She stood up on his approach and perfunctorily pecked his cheek without saying anything and then knelt again and continued to stab at the soil with a small hand-held garden fork, drawing out and casting weeds into a sieve. Swannell turned and walked back into the house.

It was, he had come to realize, all that he could now expect from family life.

Tom Ainsclough also returned home, also feeling tired but satisfied after his day's work. He entered his home in Hargwyne Road in Clapham and checked for post on the top of the table that stood in the communally owned hallway which he and Sara shared with their neighbours, the Watsons, who owned the lower conversion of the house. Ainsclough took the two letters which he found addressed to Mr and Mrs Ainsclough, both from the bank, and unlocked the door leading to the stairs and to the upper conversion. His wife met him at the door and kissed him warmly, but she was already dressed in her uniform and hurriedly leaving for work, anxious not to be late. Newly promoted to Sister at the hospital she was keen to create a good impression and to lead from the front, believing that 'good timekeeping makes good leaders'. Tom Ainsclough spent the evening channel surfing the television, wondering again if it was the constant crossing of paths with his wife as one leaves and the other returns that kept their marriage, in their cramped accommodation, healthy.

Penny Yewdall also felt a sense of satisfaction at a good day's work as she returned home. She took the train from Charing Cross and alighted at Maze Hill, from where she walked the short distance, through narrow Victorian streets, to her modest house in Tusker Road. Once showered and changed into jeans and a T-shirt, she went for a stroll in Greenwich Park and up to the observatory, where a group of foreign youth were photo-graphing each other standing astride the meridian, and was reminded of the amusing incident wherein two Argentinian women seeking the meridian had stopped her and asked, with limited but sufficient English, 'Please, where is half the world?' Upon Observatory Hill, she turned and enjoyed the vista of the

Thames and of East London beyond the river. Penny Yewdall then walked home, casually, enjoying the safety that Greenwich afforded. It was a safe place for a woman to walk alone and, being a young woman, she could still rejoice in her single status; there was time for marriage and a family yet, she told herself . . . still time and that bit is not to be hurried; perhaps, she thought, perhaps she was not the 'elective spinster' she thought she was. After eating, she retired to bed early and as darkness fell the night sky revealed a good Orion. Sometimes the constellation of Orion was stationary but at other times, as on that night, it could be observed marching across the sky. She lay quite still watching the seven observable stars of the constellation move slowly across the window pane of her bedroom, and as she laid there her mind turned to Elizabeth 'Long Liz' Petty, she of the endless legs, who would at that moment be out there, negotiating a price on the hoof in London's other meat market.

SIX

'I feel that I must confess that I find it most unnerving. Most unnerving indeed.' Davinia Bannister was, Yewdall observed, a short, auburn-haired woman of trim, almost petite figure. She and Penny Yewdall walked the athletic track on the school playing fields. Davinia Bannister had suggested that they walk 'the white lines on the green stuff' as it was the only place that they would find peace, the games field not being required at that particular time.

'Yes, I'm sorry,' Yewdall replied, 'I can well imagine how unnerving it would be to have your past tapping you on the shoulder like this, but please don't let it alarm you.'

'I can't help being alarmed.' Davinia Bannister looked sideways at Penny Yewdall. 'Though I am not fearful of any action being taken against me; I did nothing illegal. I have no fears there, but I won't be giving evidence, you may rest assured there, madam, you may rest well assured.'

'Yes,' Penny Yewdall sighed, 'unfortunately they all say that.'

'And no wonder.' Davinia Bannister was neatly, if not severely, dressed in a three-quarter length black skirt, high-necked white blouse, dark nylons and sensible shoes, and was carrying a large black handbag on her shoulder; all in complete accordance, thought Yewdall, with her position as history teacher at a large comprehensive school. 'They were, still are, very heavy boys and if you can find me, so can they. So, how did you find me, anyway?'

'Liz Petty told us about you, she said that you and she talked during that week. She recalled few details; your Christian name, that your father was a lawyer and your mother a curate.'

'She is a fully fledged priest now, the Reverend Muir.'

'I made a few discreet enquiries, mainly of the police in Reading. Davinia is not a common name; the police seemed to know your father. He does a lot of criminal work, so I found.'

'Yes.' Davinia Bannister brushed a wasp from her face. 'He

is a solicitor. He represents felons in low-end crime; the sort of stuff that is dealt with in the magistrates' court, and the police do indeed know him, even though he acts for criminals whom they are prosecuting; each doing their job, but they sit and chat to each other at the conclusion of the morning's business.'

'Yes, they would do. So one police officer did know of a Mr Muir whose daughter Davinia is a school teacher and whose mother joined the priesthood when she was in her middle years. I did assure the police in Reading that you were not a suspect and they insisted on phoning me back at New Scotland Yard to ensure I was kosher. Another phone call to the local education authority, again with the same assurances and with them phoning me at New Scotland Yard . . . and . . .'

'And here you are. So frighteningly simple.'

'Only for the police; Arnie Rainbird and his crew won't be able to do that and they know you as Davinia Muir.'

'No . . . no, they couldn't but they knew I was a secondary school teacher. They will assume I returned to my roots in Reading. Very easy for them to wait outside the school gates of every comprehensive school in this city until they see me emerge, follow me home and, if I am lucky, I'll only get beaten up. If I am unlucky, I will disappear and my little body will never be found.'

The two women walked on in silence for some moments, broken when Davinia Bannister said, 'You know we used to do this when I was at school, as a pupil, I mean.'

'Do what?'

'Walk on the athletics track chatting with my mates. It was meant to be run on with great effort, with gritted teeth, total determination. Sorry, but I was never particularly sporty when I was at school, and when other girls were shaving split seconds or minuscule distances from school records, me and two other girls would just stroll round the athletic track being overtaken by other girls working on their one thousand metres time, using it for the purpose for which it was laid out, and occasionally we'd catch the eye of the games mistress who'd yell, "Run, you three!", so we'd jog along for a few yards and then start walking again. Eventually she gave up on us as a hopeless cause and forgot about us, which suited us admirably. It suited us to perfection. We would even risk a cigarette. When we were circling on the track and were at our apogee from the games mistress we'd risk a quick drag.'

'That was risky.' Yewdall grinned.

'I'll say. Exclusive girls' grammar school, sneaking a cigarette behind the bicycle sheds during lunch break was bad enough, but smoking when purporting to be doing games, that would be akin to lighting up during maths . . . instant expulsion, and I'd really catch it at home. My mother used to be very heavy-handed, even when I was a teenager, but we got away with it, and now I am a teacher and have to keep an eye out for smoking among the children . . . what goes around comes around, as they say.'

'I grew up on a housing estate in the Potteries,' Yewdall replied. 'A corner shop was run by a kindly but partially sighted old gentleman and we could steal sweets and chocolate bars very easily. So, not anything I am proud of, and I am now a copper and catch thieves. Dare say we grow up and turn out all right.'

'Yes.' Davinia Bannister nodded her head slightly. 'Dare say that's the main thing. So what can I tell you about that so-called party?'

'We know the gist, we know some of the details, but we don't know all the personalities. Can you tell me about your lover?'

'Well hardly my lover, and he was nothing to me as soon as we arrived and I found out what was going on.'

'Yes . . . sorry, not a lover.'

'He was my sugar daddy and I was his bit on the side to visit twice or thrice a week because his wife didn't understand him. He paid the rent on my bedsit.' Davinia Bannister shuddered. 'Imagine, my father a lawyer, my mother a curate, my brother studying for a medical degree and intending to join the army as a medical officer, and me a school teacher and bunking up with a career criminal.'

'But you didn't know he was a career criminal?' Yewdall offered.

'No.' Davinia Bannister shook her head. 'No, I didn't. I thought he was a stockbroker or something of that ilk. He led me to believe that. I did think he was a little rough round the edges, but I dismissed that as being part of his self-made, local boy makes good image, and he paid the rent and bought meals, and occasionally gave me a wad of pocket money. It all made living in London possible on a school teacher's salary, especially on the salary of a newly qualified teacher. I used to feel sorry for the males or the less attractive females who had no option but to make their salary stretch. I had an easy ride until the party . . . then I paid for it.'

'Yes.' Penny Yewdall looked to her left at a stand of trees which formed the boundary of the school grounds. 'That's what Sandra Barnes described it as being like; enabled her to survive, financially speaking. Then she also paid the price.'

'Sandra . . . yes, I remember her.' Davinia Bannister kept her eyes downcast. 'She was in the same boat, a primary school teacher, so even worse off than me. I earned more as a teacher of the eleven to sixteen age range, but it took that dreadful week long orgy of sex and violence to see our sugar daddies for who they really were. So how is Sandra?'

'Doing well, living in the north . . . two children, happy with her marriage.' Yewdall did not wish to provide too much information.

'And "Long Liz" Petty?' Davinia Bannister enquired. 'I really took to her. She was a working girl but she had a naturally warm personality.'

Yewdall paused. 'She still is and still has.'

'Oh,' Davinia Bannister groaned, 'she's still working the street?'

'Yes, sadly for her,' Yewdall replied softly, 'she's still a working girl and a vodka merchant as well.'

'I am sorry to hear that. I did hope she could tear herself away from the street. I know it's not easy . . . but . . . I did hope the best for her.' Davinia Bannister looked at the low-rise angular brick building that was the school at which she taught. 'She and I talked of escaping.'

'Yes, she told me that.'

'Fanciful really, but the idea kept our spirits up a little. We would not have got far, both naked and no footwear. You have to experience that state to realize how vulnerable you are, and both so dreadfully weak through insufficient food. Picture us if you will, picking at the remains of hamburgers and carbon-encrusted sausages, not caring what we ate and talking of making a run for it. We wouldn't have got past the goons.'

'Goons?' Penny Yewdall queried.

'The guards, we called them goons like it was some prisoner of war camp. Dogs guarded the front of the house by night and gofers, the goons, by day. The back of the house was fully fenced off with that interlocking stuff you have to use your big toe to climb and that is excruciating; if you've ever tried to do it you'll know what I mean. I did it once.'

'At the party?'

Davinia Bannister smiled. 'No . . . no, another more innocent situation, but the same sort of wire. So we gave up the idea and realized that if we were going to survive the answer was docility and compliance, or as Liz said, "Look, just forget it. Keep your head down and don't kick up a fuss about anything and we'll get through this" . . . she had that sort of street girl savvy and she was right. And by then, of course, we'd seen Sandra Barnes get a slap, and such a slap I never saw before or since, then get half-drowned by The Baptist. Then these two wretched men getting pummelled with golf clubs and then handed to The Baptist to finish them off, though I confess I don't think The Baptist's skills were needed. I can't imagine anyone surviving an assault like that but Arnie Rainbird wanted to make sure.'

'You saw it all?'

'Yes.' Davinia Bannister kept her eyes fixed on the ground in front of her. 'Little Davinia Muir as I was then, all five feet nothing of me, waif-like, yet I was the only one who didn't faint. Some girls fainted at both assaults or at one or the other, but I didn't faint at either, or at the drownings or at the bonfire. I saw it all from beginning to end and it's lodged in here –' she tapped the side of her head – 'I just cannot drive the image . . . the images from my mind.'

'Who assaulted the two men?'

'Charlie Magg and Fergus McAlpine. Imagine a name like Fergus McAlpine, you'd think you'd hear him saying things like, "Am a no a bonny fighter, Jamie?" Instead, he complains in estuary English when Charlie Magg drags him off a woman before he kills her, "Leave it aht, Charlie, ah was only given her a little slap, wasn't ah? I mean gotta learn 'em right from wrong, ain't yer?"' Davinia Bannister fell silent. 'You know, Charlie Magg saved the lives of the two women whom Fergus attacked, you really should put a word in for him for that if you can.'

'I'm afraid Charlie is past helping any. He might well have rescued women but he has a number of male victims.' Yewdall savoured the fresh air of the playing fields. 'So, if you can, tell me about The Baptist, we know nothing of him.'

'Jerry Primrose was his name, probably still is; quite a nice evocative name but the character was evil; he smiled as he killed. Jerry Primrose, he owned a big house in north London and had a passion for Ferraris. Only a blood-red Ferrari would do for our Jerry. He has a large birthmark on his chest which he is self-conscious about and that explains why he kept his clothes on when he was doing his thing in Snakebite's swimming pool.'

Penny Yewdall beamed at Davinia Bannister. 'You *do* know a lot about him.'

'I should do, I was his tart. I was his to visit when he so fancied, but that was his name, Gerald Primrose. I saw his name often enough on cheques and credit cards. Kept me in a bedsit hidden away from his world and then one day out of the blue he calls and drives me up to Bedfordshire. "We're going to a party," he says, so we go to the house and he opens the car door, and drags me out by the arm. He never got hold of me like that before. The foyer of the house is full of naked women, and he drags me across the floor and plants me in front of the only woman who was wearing clothes and says, "Do everything this woman tells you and don't argue about anything", then he walks away out to the back of the house, to the garden and pretty soon I am starkers, too. The next day he half-drowns Sandra Barnes then seems to vanish. I didn't see him again until the middle of the week when he appears again and drowns those two tramps after they had been well worked over with golf clubs. I never saw him again.'

'And you are sure that you won't give a statement?' Penny Yewdall pressed. 'You saw everything. You can make a clear identification of The Baptist.'

Davinia Bannister walked on in silence. Then she said, 'I wouldn't be seen as a grass, would I? I wasn't in a gang. I wouldn't be breaking the criminal code of honour.'

'No . . . no . . . you wouldn't,' Penny Yewdall answered with a note of encouragement.

'I want to talk it over with my mother.'

'Your mother!' Penny Yewdall couldn't contain her surprise.

'Yes.' Davinia Barrister smiled. 'I'm a grown woman, I am not seeking her permission but I would like to talk to her in her capacity as a priest; it is a matter of ethics. I need guidance. I would also like to talk to my husband. He is a man of some standing in this town. The trial, if it comes, will generate a lot of publicity. He should at least have some forewarning. Neither he nor my parents know anything of that horrible week in Bedfordshire and about how I survived on a teacher's salary when I lived in London. They should hear it all from me first. Let me phone you. Give me a contact phone number and I will phone you in a day or two.'

'That was hardly legal,' Harry Vicary sighed as he and Tudy Scaly sat on a wooden bench on the Albert Embankment, with the river and the Houses of Parliament on the opposite bank behind them.

'It was all very illegal, chummy, most bent.' Tudy Scaly shrugged. 'But it got a result.' He was a tall, broad-chested man and was dressed, in Vicary's view, in a manner which could only be described as 'meticulous', with highly polished shoes, knife-edge creases in his trousers, a neat Italian cut jacket. 'It's just the way of it, Harry, my good mate; just the way the world turns.'

'It was immoral.'

'It got a good result, like I said.' Scaly glanced up at the sunlight streaming through the foliage of the trees. 'You know, my weird Christian name wasn't given to me because my parents were practising Christians and wanted to imbue me and my brother with the Christian ethic of right and wrong. We were given the names of obscure saints – he is Arwan – so we'd learn to stick up for ourselves on the sink estate we lived on because the other kids would poke fun at us because of our weird names. My old man, he was a Royal Marine Commando, and me and Arwan inherited his physique, so we could look after ourselves at that awful council school we went to. But the old man did tell us one thing: he hated the French . . . how he hated them.'

'Most English do,' Vicary said drily. 'Most of us are Francophobic.'

'Yes, but he said the French have a saying, "You can't make an omelette without breaking the egg."'

'Meaning what in this case?'

'Well, meaning if you have to do some damage to bring on a greater good then so be it. The initial damage is worth the outcome.' Scaly's eye was caught by a trim nurse in her blue uniform walking strongly and proudly towards St Thomas's Hospital. 'She will make one lucky man an excellent wife,' he commented. 'You married, Harry?'

'Yes.'

'Children?'

'No.'

'I'm divorced with three up and flown.' Scaly continued. 'So, Rainbird killed that boy and it was murder. The broken bottle picked up in haste and panic was well on the floor and the boy was putting his hands up, but Rainbird was advancing on him with a grin on his face and a blade in his paw, saying, "You shouldn't have done that to me", and slowly closed on the boy and did the business with the knife. Murder. Clear as day.'

'And you know that that was how it happened?' Vicary asked.

'Yes, Harry, we know. We spoke to the landlord of The Cross Keys, he saw everything, but it was Arnie Rainbird's pub, full of Arnie Rainbird's gang. Herron, Primrose, Magg, McAlpine, they were all there, but the boy's prints were on the neck of the bottle. Rainbird was convicted of murder but the charge was reduced to manslaughter on appeal because of those prints. So Arnie Rainbird walked after ten summers. No one saw anything but everyone saw everything.'

'So, no statements?'

'None, not a single dicky bird would sing a song. Not one.'

'So where did you find your witness?' Vicary enjoyed the gentle heat of the sun upon his face.

'We didn't. He found us.' Scaly smiled. 'He walked into New Scotland Yard as bold as brass asking to see me. He had two gofers with him.'

'Convers and Tyrell?' Vicary guessed.

'Yes, so we sat down and we had a powwow. The witness was only a witness by proxy.'

'Eddie Fretwell?'

'Eddie "The Slime" Fretwell . . . "Slimy" Eddie.' Scaly nodded slowly. 'That villain would have shopped his own mother if there was something in it for him. Anyway, "Slimy" Eddie is looking at a ten stretch for armed robbery and is not enthusiastic about the prospect. He was on bail at the time having surrendered his passport,' Scaly explained, 'hence being at liberty.'

'I see.'

'And not over the moon about being a guest of Her Majesty for the next few years, as I am sure you can imagine.'

'Yes.' Vicary watched a grey squirrel jump from one tree to another. 'That does not require a great leap of imagination.'

'Indeed, indeed. So Convers and Tyrell are also looking at a little of Goldilocks's favourite food in respect of a bungled snatch and grab at a jewellery shop. It was all very clumsy and so clearly caught on CCTV that it could have been staged for ITV London. I mean, if they had stood and posed for the images it couldn't have been better, but they had previous and so it was worth two years inside. They were also bailed pending trial.'

'I follow,' Vicary replied, taking his eye off the squirrel.

'So . . . here's the script –' Scaly turned to face Vicary – 'it turns out that Convers and Tyrell are a pair of lowlife petty thieves and they occasionally, but only occasionally, do a little gofering for "Slimy" Eddie and The Whitechapel Fleet, but they are not seen or even known to be part of The Fleet, which means they can drink on Arnie Rainbird's turf. So, were they or were they not in The Cross Keys on the night that Rainbird stabbed that boy? They were sitting at the next table; ringside seat.'

'Useful,' Vicary replied. 'I think I can see where this is going.'

'Yes . . . added to which is the great hostility between Eddie "The Slime" and Arnie Rainbird.'

'Yes, we know that.'

'OK. So the script is that Convers and Tyrell feed details about the incident that only an eye witness would know . . . clothes Rainbird was wearing, exactly when the broken bottle was dropped; all crucial to our case if we wanted a murder conviction. They feed the details to Eddie "The Slime" Fretwell.'

'He gave evidence . . . and . . .' Vicary held up his hand, 'let me guess, all the charges against Fretwell, Convers and Tyrell went away.'

'In a word, yes.' Scaly smiled. 'Neat, don't you think?'

'No . . .' Vicary growled, 'but carry on.'

'So Fretwell disappears into witness protection; he's probably John Smith living north of the Humber now. Nobody wants to go north to look for him . . . that old north/south divide . . . it keeps many people safe.'

'You can say that again. All those mammoths in the Pennines and the cave dwellers everywhere.' Vicary forced a smile, though he felt increasingly uncomfortable in the presence of Tudy Scaly.

'So Fretwell disappeared down the witness protection rathole, taking all he had in the bank with him, all ill-gotten, and he deserted his gang. With Fretwell gone The Fleet just evaporated.'

'And Convers and Tyrell?'

'Oh . . . two silly boys; they didn't want to leave old London Town, did they? Reckoned they did not need witness protection because they did not give evidence against Arnie Rainbird.' Scaly opened the palms of his hands.

'Big mistake.' Vicary shook his head.

'Very big mistake, but the evidence Fretwell gave was so detailed that Rainbird knew what had happened. His gang worked out that the only people in the pub who could not be vouched for were the two loafers in the ringside seat and the tried and tested East End telegraph started chattering. Blaggers started to talk with or without a few well-aimed kicks to the ribcage and eventually names were mentioned. So, those old bones dug up in Enfield were the remains of Convers and Tyrell? Surprised me that they were not tipped into the Old Father.' Scaly raised a thumb and indicated the River Thames behind him. 'That's where bones usually end up.'

'You're admitting perverting the course of justice, Tudy. With your encouragement, Eddie Fretwell gave false testimony.' Vicary sat forwards resting his elbows on his knees. 'He perjured himself . . . with the encouragement of the police. That is sub judice; conspiring to give false evidence.'

'Not admitting anything, chummy, not admitting anything, my good mate. Like I said, it's the way the world turns, it's the way the ball bounces . . . and this . . . this, Harry, my good and faithful friend, this is just a chat about the weather.'

'I feel unwell,' Vicary sighed.

'Don't be soft-hearted. We got Arnie Rainbird.' Tudy Scaly spoke confidently. 'We got him for just one murder but his paw prints were on many more, not just trussing up a geezer and rolling him off the roof of a twelve storey block of flats and taking his time about it; letting the geezer sweat before he was pushed. Not just tying up another geezer on the tracks in front of an express train and singing "The Runaway Train" as the rails begin to sing . . . but many, many more. Yes, we knew about those two murders well before you found out. Arnie Rainbird's victims are numbered in two figures, Harry, so it was down to the old eggshell for an omelette game if we were going to nail him.' Tudy Scaly scratched the back of his left hand. 'And Convers and Tyrell wouldn't have come to any harm if they'd taken our advice and followed Fretwell into the witness protection rathole. So hell mend them.'

'So Rainbird knew who they were more or less as soon as he was convicted?'

'More or less.'

'And left them alone until a few weeks before he was released, when he had them abducted and given a good kicking, and then kept somewhere on a starvation diet until they were dragged on to the lawn at the party, apparently looking like two shipwrecked sailors?'

'Seems like it. But they had their chance to escape . . .' Scaly paused. 'Confess East End justice can be quite inspiring at times.'

'You have no conscience, Tudy. You don't feel guilt at all?'

'None. Nothing to feel guilty about. Unlike you, Harry, unlike you.'

Vicary turned angrily towards Tudy Scaly. 'Just what is that supposed to mean?'

'Your methods might be a little more in keeping with the rules, Harry, but at what cost? Harry, my good mate, at what cost?'

'I don't follow,' Vicary replied coldly. 'What do you mean "at what cost"?'

'Well, let me explain. You know when I was in the Murder and Serious Crime Squad we had our narks, toerags giving information on other toerags for a few quid, but nothing like we get in the Anti Terrorist Squad, because no one likes people who plant bombs on underground trains and no one likes people who plant bombs on airliners. So we get a lot of stuff coming our way and because of that we probably heard what happened last night before you did, my good mate.'

'What was that?' Vicary's voice cracked. 'What has gone down?'

'Only that Arnie Rainbird's foot soldiers were down King's Cross last night and were down there in very large numbers. They were looking for girls, not just any girls, Harry, but girls who once attended a certain party somewhere.' Scaly fixed Vicary with a cold stare. 'Do you know anything about a party that had something to do with Rainbird, Harry? Anyway, girls who were at that party and who no longer work the street or who have left London completely, well, they're probably safe, but those girls who were at the party and who still work the street . . . they, on the other hand, are not safe. The soldiers apparently were controlled by a small, feisty woman who was heard to say things like, "She's one, she was at the party; grab her."' Scaly paused and looked upwards. 'You know, Harry, if you told Rainbird that the girls at that party were talking because they had seen something naughty and you did that in order to put the wind up Rainbird and his lieutenants, well, you did that all right. You frightened him, but probably not in the way you hoped or intended, no Harry, you frightened Rainbird into making a pre-emptive strike, my good mate; hitting you before you can hit him. Three girls got very badly rolled. They were dropped off on the steps of the Westminster Hospital. All three were brasses but they're still girls, Harry, still human beings. One of them will never walk again; another is still in a coma and not responding to any stimulus. The one girl that can talk said they were warned by Arnie Rainbird's soldiers not to say anything to the Filth about the party. Sounds like it was quite a knees-up, Harry, that party, quite some knees-up. The soldiers were very keen to find a brass called "Long Liz". Do you know of her, Harry? Do you? Because if you do, you need to move fast; they want her. You know what I mean?' Scaly drew his finger across the front of his throat. 'She's on borrowed time, if it isn't already too late, Harry. She was seen talking to the Filth in a pub in Canning Town. I mean, Arnie Rainbird's spies are everywhere . . . everywhere and he has tentacles which are both long and numerous. Talk about being indiscreet. You're not the brightest button in the box are you, Harry, my good mate. In fact, you're well short of the full shilling, if you ask me, well short, and you climb on your moral high horse because I bent a rule or two to get Arnie Rainbird put away . . . do me a favour.'

Vicary's stomach felt hollow. His jaw sagged.

'You've come over all pale, Harry, do you know that?' Tudy Scaly stood. 'Your little old face has suddenly lost all its lovely colour. Do you want me to call a cab for you, Harry? Do you want me to get a cab to take you home?' Tudy Scaly turned to walk away, but looked back and said, 'I'm serious, Harry, don't wag your little moralizing finger at me. So I broke a rule, but I put a very nasty man where he belongs, and if Convers and Tyrell had taken the advice I gave them . . . and strongly gave them, I might add, they would still be alive and no one would have got hurt. But you . . . going by the book . . . well, there's three women in the Westminster Hospital. All three are still south of thirty years old, all three have eclipsed life ahead of them, a sort of half life; go and listen to what they have to say to you. Go and listen to what they are likely to tell you to do with your rule book, Harry . . . go and listen to them . . .'

'All right. Thank you.' Harry Vicary put the phone down. 'That was Canning Town Police; Long Liz isn't at home. It was fanciful to think we might have been in time. Penny, Tom . . .'

'Sir?'

'Go and talk to her neighbours, someone might have seen something.'

'Yes, sir.'

'Frankie . . .'

'Sir?'

'You have something?'

'Yes, sir. Alex Montgomery.'

'Remind me.'

'He's the glazier whose premises occupy the site once owned by the Cole brothers, the builders.'

'Ah, yes.'

'Turns out that Montgomery has previous for violence. He's known to McAlpine and Charles Magg, and probably to others in Arnie Rainbird's crew.'

'So he's no glazier?' Vicary leaned forward.

'No, sir. He's sitting the land to keep the squatters off . . . and the land, according to the Land Registry, belongs to A. R. Holdings.'

Vicary groaned. 'Don't tell me the A. R. being Arnold Rainbird?'

'Yes, sir. I'd like to take a run out to see Mr Cole. I am certain he's a victim of some scam and he didn't tell Penny and Tom here the full story when they called on him, probably out of fear.'

'Yes, do that, have another chat with him. Thanks, Frankie. Are you happy to go alone?'

'Yes, sir, it's a one-hander.'

The three officers stood and walked towards the door of Vicary's office. Penny Yewdall, the last of the three to reach the door, stopped and turned around. 'Hindsight is a wonderful thing, sir; we should all have seen what Rainbird would do.'

'Possibly . . . possibly.' Vicary reclined in his chair. 'But I should have seen it more than anybody and before anybody else. All right, thanks, Penny, but go and see if you can rescue anything from this mess.'

'I saw her get taken away, so I did.' The woman opened the door to her house just an inch and kept the security chain in place. 'About six o'clock this morning. I was awake and I looked out from my bedroom window which is opposite her house. Didn't give her no time to dress they didn't, just in a red T-shirt, nothing else . . . no shoes . . . nothing. Such long legs she has, long legs.'

'Who took her?'

'You did, the Old Bill. You're the Old Bill, aren't you?'

'We did?' Penny Yewdall gasped. 'Yes, we're the Old Bill.'

'Yes, they was police, four of them. Four big geezers.'

'How did you know they were police, madam?' Tom Ainsclough asked.

'Cos they had her in . . . what are those things? Handcuffs, they had her in handcuffs.'

'You can buy handcuffs from a toy shop!' Yewdall could not contain her anger.

'Were her hands cuffed in front of her or behind?' Ainsclough fought to contain his annoyance.

'Behind,' the woman replied. She was timid. Elderly. Dark-haired.

Tom Ainsclough sighed. 'They were not police officers; we would not handcuff a female DP with her hands behind her back.'

'DP?' The woman asked.

'Detained Person,' Yewdall replied coldly. 'What sort of vehicle did they have?'

'Red van, dearie, just a red van; she went in the back with three of the men.' The woman shut her front door.

Yewdall and Ainsclough looked at each other. 'Now what?' Yewdall said softly. 'Now what do we do?'

'We built the business up from nothing, me and my brother.' Roy Cole received Frankie Brunnie on the south-facing porch of his modest, paint-peeling, bungalow where he had received Yewdall and Ainsclough a few days earlier, and similarly Brunnie found himself sitting adjacent to a plethora of colour and abundance of flora, with bees humming and birds in song. 'We had both left school with no qualifications and we were walking near our house one day, two sixteen, seventeen-year-old lads, and there was a team of blokes digging a trench along the pavement. So there were a couple of spades standing propped up against the wall and me and my brother, well, we just grabbed one each and pitched in. We grafted with that crew all day and went home when they knocked off, and the next day we went back to the trench and worked with them like a pair of Trojans, and at the end of that day the boys said to the gaffer, "Set 'em on, boss", and we were set on and we worked with that crew for the next year and a half, and we got to know the building trade. We got known, got offered jobs and the work just kept coming in, and over the years we became established. Then, a few years ago, we got word of an odd parcel of land which was up for sale and we bought it because it was next door to our premises. I mean, it was the next field. We owned two acres, more than we needed, and the field next to us suddenly sprouted a "For Sale" sign; that field was ten acres. Now ten acres with planning permission . . . that land would then be worth something. So we bought it without planning permission, and if we threw in our two acres and then applied for planning permission for houses on a twelve acre site, that was retirement money for me and my brother. I mean low to middle seven figures; North London, a green field site . . . it was valuable with planning permission.'

'I can believe that,' Brunnie commented.

'So we applied for planning permission, achieved interim status, not full permission, but we lodged the application. It was received and we had it progress to the "pending" stage, when we were visited by a man who offered us what the land was worth without planning permission.'

'Which you declined?'

'Of course we did. So then the guy says, "I am representing a gentleman who always gets what he wants. This way you stay alive. So you are offered a fair two hundred thousand pounds for the twelve acres. If you refuse the offer you will meet with an accident, you'll just vanish." To which I said, "Don't threaten us like that!"'

'Yes.' Brunnie nodded his head. 'As you would.'

'To which he replied, "I am not threatening you, Mr Cole, I am making you a solemn promise." So we had warnings; our yard was vandalized, our vehicle set on fire. We would come home and some soul's clearly beloved cat or dog would be on our doorstep with its neck broken. I don't mean a stray but a well-fed pedigree with an owner's collar, that sort of thing. Then one day my brother got attacked, they broke his legs. Then I got a phone call at home and the voice said, "You're next." Eventually we sold it all for a quarter of a million pounds, we managed to negotiate an increase of fifty thousand. The people who bought it still have it; they haven't built on it but they now have the planning permission we applied for. The planning permission went through. It's now worth about five million pounds with clear planning permission for an estate of sixty houses plus amenities. The building trade is in a depression at the moment so those guys are clearly waiting for things to pick up again, then they'll sell it and make a killing. If we had kept our mouths shut me and my brother would have shared five million pounds between us instead of a quarter of a million.'

'Who did you talk to, Mr Cole?' Brunnie glanced at the multitude of colours that was the small garden in front of Roy Cole's modest house.

'Only the men we employed as builders,' Cole explained. 'We told them that we had bought the field next to our depot and had applied for outline planning permission, and if we got full planning permission then there would be at least twelve months' work for them. There was nothing on the land at all; just an old wooden hut which looked like it had been there since Victorian times, so one of them, one of our crew, told someone, who told someone . . . or one of our builders was probably known to the proprietor of A. R. Holdings, being the people who now own the land.'

'So who is the glazier who occupies your old site, Mr Montgomery?'

'He's no glazier,' Roy Cole snarled as he brushed a fly from his face, 'he's just keeping an eye on the land, occupying it in case travellers find it. It doesn't sound like A. R. Holdings will have any problem getting a bunch of travellers off their land, but probably, sensibly, they don't want them there in the first place.'

'I am sorry.' Brunnie stood. 'That is not a clever story.'

'It's done now,' Roy Cole sighed. 'I live here, modestly. My brother lives in Spain, modestly, but we are alive and we have been left alone.'

'Long Liz' Petty pulled on the length of chain but it was soundly fastened. Outside, it was silent apart from the birdsong. She sat against the wall of the hut and tried to calm herself, breathing the hot, stale air with difficulty; adjusting her eyes to the gloom. She felt about her with her fingertips and eventually found a section of floorboard which was loose and could be lifted up. Below the section of boarding she felt a small enclosed space. She tugged at her scalp hair, pulling out as many strands as she could, and then rolled them into a tight ball and placed them in the space. She then replaced the small section of flooring.

'One day, one day, someone might just find them,' she said quietly to herself.

She sat against the wall of the hut and thought of her life, the escape from Basingstoke to the not much better existence of nights in King's Cross and daytime sleeping in cramped bedsits in East London . . . and her death . . . tomorrow . . . battered half to death with golf clubs before being drowned in Snakebite's swimming pool, her body incinerated, her bones dropped into the river at still not thirty years old.

If only she had accepted the witness protection offer. If only she hadn't gone for a drink with a copper in the pub in the middle of the day . . . if only . . . if only . . . if only . . .

Harry Vicary sat on the settee clutching the bottle and grinned inanely as his wife entered the living room.

'Harry!' Kathleen Vicary strode forward and grabbed the half-empty bottle of whiskey from her husband's hand. 'Why? Why now? You've been so good. You know your job depends upon you staying off the bottle. Heavens, Harry, why? This is going down the sink . . . but Harry, why?'

'Why?' Vicary slurred his words. 'Why? You ask why? Well, three women, that's why. Three young women . . . one's a raspberry ripple . . . a cripple.'

'Yes, I know what a raspberry ripple is. I am a nurse! Remember.'

'Another is in a coma and the third looks like she's been run over by a steamroller, that's why . . . Oh . . . there's a fourth, she's been abducted and she is going to be murdered if she hasn't already been iced.'

'So, is that your fault?'

'Yes,' Vicary replied quietly, 'yes, it is . . . all of it, all my fault, all because of my stupidity.'

Penny Yewdall lay in her bed again watching Orion track really quite rapidly, she thought, across the sky.

She sat upright. Staring straight ahead. She said to herself, 'I know where she is.' She leapt out of bed and pulled on a pair of jeans, a T-shirt and a pair of sports shoes. She left her house quite calmly, ensuring that the door was locked behind her, then she got into her socially responsible grubby car, which was good for London but not any further afield, and drove slowly and steadily away, towards the Dartford Tunnel. She knew the value of taking her time.

It was a night of a full moon and once clear of the city, and off the main road, the landscape was bathed in moonlight. Switching off her car's headlights, she found that she could see clearly for a distance of about, she guessed, half a mile in all directions. She halted the car at the entrance of the first field and then, expediently, turned it around so that it faced back towards London. She opened the door slowly and quietly and let it remain open.

An owl hooted.

She crept stealthily onwards between the glazier's lorry and the first hut, and saw, clearly, the second hut standing as if forlorn in the second field. She halted at the entrance of the second field, recalling advice given to her in her childhood, "Don't go into that empty field because that empty field might not be so empty . . . search, search the shadows." So she searched the shadows as the owl hooted once more. Then she crept forward, approaching the second hut, and then she halted at the door. She tapped on it. 'Liz . . . are you in there?'

There was no answer.

'Liz . . . Liz . . . it's Penny.'

There was still no reply. Yewdall examined the hasp and padlock . . . it was small and screwed into rotting timber and would, she guessed, be easily broken. She returned to her car, moving more speedily by then, and took a large screwdriver from the tool kit and returned to the shed, confident that she was the only person in the vicinity. At the shed once again, she forced the screwdriver behind the hasp and levered it towards her. The hasp tore away from the rotting wood of the shed and she opened the door.

The shed was empty.

There was though, as if by some compensation, a sense felt by Penny Yewdall of someone having recently been within the shed, not dissimilar, she thought, to returning to one's hotel room after room service has called . . . There was a definite presence in the confines of the wooden structure, and she saw in the moonlight a length of silver chain which lay on the floor of the shed, with one end affixed to a ring bolt set into the frame.

She had been here. 'Long Liz' Petty had been here . . . Penny Yewdall had been correct . . . and she had also been too late.

Yewdall returned to her car . . . disconsolate . . . even the owl's hoot then seemed to have a spiteful, mocking tone. In the distance she saw the vast spread of the lights of north-east London; to her left and behind her, all was darkness. She knew then that Long Liz Petty was out there . . . anywhere. Anywhere at all.

'Long Liz' Petty lay on the grass shivering in the early morning, wearing only the red T-shirt she had on when she had been abducted by the men who had woken her up by knocking on her door and shouting, 'Police, Miss Petty, open up . . .' She looked about her. The house hadn't changed much, if at all, so far as she could see; the large lawn, the swimming pool, the barbecue area, the Leylandii, taller now, and doubtless still concealing the impossible to climb high wire fencing, which, she assumed, was the only reason why she had been left on the lawn unsupervised and unrestrained . . . There was just nowhere for her to go . . . she was like an animal in a huge cage . . . all she could do was wait.

'Rainbird won't have her at his house . . . he's too fly for that . . . he'll keep that drum very clean, you can bet on that,' Frankie Brunnie offered to the group who sat in front of Harry Vicary's desk; Swannell, Ainsclough, Yewdall and, behind the desk, Harry Vicary himself, and with each person in front of the desk noticing Vicary's heavily bloodshot eyes, and smelling the vapour of strong mint on his breath, which did not fully smother the under odour of stale alcohol. Each person thought, 'Come on, Harry, pull through, pull through, you can do it, you've been doing so well . . .'

'Where?' Penny Yewdall turned to Brunnie. 'Where, Frankie . . . ?'

'The big house up in Bedfordshire, Snakebite's drum . . . it's the place they used to execute people before. That back garden has probably seen quite a few lives snuffed, many more than the two we know about.'

'Yes.' Vicary nodded. 'It's the only place she can be . . .' He reached for the phone on his desk.

Ainsclough stood and grabbed the phone. 'Let me do the talking, Harry . . . you'd better get home . . . lie down . . .'

'No. I am staying.' Harry Vicary sank back in his chair, but he allowed Ainsclough to make the phone call.

'Bedfordshire, isn't it?' Ainsclough dialled a four figure internal number.

'Yes.' Harry Vicary put another strong mint into his mouth. 'Ask them to get there asap. Tell them to batter their way through that front gate . . . a Range Rover should be able to cope with that. If we leave now, we'll arrive at about the same time . . .'

'Yes, boss,' Ainsclough replied. 'But one of us will drive . . . you'll be in the passenger seat . . . We'll go in two cars in fact. Switchboard? Hello, can you please put me through to the Bedfordshire Constabulary . . . in Luton. Yes, I'll hold . . . thank you.'

'Long Liz' Petty stood slowly as the three men walked purpose-fully side by side towards her.

Snakebite, who carried a golf club, Rainbird, and the man they called The Baptist. They had, she noted, aged a little, as was to be expected, but they were definitely the same three men whom she had first seen, amongst other men, at that dreadful party nearly ten years ago.

'You're not going to run?' Snakebite asked coldly, as the three men stood in front of her. 'Pity.'

'Pity?' Petty asked. 'What's the pity about?'

'We thought we'd be having a little fun with you . . . chasing you round the lawn till we caught you . . . so . . . pity.'

'Well, sorry but you're not going to have any fun . . . not with me.'

'You've got bottle, I'll say that for you,' The Baptist commented. 'Me . . . I reckon I'd try to make a run for it.'

'There's nowhere to run to.' Petty lowered her head. 'Just make it quick . . . no need to spin it out; there's no audience . . . not like the last time.'

'That wasn't the last time.' Rainbird smirked. 'It was the last time you saw anything . . . but we've been quite busy over the years . . . our little system . . . golf club, swimming pool . . . bonfire . . . now it's your turn. Talking to the law . . . you should

have stayed shtum . . . and you a street girl . . . you should have
known better.'

It was then, 'Long Liz' Petty would later recall, just as Rainbird
and The Baptist were stepping backwards to allow Snakebite
room to swing the golf club, that the air was rent by the sound
of klaxons, of barking dogs, of shouts, of squealing tyres. The
three men turned away from Petty and looked towards the house,
and Petty also turned and ran . . . instinctively realizing there
was then some hope of escape. She ran beyond the remnants of
the fire to the very bottom of the garden and then turned. She
saw police officers in uniform and also in plain clothes spill out
of the rear door of the house and on to the lawn . . . amongst
them she recognized Penny Yewdall.

She saw Snakebite lift the golf club as if to strike at the officers
. . . and continued to watch as The Baptist slowly took it from
him and dropped it on the grass. She saw a police officer, a male,
step forward and approach Rainbird, and she was able to read
his lips as he said, 'It's over . . . Arnie. It's all over.'

EPILOGUE

Six months later

'**M**eet Alice Adnam.' Liz Petty smiled as Penny Yewdall sat on the bench beside her.

'Hello, Alice.' Penny Yewdall returned the smile.

'They're not very friendly in here.'

'They think you're a criminal,' Yewdall explained. 'The majority of people who go into witness protection are criminals who have turned Queen's Evidence to avoid prosecution, so don't take it personally. It's better if as few people know your real identity as possible, including police officers, so let them think you're a crim.'

'OK.'

'So why Alice Adnam?'

'They showed me a list of names and asked me to choose one. It was in alphabetical order so I just took the first one. Tell you the truth, I am getting to like it. I'll get a new social security number. If I want a passport I'll have to use my real name. They explained that I can't be issued with a replacement birth certificate.'

'That is the one proviso of a new identity, so don't plan any long distance travel for a while.'

'Yes.' Long Liz sighed. 'Penny, if you lot hadn't rescued me . . .'

'You're safe now.' Penny Yewdall looked at the room; it was large and cavernous like a small aircraft hangar, she thought. Two uniformed police officers stood by a car with a plain-clothed driver waiting to drive 'Long Liz' Petty into her new life, as Alice Adnam.

'I'm going to the south-east,' Petty said.

'You don't have to tell me,' Yewdall cautioned. 'In fact, you shouldn't.'

'Well, I'm a soft southern flower and I won't do well in the cold north and I want to learn to speak French.'

'French?'

'I'm going to do what you suggested, Penny. Take evening classes; French for Beginners. I might meet someone. If I do, I won't hide my past.'

'Good. Always the best policy.'

'And if I live near Dover or Ramsgate I can get a ferry across to France for the day, once I have the basics; see if I can go into a café and order some food. I don't need a passport to travel within the European Community.' Petty reclined on the hard bench.

'You have it all planned,' Yewdall observed. 'It's a good sign.'

'It is?'

'Yes . . . positive attitude.'

'I dare say. So it was what you wanted?'

Penny Yewdall smiled. 'Yes, it was a good result, a very good result. Rainbird, Herron, Magg, McAlpine, Primrose and Harley all with multiple life sentences . . . Pearl Holst, with ten years for conspiracy to murder, with four years for procuring for the purposes of prostitution swallowed up in that. I dare say that that will please her family no end. Your testimony and Davinia Bannister's testimony, and you putting your hair in the shed where Convers and Tyrell had done the same thing seven years earlier – nice DNA profiles to be had there to match the bones dug up in a wood in Enfield. And the Forensic Accountants are looking at their assets, Rainbird and Co.'s assets, I mean. Anything that cannot be proven to have been obtained lawfully, or bought with lawfully earned money, will be seized and sold off as proceeds of crime and the money donated to the public purse. So, if they come out, they'll come out to very little at all. A very nice result all round.'

A stern and stoutly built woman police constable approached and handed 'Long Liz' Petty a padded envelope. 'Your documents.' The constable spoke in a cold, detached manner. 'Your new National Insurance Number, a Post Office savings account book in your name, with five hundred pounds credited to your name to start you off. Anything else you earn or claim as being unemployed. Do not make contact with the Metropolitan Police for any reason. If someone from your past finds you and threatens you, you must walk into the nearest police station and explain the situation; let them contact the Metropolitan Police, and you'll be given another new identity.'

'Long Liz' Petty nodded. 'Understood,' she said.

'If you'd like to get in the car, please?' The WPC turned and walked away. 'Long Liz' Petty and Penny Yewdall stood.

'Well, I suppose this is it . . .' Long Liz said. 'I'll send you a postcard from time to time.'

'Yes, I'd like that . . . care of the Murder Squad, New Scotland Yard. Send me one when you arrive, and one each year after that.'

'Miss Adnam!' The woman police constable stood indignantly by the car holding the rear door open. 'We can't wait.'

'Gotta go . . .' Petty began to walk to the car 'Gotta new life to catch.'

The room was hushed. The man and woman stood up together, holding hands. The man said, 'Hello. We are Harry and Kathleen and we are alcoholics.'

And the people in the room chorused, 'Hello, Harry and Kathleen.'

m

NE   1-13